For my son Cass—with thanks for the title

ANTHONY HOROWITZ

PHILOMEL BOOKS

An Imprint of Penguin Group (USA) Inc.

This is a work of fiction. Names, characters, places, and incidents are either the product of the author's imagination or are used fictitiously.

PHILOMEL BOOKS

A division of Penguin Young Readers Group.
Published by The Penguin Group.
Penguin Group (USA) Inc., 375 Hudson Street, New York, NY 10014, U.S.A.
Penguin Group (Canada), 90 Eglinton Avenue East, Suite 700, Toronto, Ontario M4P 2Y3, Canada (a division of Pearson Penguin Canada Inc.).
Penguin Books Ltd, 80 Strand, London WC2R 0RL, England.
Penguin Ireland, 25 St. Stephen's Green, Dublin 2, Ireland (a division of Penguin Books Ltd.).
Penguin Group (Australia), 250 Camberwell Road, Camberwell, Victoria 3124, Australia (a division of Pearson Australia Group Pty Ltd).
Penguin Books India Pvt Ltd, 11 Community Centre, Panchsheel Park, New Delhi—110 017, India.
Penguin Group (NZ), 67 Apollo Drive, Rosedale, North Shore 0632, New Zealand (a division of Pearson New Zealand Ltd).
Penguin Books (South Africa) (Pty) Ltd, 24 Sturdee Avenue, Rosebank, Johannesburg 2196, South Africa.
Penguin Books Ltd, Registered Offices: 80 Strand, London WC2R 0RL, England.

Published simultaneously in Canada. Printed in the United States of America.

Text set in 11-point Palatino.
Library of Congress Cataloging-in-Publication Data
Horowitz, Anthony, 1955–   Bloody Horowitz / Anthony Horowitz.   v. cm.
Contents: Why horror has no place in children's books—The man who killed Darren Shan—Bet your life—You have arrived—The cobra—Robo-Nanny—Bad dream—My bloody French exchange—sheBay—Are you sitting comfortably?—Plugged in—Power—The X Train—Seven cuts.
1. Horror tales, English. 2. Children's stories, English. [1. Horror stories. 2. Short stories.] I. Title.
PZ7.H7875Bl 2010   [Fic]—dc22   2009044748   ISBN 978-0-399-25451-2

1 3 5 7 9 10 8 6 4 2

CONTENTS

WHY HORROR HAS NO PLACE IN CHILDREN'S BOOKS

by Professor Wendy Grooling

Yes, we want young people to read. But do we ever ask ourselves *what* we want young people to read?

It is undoubtedly true that the success of the Harry Potter books has led to what many would call a "golden age" of reading. I, myself, am a great admirer of many of the new wave of children's writers and in particular Philip Pullman (a lovely, wise man), Geraldine McCaughrean (so warm and delightful!) and David Almond (a genius . . . nothing more to be said). And let's spare a thought for dear J. K. Rowling herself. It's all too often forgotten that she has single-handedly taught an entire generation the value of reading, and what is so wonderful is that she has asked for absolutely nothing in return, except for a few billion dollars.

But the question we have to ask ourselves is—are all books of equal value? On the one hand, we have Alice who has such cheerful and blood-free adventures in Wonderland with the white rabbit and the naughty Knave of Hearts. But on the other, there are books like *Bloody*

Horowitz (what a rude title!), which seem to delight in cruelty and bloodshed. And so we have to ask: Are there perhaps some authors who are just leaping on the band-wagon, writing books that, far from educating or enlightening, are more likely to harm a vulnerable mind?

As you will have gathered if you have read this far—and I very much hope you have—I am thinking, in particular, of horror writers.

Now don't get me wrong. I'm no fuddy-duddy. Indeed, in the past I have been described as a friend of horror or, so to speak, a bloody-buddy. But it seems to me that we are in waters that can become too easily muddy. But if I may put it simply, and in capital letters, IS HORROR GOOD FOR CHILDREN? And here is my answer: No, no, no, no, no.

It is well known that children have a much more active imagination than adults. You or I may be scared of, for example, spiders. I am so scared of finding a spider in the bath that I haven't actually had a bath for twenty-seven years. But the point is, we can live with this. Because we are adults, we know how to make the correct judgments. But let us consider the description of a spider in a book. Perhaps a spider crawling out of the eye of a rotting corpse, lingering for a moment on the white, glistening cheek before scampering forward to begin feasting on what remains of the decomposing flesh . . . That sort of description could do permanent damage to a young mind.

Films like *Beyond the Grave* and *Zombie Stranglers* come with a little letter attached to them—R—which means that they cannot be seen by anyone under seventeen. Books, unfortunately, do not have this protection. Indeed, many quite reputable publishers will make their covers as gruesome as possible to attract younger and younger children, driven only by their desire to sell books. I have to say, these people make my blood boil, and if I had my way I would sneak into their offices in the middle of the night with twenty gallons of gasoline and set the whole building ablaze. But first I would make sure that the publishers, and the writers, were tied to their chairs, unable to move, so they would be able to see the flames approaching and, in their last moments before they died in hideous agony, perhaps they would begin to regret their irresponsible behavior.

Of course, publishers would argue they are only giving children what they want. But do children know what they want? They are, after all, only children. They play computer games and they run around shouting all the time. Really, they don't know anything at all.

So I am shocked, really quite shocked, when I visit well-known bookshops and see them advertising horror stories in departments that are clearly designed to be for children. What do they think they're doing? Don't they realize there are likely to be children as young as six or seven on the premises, innocently searching for Postman Pat or Fireman Sam? And while I'm on that subject, I might mention that these books have sold millions of copies without any severed limbs, exploding eyeballs or blood jetting out of severed arteries. As far as I can recall, Postman Pat has never once been savaged by a rabid dog, while Fireman Sam has also never been called upon to give mouth-to-mouth resuscitation to a victim with hideous third-degree burns.

How do our bookshops get away with this? I think I would be perfectly justified in concealing a small meat-ax in my handbag and attacking the shop assistants, perhaps lopping off a few of their fingers or toes. That would teach them to corrupt our young people.

I would certainly like to kill Anthony Horowitz. Yes, I know that would mean no more Alex Rider books (although I'm sure Charlie Higson could be persuaded to write some if he was paid enough money), but it would also mean no more of his repellent horror stories. Now that I come to think of it, there are quite a lot of writers I would like to kill. That man who does the Goosebumps series for a start, although they're so badly written that maybe I'd let him get away with a good spanking.

And although there are many who might think I'm

being a bit extreme, maybe it would be a good idea to start murdering children too. I could stand outside the bookshop, and if I spot anyone under the age of eighteen buying a book that is not suitable for them, I could follow them home with a huge net and then throw them into a swimming pool filled with poison. In fact, I've got an even better idea. We cannot allow young brains to be corrupted. Much better to saw off the tops of their heads and scoop them out with a spoon or, alternatively, insert a fish-hook up their little noses and pull them out that way, a method used, incidentally, by the ancient Egyptians.

Kill, kill, kill, kill, kill, kill, kill, kill . . .

• • •

Professor Wendy Grooling is herself a successful children's author and a world expert on teenage literature. She is also the founder of Read This or Die, a charity that encourages young people to discover new books. This article originally appeared in *Straight Talk, Straitjackets,* the house magazine of Fairfields, the East Suffolk Maximum Security Hospital for the Criminally Insane.

THE MAN WHO KILLED DARREN SHAN

Looking back, Henry Parker could honestly say that he never wanted to hurt anyone. Certainly it never occurred to him that he would one day plan and then execute the perfect murder of an internationally well-known children's author . . . even if that was what actually happened. To begin with, all Henry wanted to do was write.

Even as a boy he had dreamed of being a writer. No, not just a writer, but an Author with a capital A— published, with a fan club, his book in every bookshop window, his photograph in the Sunday newspapers and a great pile of money in the bank. And what sort of writing was going to make his name and put that name on the front of a million books?

Henry loved horror. To him, the only good story was one that had people dying, knives cutting into flesh, brains exploding and blood dripping from every paragraph. In "Verbal Abuse," written when he was just sixteen years old and still at school, a boy was actually crucified by his Latin teacher for talking in class, while another work, "Tooth Decay," told of a Birmingham dentist being torn to shreds by one of his patients, who turned out to be a werewolf.

Having written these stories, Henry wasn't sure whom to show them to. His wealthy parents were abroad most of the time and didn't seem to have a lot of interest in their only son. He didn't really have any friends. In the end, he went to his English teacher and asked him to look at the neatly bound manuscript that he'd carried to school in his backpack.

"I'd be very grateful if you would tell me what you think, sir," he said. "Although, personally, I think they're very good."

The teacher, whose name was Mr. Harris, accepted the task with pleasure. He was always glad when any of his young students showed initiative in this way. However, after reading the pages at home, he wasn't quite so sure.

"Your work does show promise, Henry," he muttered uncomfortably. "But I have to say, I did find some of your writing a little . . . over-the-top?"

"What do you mean, sir?" Henry asked.

"Well, do you really have to be quite so explicit? This paragraph here, where the dentist's heart is pulled out and then minced. I read it after dinner and felt quite ill."

"But it's a werewolf!" Henry protested. "Werewolves enjoy mincing human organs. It's well known."

"And in this other story . . . the boy being nailed down in that way. Wouldn't it have been better to leave a little to the imagination?"

"My readers may not have any imagination," Henry replied.

"I'm sure that's not true." Mr. Harris sighed. "Have you considered writing any other genre? Romance, for example. Or perhaps a spy story?"

"I prefer horror."

"Well, I don't want to discourage you. It's very good to see you taking an interest in anything at all. But I don't think you're going to succeed unless you tone it down a little. Scaring people is one thing. Making them feel sick is quite another."

That night, Henry began a new story in which a stupid English teacher named Mr. Harris was captured by cannibals and eaten alive.

Two years went by. Inevitably, Henry wrote less as his high-school exams took over his life. He did not get brilliant results, managing only two C's and a D. His worst marks were for English Literature. In one essay he wrote five thousand words describing the murder of Duncan in Shakespeare's *Macbeth*. The woman who marked it resigned from the examinations board the very next day.

Henry didn't go to college. By the time he left school, he felt he had learned more than enough and that four more years of education would only get in the way of his becoming a world-famous author. His parents owned a large house in Reading where he could live. He was fairly sure that his father would support him while he wrote his first full-length novel. He already had the beginnings of an idea. Fame and fortune were surely only around the corner.

But then two things happened that changed everything. First, his parents died in a bizarre accident. They had gone to a circus outside Munich—Henry's mother had always been fond of trapeze artists—and they'd been having a wonderful time until the time had come for the human cannonball to perform. Something had gone wrong. Instead of being fired into the safety net, the human cannonball had been blasted, with some force, into the third row of the seats, killing Mr. and Mrs. Parker instantly.

The second disaster was that Henry discovered that

his parents had left him no money at all. In fact, it was even worse than that. In recent years, their business (in dental equipment) had taken a distinct downturn and their borrowing had grown so out of hand that their home and all their possessions had to be sold off to meet their debts. And so, at just nineteen years of age, Henry found himself broke and alone.

Somehow, he needed to earn a living. With such poor grades and no college degree, that wasn't going to be easy, but a friend of his parents took pity on him and managed to get him a job as a real estate agent. This involved showing people around properties in Battersea, in south London—and he hated it. He sneered at the other real estate agents and he was jealous of the young couples moving into houses that he himself couldn't possibly afford. He was now renting a single room that backed onto the main railway line from Victoria station.

But he still had his dream. More than that, he had the use of a desk, paper and pens, the office computer. And so, every evening, once the agency closed, he would stay behind, tapping away into the small hours. He was writing his novel. Two thousand words a night, five nights a week—Henry figured it would be finished in less than three months.

In fact, it took him eleven years.

Writing is a strange business. You write a sentence and

then you read it and one word leaps out at you. Or should that be *jumps* out at you? Or *bothers* you? And then you go over and over it and by the evening you find you haven't written two thousand words at all. You've only managed a couple of sentences and even they don't strike you as being quite right. So you start again and again, crossing out and crumpling the pages into balls, and no matter how hard you try you never quite reach the two words you're most keen to write: THE END.

That was how it was for Henry. Eleven long years of showing people around properties, working through the night and sleeping right through the weekends certainly took their toll. By the time he was thirty, he had lost most of his hair and much of his eyesight. He wore thick glasses and sat with a stooped back. A poor diet and lack of exercise had both hollowed him and drained much of the color from his skin. The honest truth was that if he had gone to a funeral, no one would have known if he was the undertaker or the corpse.

But at last he finished the novel. And reading it—while chewing on a cheese rind, which was all he had been able to find in the fridge—he knew that he had created a masterpiece. A horror novel for children, one hundred thousand words long and like nothing anyone had ever written before.

Curiously, it was the death of his parents that had inspired him. Although he had been shocked by their sudden end, and even more so by the disappearance of their wealth, Henry had never really missed them. His father had always been bad tempered and his mother too busy to look after him. But the way they had died had given him the idea of a story that would begin in a circus; not an ordinary circus, but a world inhabited by strange creatures . . . freaks.

His book was called *Ring of Evil* and it told the story of a young boy who ran away from home and got a job in the circus, only to find himself surrounded by ghosts, werewolves, witches and vampires. Henry described in loving detail how the vampires would chase members of the audience, tear their throats open and drink their blood. The hero's name was Justin and in Chapter Five he was turned into a vampire himself. He then spent Chapters Six, Seven and Eight killing people, gradually discovering that being a vampire was fun . . . certainly more fun than being a schoolboy. Eventually, Justin teamed up with the ringmaster—who was called Mephisto and who turned out to be the son of Count Dracula himself—and the two of them set off on an adventure that brought them into contact with two vampire armies fighting for control of the world.

The final chapter was set in New York and finished with the whole of Fifth Avenue turning into a river of blood. At least a thousand people were killed as the two vampire armies joined battle in the subway system. Mephisto himself was impaled on a metal spike, and Justin returned to England and took over the circus.

THE END.

Henry typed the words in bold and underlined them twice.

That evening he left the office at the same time as everyone else and bought himself a half bottle of champagne, which he sipped, on his own, in his room as the trains rumbled past outside. He had spent twenty dollars having the manuscript photocopied and bound, and he couldn't stop himself from flicking through the pages, running his hands over the cover, reading his favorite paragraphs again and again. He had absolutely no doubt that *Ring of Evil* would be a huge international success. He went to bed that night working on the speech that he would make when he won the Carnegie Medal, which was only awarded to the very greatest writers. The book was everything he had hoped it would be . . . and more.

The next day he put the manuscript in an envelope and sent it to one of the most famous publishers in London. He had noticed their name on a number of bestsellers and guessed they must know a thing or two about children's fiction. Three days later, he received a polite note, thanking him for the manuscript and assuring him that the publisher would contact him shortly. The next month was a nightmare. Henry was in a state of such nervous excitement that he couldn't eat or sleep. When he showed potential customers around houses, all he could think of was blood and vampires, book signings and VIP travel around the world. The next month was just as bad. By the third month he was beginning to wonder just how long the famous publisher needed to read one hundred thousand words.

And then the letter came.

Dear Mr. Barker . . .

It was a bad start. They hadn't even gotten his name right.

Thank you for sending us your novel, Ring of Evil. *Although your work shows a great deal of imagination and energy, I regret to say that I do not think it is suitable for publication.*

You say that this is a work for children, but I would be very concerned, personally, by the levels of violence and bloodshed. I think you would find that most teachers and librarians would not want this on their shelves. At the same time, the book is clearly not adult enough—particularly with a hero who is only twelve.

I'm afraid, therefore, that I am returning the man-

uscript. I hope you won't be too discouraged and wish
you luck elsewhere.

Yours sincerely,
Hilary Spurling
Senior Editor

Henry read the letter once. Then he read it again. He felt
a rush of different emotions. The first was disbelief. *Ring*
of Evil had been rejected! That was followed by dismay.
All those hours of work, the weeks and the months—for
nothing! Then came anger. Who was Hilary Spurling?
What did she know? How could she be so shallow and ar-
rogant, to dismiss his one-hundred-thousand-word manuscript with a letter that didn't even reach a dozen lines?
Muttering a curse, Henry reached for a second envelope.
There were plenty of publishers in London. A few weeks
from now, Hilary Spurling would be weeping bitter tears.
And she would be a senior editor no longer, fired from her
job for missing the biggest bestseller of the decade when it
had been sitting right there in her hands.

In the next twelve months, *Ring of Evil* was rejected by
another eight London publishers as well as three literary
agents. By now, Henry had left the real estate agency. Everyone in the office knew that he'd been writing a novel
and he couldn't bear to tell them that he hadn't managed
to sell it. He got a job in a warehouse in Shoreditch, sup-

plying chemicals to laboratories around London. There was no computer here for him to work on after hours. Nor did he want one. If his first book—his masterpiece— wasn't going to be published, why should he even think about writing a second?

And that might have been the end of it. Henry could have ended his days bitter and defeated, unhappy, un- married and alone. Perhaps he'd have been found in the corner of his local pub, propping up the bar with one whiskey too many, dreaming of what might have been. He could have worked at the warehouse until he retired and then, after a couple of years in a dreary old people's home, quietly died.

But everything changed one day when he walked into a bookshop near Victoria station. He hadn't even gone in there to buy a book. He had just needed somewhere to shelter from a sudden violent storm. But while he was in- side, waiting for the rain to die down, his eye was caught by a pile of books on the front table. He picked one up. The book was called *Cirque du Freak* and it was written by someone named Darren Shan.

The back cover told him everything he needed to know. The hero was a boy named Darren Shan—it was strange that he had the same name as the author—who snuck away from home to visit a traveling freak show. Henry flicked through the pages. The book struck him as very short. Every chapter was topped with a picture of a skull. Before he had even left the shop, he had the general idea of the story. Darren Shan's best friend got bitten by a spider, and in order to save him, Darren had to become a vampire and . . .

It was his story! There could be no doubt about it. Of course, not all the ideas were the same. But the circus, the freaks, the vampires, the child hero, even some of the names were too similar to be pure coincidence. For example, there was a character named Mr. Crepsley in Shan's book—almost the same name as one of the clowns (Mr. Crispy) in Henry's. Shan's best friend was named Steve. In *Ring of Evil* a character named Steve was murdered in Chapter Twenty-seven. Henry looked at the cover. As he gazed at the name of the publisher, a black fury rose up within him. The same publisher had turned *Ring of Evil* down.

He bought the book and took it home and that night he spent several hours reading *Cirque du Freak*, underlining passages in red and circling words. As the sun rose, he was one hundred percent certain. The publisher had taken his manuscript and given it to another author. This author, Darren Shan, had copied the best bits and published the book as his own. He had stolen the result of eleven years' work!

And to make things worse, Shan was getting brilliant

reviews. The next day Henry called in to say he would be late for work. He scuttled off to an Internet café down the road and Googled everything he could about *Cirque du Freak*. The critics were unanimous. Here was a well-crafted and completely original story that would attract even the most unwilling readers. There were another fourteen volumes planned and publishers were snapping them up all around the world. A major Hollywood film was on the way. Overnight, Darren Shan had become a star.

Henry went straight back to his room, sat down and composed a letter, writing with a pen that kept leaking ink, in jagged handwriting that lay on the page like dead spiders.

Dear Mr. Shan, he began.

> *I have just read your book "Cirque du Freak" and have noticed many similarities to a book of mine, "Ring of Evil." My book is set in a circus, just like yours. My book has vampires in it, just like yours. My book also has a boy hero who is only two years younger than yours. I could also point to several phrases in your book which also appear in mine. For example, on page 33, you say "It was Friday evening, the end of the school week . . ." Almost exactly the same words— though in a different order—appear on page 297 of my manuscript! Again, on page 124, you describe your*

teeth as "clattering." That description is obviously
taken from page 311 of my book, which describes window shutters in exactly the same way.

I could give you a hundred more examples.

I would like to know who it was at your publisher
who showed you my manuscript and whose idea it
was to steal it and make it your own. We will discuss
how much money you should pay me later.

Yours sincerely,
Henry Parker

It took three weeks for Henry to receive a reply, and when
it came, it wasn't from Darren Shan at all. It was from
someone called Fenella Jones who worked at the publishing house. It read:

Dear Mr. Parker,

Thank you for your letter. I can assure you that
Cirque du Freak is a completely original piece of
work. Mr. Shan wrote it without any discussion with
us and we are very proud to have published it.

I am sorry if you feel that there are similarities to
your own book.

With best wishes,
Fenella Jones
Editorial Assistant

And that was it. No apology. No explanation. No promise of money. Just a few lines dismissing him as if he would simply crawl away and forget the whole thing.

Over the next six months, Henry wrote nine more letters, and when *The Vampire's Assistant*, the second book in the series, was published and was even more successful than the first, he wrote eleven more. He got no reply to any of them. It seemed that Darren Shan and his publishers had decided to pretend he didn't exist.

As The Saga of Darren Shan grew and became ever more popular, Henry bought all the books and went through them, not once but several times, making notes in a pile of notebooks that he kept by his bed. Of course, it was easy enough to convince himself that certain words and phrases had been copied from him, and even when the saga went off in a completely different direction from his own *Ring of Evil*, he was able to convince himself that Shan had changed his plans because he was afraid of being sued. Or maybe he was stealing his ideas now from somebody else.

At the same time, Henry began to collect as much information as he could about Darren Shan. He learned that the writer was surprisingly young and lived in Ireland. He cut out pictures of him from newspapers. Shan was short and stocky with a face that was as round as a pumpkin and closely cut hair. Henry thought he looked more like a soccer player than a professional author. It seemed he had once worked as a teacher. He visited Shan's website and began to follow his progress through Britain and around the world. It soon became clear that there wasn't a country on the planet where the books weren't doing well. And all the time he could feel a jealousy, like a cancer, creeping through him. *Cirque du Freak* was *his* book. It was *his* idea. He should have been the one enjoying the fame, the wealth, the jet-setting life.

Henry would never be able to remember the exact moment that he decided to murder Darren Shan. It wasn't an idea that simply arrived, a sudden inspiration. It was more like a growing awareness that murder was the only answer. He wanted to punish the successful writer. But more than that, he needed to get rid of him, to stop him from existing. As far as he could see, it was the only way to allow his own life to continue. Without Shan, there would be no more *Cirque du Freak*. And then, just possibly, there might be room for *Ring of Evil*. But the truth was, Henry no longer cared if his own novel was published or not. He had fallen into a quicksand of hatred and despair. He wanted to lash out one last time before he was sucked under completely.

But how to do it?

Shan made occasional appearances in London, where he would sign books for long lines of his devoted readers.

It would be easy enough to join the line with some sharp implement concealed beneath his jacket. That would be appropriate. There was plenty of blood in Shan's books already. Henry would add a few pints more.

But despite everything, he didn't want to go to prison. It wouldn't be fair. After all, he was the victim here and he would only be giving Shan what he deserved. And he certainly didn't want to spend the rest of his life surrounded by common criminals. Henry thought about it and decided. He was an artist. He would use his talents to commit the perfect murder. And one day, maybe, he would write about it. Yes. He would have to change a few names and places, but killing Darren Shan might actually make a good subject for a book.

It wasn't going to be easy. Henry had to kill someone he had never met before and probably never would meet. He had to do it from a distance. Almost at once an idea began to take shape in his mind.

Like many successful authors, Shan received fan letters and mentioned on his website that he tried to reply to as many as possible. Henry had already written to him once and had received a reply from some editorial assistant. But suppose he were to write again, pretending to be a twelve-year-old boy? Shan would have to write back. And that would be it. It would be easy. Nobody would ever be able to pin anything on him.

The very next day, Henry stole a pair of rubber gloves from work—the sort used to protect workers' hands from dangerous chemicals. He would need them to make sure he didn't leave any fingerprints. He bought a cheap pen and some writing paper—choosing a common brand. Then he sat down and composed his letter.

Dear Mr. Shan, he began. He was careful to disguise his writing. He used large, looping letters to make it look as if the letter had been written by a young boy.

> *I am a huge fan of your work. I think you are a great writer. I have read all your books but my favorite was* Vampire Mountain, *which I thought was briliant.*

He misspelled *brilliant* on purpose. He was meant to be a schoolboy.

> *I would be very grateful if you could send me an autograph. I know you are busy so I am enclosing a stamped, addressed envelope. Right now I am in a hospital and the doctors are very worried about me. So your autograph means a lot to me. Please send it soon.*

> > *Yours sincerely,*
> > *Steve Lyons*

• • •

The fake name was based on the character Steve Leopard that he had read in Shan's book. He was particularly pleased with the lie about being in a hospital. It made it doubly certain that he would get a response. But the most briliant—or *brilliant*—part came next. With his work in the Shoreditch warehouse, Henry regularly came into contact with poisons and dangerous chemicals. It wasn't all that difficult to steal a small vial of liquid that was colorless, odorless and totally lethal. He mixed this with glue, then, using a paintbrush, applied it to the inside flap of an envelope that he addressed to Steve Lyons at a false address in Brighton.

The trap was simple. Shan would read the letter asking for his autograph. He would sign his name on a card and slip it into the stamped, addressed envelope. And when he licked it, he would seal his fate. Henry reckoned he would be dead before he reached the nearest mailbox, and with a bit of luck the police wouldn't even be able to work out how the poison had been administered.

Finally, just to be on the safe side, Henry took a train to Brighton and mailed the deadly letter from there. With no fingerprints, a false name and no giveaway postmark on the stamp, he was confident that nobody would ever trace the letter back to him.

He sat back and waited. The next few days passed with a sense of continual excitement . . . almost, in fact, like reading a good book. Every evening he hurried home to his single room to catch the six o'clock news on his television, the picture flickering each time a train went past. He couldn't wait to hear it . . . "And after the break, the children's author who took a tumble. Darren Shan's painful end . . ."

But in fact it was the newspapers that gave him the story he most wanted to hear. It was as he was leaving the warehouse, on his way to Shoreditch station, that he saw the words in bold type, hanging on the side of the kiosk.

CHILDREN'S AUTHOR MURDERED

Just three words—but it was the most brilliant sentence Henry had ever read. He fumbled in his pocket for cash and bought the paper, and there it was, on the front page.

POLICE SUSPECT "POISON PEN LETTER"

Darren Shan, the moderately popular children's author, died shortly after being admitted to a hospital this morning. Shan, 38, had been answering his fan mail when he was suddenly taken ill. His assistant, Fenella Jones, called an ambulance, but despite their best efforts, paramedics were unable to revive him.

Shan, whose Cirque du Freak series topped bestseller lists all over the world, was in the middle of a second series known as The Demonata, and fans have already begun a candlelit vigil outside his Limerick home. At first it was believed that he had succumbed to an attack of food poisoning, but police are now examining mail that he received in the morning post. Detective Superintendent John Dervish said, "It is possible that Mr. Shan was the victim of a fan—or a madman pretending to be a fan. At the moment we are looking at every possibility."

The story went on over the page and there was a picture of Shan signing books, surrounded by children. Henry read the article with a mixture of emotions. Of course, he was delighted that his plan had succeeded. But at the same time he was a little nervous that the police had arrived so quickly at the murder method . . . the poison pen letter, as the newspaper had put it. In a way, he was glad—he wanted the world to know that the writer had been punished, not just struck down by a piece of bad chicken or fish. But if they had found out this much, this quickly, might their investigation lead them to him? No. Neither the paper nor the envelope could be traced to him. The letter had been postmarked in Brighton, miles away. He had been careful to avoid leaving fingerprints. And even the poison that he had used was fairly common. There were plenty of people who could have gotten hold of it.

Henry watched the six o'clock news with a sense of growing confidence. He watched the news again at ten o'clock and eleven o'clock, and each time the report was the same. The death of the young writer was a tragedy. The police were looking into it. But so far they had no clues, nothing to report.

Henry went to bed that night fairly certain that he had gotten away with it. It didn't even occur to him that he had taken a human life, that he would have left behind a grieving family . . . not to mention several thousand fans. As far as he was concerned, what he had done had been well executed. Nothing more, nothing less. It was as if the murder was a story that he had plotted, one with a happy ending.

It was by now the end of November and the weather had recently turned cold. There was only one radiator in Henry's room, and although it was turned on full, it never seemed to give out much heat. The window frame was cracked and there were some nights when the wood rattled and cold breezes danced around the room. This was just such a night. More than that, a mist seemed to have risen around Victoria. There was a full moon but it seemed pale and yellow, unable to penetrate through the clouds.

Henry tried to sleep but he couldn't. Though he pulled the duvet over his head, the chill still got in. He could feel it around his neck, creeping down his spine. His room was always a little damp, but tonight he could almost see the moisture glistening on the walls. He was annoyed with himself. This was supposed to be his night of triumph. Maybe he should have gone out and bought himself a drink . . . or several. He had committed murder and gotten away with it! Surely that was something to celebrate.

"Henry . . ."

The voice came as a whisper out of the darkness. He had dreamed it, of course. It was a ghost voice, like something out of a horror film, rising up from a swamp or out of a ruined castle. Only, how could he have dreamed it when he wasn't yet asleep?

"Henry . . ." The whisper came again, louder this time and filled with venom.

Henry hunched himself up in bed, drawing his knees into his chest, looking around him. There was a strange green glow outside his window. His room looked out onto a strip of wasteland with the railway just beyond.

Normally, he could see walls covered with graffiti and topped with broken glass and barbed wire. But the mist had grown thicker. It had smothered the outside world. And as he watched, wide-eyed, he saw it trickling under his door, filling the very room where he lay.

"Who is it?" he whimpered.

The door crashed open. It seemed to have torn itself out of the frame, for there was nobody on the other side. More mist rolled in and Henry smelled something thick and horrible, like rotten, decaying meat. At the same time, he heard footsteps echoing along the corridor. He wondered what had happened to his landlady. She had a room on the floor above and must surely have heard all this. He tried to call out her name, but his throat seized up. He was petrified. No words came.

A figure formed in the half-light, then stepped into the room. Henry stared. He raised a hand, the fingers twisted as if broken, like an animal claw. He knew what he was was seeing. He couldn't believe it. But he had to accept it.

Darren Shan had come for him.

The children's writer had been dead for at least twenty-four hours. His skin was a hideous shade of white—it was obvious that not a drop of blood was being pumped through his veins. His eyes were also white and lifeless, as if covered in cataracts. At some time, blood must have gushed out of his mouth and over his chin, for it was still there, dried now, a hideous dark brown stain. His clothes were stiff with it. He was wearing a strange nightgown, but Henry recognized what it was. A shroud. He would have been wearing it in his coffin.

How could this be happening? Henry was trembling so hard, he was making the bed shake. Tears of sheer terror trickled down the side of his face. At the same time, a terrible thought was working its way through his mind. Darren Shan was a horror writer. In *Cirque du Freak* he had even claimed he was a semi-vampire. Well, suppose it was true. Suppose he was in some way in touch with dark forces, with the ghosts and the monsters that inspired him? Shan was dead. Henry had seen it on the television and read it in the newspapers. And now he had come back from the grave, continuing his life's work even after that life had ended.

"You killed me," the creature rasped, its voice rattling in its throat. And as it spoke, Henry saw that its tongue had gone green and there was some dark-colored liquid dribbling over its lower lip.

"No!" Henry replied. He wiped away his tears, but more instantly followed. "How did you find me?" he whimpered. "How did you get here?"

"You wrote to me." Darren Shan shuddered. "You made me reply. And when I licked the envelope . . . the pain! It was you, Henry Parker."

"Go away! Just go away!" Henry closed his eyes, hoping this was just some sort of hallucination. But when he opened them again, Shan was still there. "You stole my idea!" he screeched. He couldn't help himself. And at the same time, he had a sudden, crazy thought. This could hardly be better. He had spent months and months waiting to tell Darren Shan what he thought of him. Well, now Shan had returned from the grave to hear it. What was he going to do about it? He was a phantom! If he wanted to contact the police, he'd have to do it with a Ouija board.

"You stole *Ring of Evil* from me. I sent it to your publisher and they gave it to you. You took my story and my characters and you made millions of dollars, and I got nothing. Well, now I've shown you. I came up with the perfect murder. Yours! And soon you'll be forgotten, but I'll write another book and nothing will stop me . . ."

"You killed me!" Shan wailed.

"Yes. I did. It was so easy. A little potassium cyanide mixed with the glue on the envelope. And you were such an idiot, you fell for it. I'd love to have been there when you licked it. You thought you were writing to some sick kid who loved your books, but in fact it was me."

Henry began to laugh. He was still laughing when the lights in his bedroom flashed on and half a dozen policemen ran in and dragged him out of bed.

"Thank you very much, Mr. Shan," one of the policemen said.

"It was my pleasure," Darren Shan replied.

It was only then that Henry saw what should have been obvious all along. He had been tricked. Darren Shan was very much alive. Somebody had given him some clever makeup, turning his skin white. There was red dye in his mouth and he was wearing contact lenses. The smoke and the sewage smell were being pumped into the room by a machine just outside the door. And Shan was holding a tape recorder. There was a microphone attached to his shroud. Everything that Henry had said had been recorded and would be used against him when he went on trial.

"No!" Henry howled as he was bundled out of the room and down the stairs. It wasn't fair! His plan had been perfect. What could possibly have gone wrong?

They answered that question when they interviewed him at Paddington Green police station. He was interviewed by two grim-faced detectives. The man in charge was named Jack Grest. He was a big man stuffed into an ill-fitting suit.

"You might like to know," he muttered, "that my son is a big fan of Darren Shan. He's got all his books. I don't know how I'd have been able to break it to the little lad if you'd murdered his hero."

"I—I don't understand," Henry stammered. He was crying again, still unable to accept what had happened. "How did you find me? What went wrong?"

"I'll answer that, you swine," the other detective said. "Mr. Shan has an assistant who helps him with his fan mail. Her name was Fenella Jones and she was the one who licked the envelope you sent."

"She was the one you murdered," Grest continued.

"But how did you know it was me?"

"We didn't. You covered your tracks well. But the thing is, publishers keep copies of all the crank letters they receive, and they had your name on file. You had every reason to want to harm Mr. Shan—even though he never copied a word of your ridiculous book. And when we found out you were working in a chemical warehouse—"

"But you still didn't have any proof!"

"That's right. Which is why we planted the news story and asked Mr. Shan to help us with that little charade. We knew you'd confess to everything if he walked into your room in the middle of the night dressed up like that. And it worked! You were a complete idiot to fall for it and now you're going to have plenty of time to think about how stupid you've been."

He *had* been stupid.

Henry realized that, sitting on his own in a maximum-security cell in the middle of the night. He had a bunk, a blanket and a toilet built into the wall. He was still wearing the robe and pajamas that he had been arrested in, although they had taken away the cords. He had been very, very stupid indeed.

How could he possibly have believed, even for one minute, that Darren Shan was a ghost? Henry was a writer! He knew, better than anyone, that ghosts didn't exist. They were made up by people like him, simply to scare the people who read the books. Horror stories were nothing more than that . . . stories! He had been caught by surprise and had allowed his own imagination to get the better of him. An Irish writer covered in white paint had outwitted him. He should never have allowed it to happen.

There were no such things as ghosts. Or vampires. Cirque du Freak, indeed! Cirque du Complete Nonsense.

It was very cold in the cell.

In fact, it seemed to have grown colder and colder in the last few minutes. Henry looked at the door and saw, to his astonishment, that a thin white mist was seeping in, spreading across the floor. And that horrible smell was back. Rotting meat and damp graveyard soil. It was one of the policemen! They had turned on their wretched machine again to frighten him.

"Go away!" he shouted.

His breath frosted around his mouth.

And then something formed in front of him. It didn't walk in as Darren Shan had done. It seemed to piece itself out of the half-light, the molecules rushing together in the middle of the room. The figure solidified. It was a woman, hideous beyond belief, her face distorted by pain, her eyes bulging out of their sockets, her mouth twisted in a death's-head smile. She was short and muscular and her hands, stretching out in front of her, seemed too big for her arms.

This wasn't a trick. This was real. Henry knew.

"Who are you?" he whimpered.

The woman reached out for him. Her fingers clamped down on his shoulders, holding him in place. "Who do you think I am?" she replied, and he smelled the poison on her breath. "I'm Fenella Jones."

Her teeth closed in on his throat.

BET YOUR LIFE

It was the last night, the grand finale of the quiz show that for three months had, in the words of the *TV Times*, "gripped the hearts, the minds . . . and the throats of the nation." Thirty-three million people had watched the semifinal in Great Britain. Even the funeral of Princess Diana had attracted fewer spectators.

"There has never been a program like *Bet Your Life*," the *TV Times* had continued. "Forget *X Factor*. Forget *Big Brother*. This is reality TV taken to new limits, smashing through the barriers, thrilling audiences in a way that they have never been thrilled before."

It was filmed at Pinewood Studios near Iver, northwest of London, and security guards had taken up their positions twenty-four hours before, hundreds of them armed with sunglasses, walkie-talkies and canisters of pepper spray to keep back any unruly fans. The program would be seen in thirty-seven countries. But the studio was only big enough to hold a live audience of four hundred people, and competition for tickets had been intense. One ticket had changed hands on eBay for ten thousand dollars. A multimillionaire in Orpington had offered double that sum in an advertisement he had placed in the national press.

As the sun began to set and seven o'clock approached, helicopters buzzed over the studios, huge spotlights were wheeled into place, the world's press corps made final checks in their mobile broadcasting units and two thousand people gathered around the giant plasma screen that had been erected outside to allow them to watch the show live.

Inside the studio, in his makeup room, Danny Webster was feeling surprisingly calm. At sixteen, he was the youngest ever contestant, but even so, one or two of the bookies had made him a favorite to win. He was sitting in front of a mirror, looking at his own face, as a makeup girl dusted his forehead with powder to stop the sweat showing in the hot lights.

With his long brown hair, blue eyes and still very boyish face, Danny was unusually good-looking, and all the newspapers agreed that, if he won, he would certainly have a career in TV, either as an actor or as a presenter. But that, of course, was only the secondary prize. Danny tried not to think of the black attaché case containing ten million dollars' worth of diamonds that would be presented to the winner in less than two hours' time, by far the biggest prize in television history.

Danny had always been good at general knowledge. In fact, it was rather more than that. From the earliest age he had demonstrated a photographic memory. He had been able to speak fluently before he was two. He had won a scholarship to a private school and had sailed through all his exams. Although he had never been strong at creative thinking or writing, subjects that essentially required a grasp of facts—biology, physics, geography, math—had come easily to him and he had scored effortless A's throughout.

It had been his father's idea to enter him onto *Bet Your Life* when, for the first time, the entry age had been lowered to sixteen. Gary Webster had been a postman until a back injury put him out of work. Since then, he had lived on benefits, punctuating the day with visits to the pub and the betting shop. His wife, Nora, worked as an office cleaner, but this only brought in a small amount of money. The three of them lived in a cramped, unattractive apartment in a high-rise block in Notting Hill Gate. A prize of ten million dollars would completely transform their lives.

Gary had used a mixture of threats and promises to

persuade his son to put his name forward. The trouble was that Danny was quite shy and didn't like the idea of seeing his name and photograph splashed across the world's newspapers. And there had, of course, been the fear of losing. But in the end, he had agreed. He was a quiet, rather friendless boy. Perhaps his astonishing brainpower, his instant recall, had put other kids off. He didn't like his school very much and, like his parents, he dreamed of a new life. His father spoke of a house on the Isle of Wight. The money would make that possible . . . and more. For his part, Danny wanted to go to Cambridge *(Britain's second oldest university, founded in 1209).* He dreamed of becoming a librarian, perhaps in the British Library *(designer: Sir Colin St. John Wilson)* itself. He would read—and remember—a million books. And maybe one day he would compile an encyclopedia, a compendium of everything he had learned.

How many people stood between him and his ambition?

To begin with, there had been thirty-five of them. Now just four remained. There was a copy of the *TV Times* lying in front of the mirror and Danny flicked it open. "Know your enemy," as the ancient Chinese warrior Sun Tzu had written in his great book, *The Art of War (sixth century B.C.).* And there they were. Each one of them had two full pages, with a color picture on one side and background details on the other.

RICHARD VERDI (44). He was the man that Danny most feared. Round-headed and bald apart from a narrow strip of black hair around his ears, always wearing black-rimmed spectacles, he was a professor of history at Edinburgh University. He was very serious, completely focused. Nothing ever rattled him. Most of the bookies had made him the favorite to win.

RAIFE PLANT (30). The newspapers loved Raife. He was a thin, curly-haired man with a roguish, handsome face despite his broken nose and crooked teeth. Raife had been sentenced to twelve years in jail for armed robbery. The trouble for Danny was that he had spent that time taking an Open University degree and reading hundreds of books. He was a huge fount of knowledge and—with his unconventional background—he was definitely the housewives' choice.

MARY ROBINSON (49). The oldest contestant, and the only female, was a computer programmer from Woking. Her photograph showed a slim, unsmiling woman with dark hair swept back and very simple gold earrings. Nobody was quite sure how Mary had amassed her astonishing general knowledge. She gave away very little about herself, although she had let it be known that, if she won, she wanted to become a man.

BEN OSMOND (27). Ben was the only contestant that Danny actually liked. They had met during the audition process and had struck up a sort of friendship. Ben's grandparents had come from the West Indies and from them he had inherited a sunny, easygoing manner, treating the quiz—like the rest of life—as a bit of a joke. He had written poetry, climbed mountains, studied in a Tibetan monastery and campaigned for animal rights. Now he was doing this. He seemed to be enjoying it.

Just four faces left. Five, including his. Danny thought about all the contestants he had met along the way. There had been Gerald, the fat, jolly headmaster from Brighton. Abdul, the taxi driver who had been so certain he would win. Clive in his wheelchair, hoping to claw something back in a life that had been wrecked by a car accident.

Susan, who had complained when she had been asked to share a makeup room. So many different people. But they had all gone now.

And in a couple of hours, there would only be one left.

There was a knock at the door and the soundman came in with the little microphone that he would clip to the collar of Danny's shirt. Danny had chosen jeans and a simple open-neck shirt for the final, although he had been told that the other contestants had been offered thousands of dollars to wear—and promote—designer labels. He had briefly considered it himself, but he felt comfortable in his own clothes and that was important. Staying relaxed was half the battle.

"How are you feeling?" The soundman was cheerful as he slid the microphone into place. Theoretically, the technicians weren't meant to talk to the contestants, but Ed didn't seem to care about the rules.

"I'm okay."

"Good luck. I'll be rooting for you."

The makeup girl left with the soundman, and for the next twenty minutes Danny was on his own. He knew he was nervous. He could feel his heart beating. It was hard to swallow. There was a tingling feeling in the palms of his hands. He forced himself to empty his mind and stay calm. A certain amount of nervousness was perfectly understandable. He just had to control it. That was all. He couldn't let it knock him off course.

At last the floor manager arrived. She was a big, smiling woman in her twenties, always carrying a clipboard and with a large microphone curving around her neck.

"We're ready for you!" she said cheerfully.

Danny stood up.

He hadn't let his parents wait with him. They were even more nervous than he was and he hadn't wanted to be distracted. He knew that he wouldn't see the other contestants as he made his way to the set. The studio had been specially designed that way. Just for a moment, he felt very alone, following the woman down a tatty, cream-painted corridor with neon lights flickering overhead. It was more like a hospital than a television studio, he thought. Perhaps that was deliberate too.

But then they turned a corner and went through a set of double doors. On the other side, everything was dark and Danny could make out the great bulk of a wall, made of wood, hammered together almost haphazardly. There were cables trailing everywhere, fastened to the floor with lengths of duct tape. He knew he was looking at the back of the set. Through the cracks, he could make out the studio lights. The floor manager rested a hand on his arm.

"Ten seconds," she said.

The familiar music began. Danny had heard it a hundred times, playing at the start of the show. Although, of course, it had never come up as a question, he knew that it was an adaptation of a piece by Wagner (*the German composer born in Leipzig on May 22, 1813, and who died in 1883*). The music stopped. There was a round of applause. Danny felt a hand tap him on the shoulder and he moved forward, into the light.

And there was the set of *Bet Your Life*, with five metal lecterns arranged in a semicircle around a central control panel—looking like something out of a spaceship—where the question master would take his place. The lecterns could have been designed for a politician or a lecturer to stand behind when giving a speech. Each one stood on a low, square platform and came up to the contestant's waist, with a television monitor built into the surface. Every question was written out as well as spoken and the screens would also be used if there was a picture round. The lecterns were black, and polished so that they reflected the studio audience sitting in long rows, facing them. They looked somehow dangerous—but of course, that was the whole idea.

On one side of the stage, there was a giant television screen. On the other, a strangely old-fashioned clock face would count down from fifteen to zero. Inside the zero was a cartoon of a human skull.

Danny had already been told which platform was

his. The numbers had been drawn the evening before so that nobody would have a psychological advantage. Raife Plant was number one. Richard Verdi was two. Mary Robinson was three. Ben Osmond was four. Danny was on the edge at number five. He was glad to have Ben next to him. He had studied recordings of the other contestants, trying to find out as much as he could about them, the way they played the game. The professor and the computer programmer had been the most worrying. He had been struck by how grim and professional they were. Raife Plant, with his easy smile, seemed somehow untrustworthy. He would feel less intimidated next to Ben, who was, after all, the closest in age to himself.

All five of them were appearing at the same time, walking in through separate entrances, dazzled by the studio lights that formed a barrier between them and the audience. Danny could just make out the security guards in their silver *BYL* anoraks. There were half a dozen of them, huge men, standing with their backs to the stage, their arms crossed, their job being to make sure that nobody came close. The Wagner was playing, pounding out of a bank of speakers. Danny could sense the tension in the air. He could smell it. The heat of the lights was unforgiving, sucking out all the emotions of the crowd and keeping it trapped in the closed, windowless place.

He reached his platform and climbed onto it. At once,

one of the floor managers—a young man in a black T-shirt—came forward and shackled his ankles into place. Now he couldn't move. He would be forced to stand in front of the lectern until the game, or his part in it, was over. In the beginning, this had worried him. Now he was used to it. He moved one foot and felt the steel chain jangle against his shin. The other four contestants had been locked in place, just like him. He didn't look at them. He didn't want to meet their eyes.

The music changed. A circular trapdoor had slid open in the middle of the stage and clouds of white dry ice were pouring out. As the audience increased their applause, many of them whistling and cheering, a figure rose up from below, carried by a hydraulic lift. He was dressed, as always, in a black suit with a black shirt and a silver tie. His black hair was slicked back and his black beard neatly trimmed. Against all this, his skin was unnaturally pale. His teeth, a perfect white, seemed almost electric. Wayne Howard, the host of the show, had arrived.

"Good evening, ladies and gentlemen," he began when the applause had finally died down. "And welcome to the final episode of the most dramatic, the most exciting quiz show on TV. The five men and women who stand before you tonight have completed an epic journey, but only one of them can walk away with the biggest prize ever offered by any television program anywhere in the world. And just to remind you what it is, let's take a look. Ten million dollars in diamonds. Bridget . . . bring them on!"

A blond-haired woman, dressed only in a silver bikini with thigh-high boots, walked out of the wings carrying a simple leather attaché case. She stopped next to Wayne and opened it. As one, the audience rose to their feet. The diamonds seemed to catch the light and magnify it a thousand times so it was as if Bridget had opened a portal into another world. There they were. A scattering of stones, each one a different cut and a different size, glittering brilliantly on a cushion of dark velvet.

"These stones can be carried anywhere in the world," Wayne explained. He had said the same many times before. "They can be spent anywhere. And tonight, one person is going to walk out of this studio carrying them. Will it be Mary, who hopes very soon to change her name to Melvyn? Will it be Richard, whose career as a professor could soon be history? Will it be our poet and friend of the animals, Ben? Or how about Raife? We know he's gone straight. But is he going straight to the diamonds? And finally, there's Danny, our youngest contestant, just starting in eleventh grade. Could he be the one? It's time to find out on . . . *Bet Your Life*!"

More music. Searchlights sweeping back and forth. Wayne Howard took his place behind the central control desk, facing the contestants. The quiz began.

The format was actually very simple. Each round was a series of questions on a specialist subject randomly generated by a computer and fed to Wayne. Each contestant had fifteen seconds to answer, and if they didn't know, they had three lifelines. The first of these was a "pass," which meant that their question was passed on to the person standing next to them. One was a "second chance," which they could play once the question had been asked. It meant that if they guessed incorrectly, they could try again. The last was called "toss of the coin," where they would be fed two possible answers and would have to choose between them.

Wayne reached out and pressed a button on the console. The single word SCIENCE came up on a giant screen above the stage. Danny smiled to himself. Science was one of his favorite subjects. It was a promising start.

"And the first question is for Raife," the quizmaster exclaimed. "What chemical with the symbol NaCl is found in the sea and in the kitchen?"

Danny knew the answer to that one. It was sodium chloride—or common salt. Unfortunately, Raife knew it too. But that was hardly surprising. All the questions in the first round were deliberately simple. They would become harder as the evening went on. Sure enough, all five contestants answered their questions on science without any trouble.

The next round, ENTERTAINMENT, passed without much incident, but in the one after—POLITICS—there was a moment of drama when Ben had to use his pass. He had been asked who became president of the United States in 1969, and for some reason he couldn't think. The same question went to Danny, who suddenly found himself sweating as the hand of the clock began its journey. He had just fifteen seconds to find the answer, the time pressure making it all the more difficult. Thinking on his feet, he decided to play his second chance lifeline. And it was just as well he did. His first attempt, John F. Kennedy, was wrong, but that didn't mean he was eliminated. With four seconds left, he remembered the correct answer. Richard Nixon. His mouth was so dry by then that he had to force himself to spit out the words.

Richard Verdi had a bad round with FOOD AND DRINK, using his own second chance to answer the question "What alcohol is used as the basis of a *mojito*?" The answer, which he got right the second time, was light rum. He also had to use a pass in the next round, WILD ANIMALS, so that after fifteen minutes (and the first advertising break) he was looking distinctly rattled. Danny noticed that so far the computer programmer hadn't so much as hesitated. She could have been reading the answers straight out of a book.

The first upset came in the next round—FAMOUS FILMS.

It was Raife Plant who was asked the question "Who had the title role in the 1931 film of *Frankenstein*?" And with a trademark wink and a grin, he answered immediately: "Boris Karloff."

There was a long pause. Then Wayne Howard shook his head and at once the audience broke into a mixture of gasps and whispers. It was the wrong answer! Danny realized at once what had happened. This was one of the traps that the quiz program was famous for. It was absolutely true that Boris Karloff had starred in the film as the monster created by a mad inventor. But the film had been named after the inventor, Dr. Henry Frankenstein, not the monster, which actually had no name at all. And he had been played by a much less well-known actor named Colin Clive.

"I'm sorry, Raife," Wayne said. He reached down.

Behind him, the audience began a chant, as they always did. "Go, go, go, go, go . . ." Wayne brought out a submachine gun. It glimmered in the spotlights as he checked that it was loaded. Then he rested it against his shoulder and fired a hundred rounds into the unfortunate contestant.

Danny could only watch in silent horror. Raife, chained to his lectern, seemed to be trying to leave the stage in six directions at once. He was almost torn in half, blood splattering everywhere. The noise of the bullets was horrendous. The stench of gunpowder filled Danny's nostrils and throat. At last it was over. The audience shouted and clapped its approval. Raife slumped forward, his hands hanging down. Silently, his lectern was lowered out of sight, carrying the corpse with it.

So now there were just four left.

Forcing himself to turn his attention away from the square opening in the stage—Raife Plant's grave—Danny searched for his mother and father in the audience. They had been given VIP places in the front row. Gary Webster was trying to smile, feebly waving a hand at his son. It looked as if his mother had been sick. She was slumped in the seat next to him. Her face was pale.

Richard Verdi answered the next question correctly. So did Mary Robinson. When it came to Ben Osmond's turn, he seemed rattled after what had just happened and hesitated—"What was the name of the character played by Ian McKellen in the three *X-Men* films?"—and only came up with the right answer, Magneto, with seconds left.

Danny liked films, but he was forced to use his precious pass when his turn came. "Who directed the original version of *The Italian Job*?" In the back of his mind he knew—somehow—that the remake had been made by someone named F. Gary Gray. But the original had been shot in 1969, almost thirty years before he had been born. The question went to Richard Verdi.

And with a thrill, Danny realized that the history professor also wasn't sure. He could, of course, have passed the question on to Mary Robinson, but he had already used his pass in the WILD ANIMALS round. Would he use his last lifeline, toss of the coin? Danny glanced his way and saw the beads of sweat on the bald man's head.

"I need an answer," Wayne Howard said.

The clock was ticking. Five . . . four . . . three . . . two . . .

"It was Robert Collinson!" the professor exclaimed at the last second.

There was another pause. Pauses were what everyone feared.

"I'm sorry," Wayne Howard said. "The correct answer is *Peter* Collinson."

"Go, go, go, go, go," the audience began.

"But that's not—" Verdi began.

He never finished the sentence. Wayne Howard flicked a switch on his console and twenty thousand volts of electricity coursed through the leg irons and also through the man who was connected to them. In less than five seconds, Richard Verdi was carbonized. Flames burst out of his ears and eyes. There was a terrible smell of burning meat. Then he crumpled and disappeared behind his lectern. Once again the stage opened and swallowed him up. The audience was cheering. Two women in the back row were holding up a banner that read GIVE HIM THE JUICE, WAYNE. It seemed that their wish had been granted.

There were just three contestants left.

Danny had to force himself not to lose his composure. He had passed on the film question and so, in a way, he was responsible for what had happened. He had used the second of his lifelines, and worse still, he had to play toss of the coin in the next round, GREEK MYTHS. The question should have been simple. Who was the first wife of Zeus? But with the heat of the lights, the ticking clock, the growing tension, his brain had failed him. Two names came up on the screen. Hera or Metis. For a second, he was tempted to go with Hera. It had to be her, surely. But then he remembered. She had been Zeus's third wife.

"Metis," he said.

A pause. The audience waited.

"That's the correct answer," Wayne Howard said.

Danny almost fainted with relief. At the same time, he noticed Mary Robinson sneering at him, telling him that she had known the correct answer all along.

And now he had no more lifelines left.

Two more rounds—CURRENT EVENTS and THE BEATLES—and not a great deal had changed. Ben had used one pass. So had Mary. Danny was in the weakest position. With the contest almost over, any one of them could still win, although if Danny had been allowed a bet, he would probably have put his money on Mary.

And then came a round entitled UNLUCKY DIP. The audience cheered when they saw the two words on the screen. It was well known that these questions would be particularly fiendish, designed to catch the contestants out. And in this round, no lifelines were allowed.

Wayne Howard looked more devilish than ever as he read out the first question.

"The Smith family has six sisters and each sister has one brother. Including Mr. and Mrs. Smith, how many people are there in the family?"

It was Ben Osmond's turn to answer.

"There are fourteen people," he said.

Danny's heart sank. He knew exactly how Ben had arrived at the answer. He had added six sisters to six brothers, making twelve. Then he had added Mr. and Mrs. Smith, bringing the total to fourteen.

But he was wrong.

In fact, the six sisters only had one brother among them. There were just seven kids and with the parents, the correct total was nine.

"Bad luck," Wayne muttered.

"Go, go, go, go . . ."

What had happened? Had Ben let his concentration slip? Had he been tired? Or had he simply wanted the whole thing to be over? Either way, the result was the same and the answer was no sooner out of his mouth than he seemed to realize what he had done. He turned to Danny. "I'm sorry, little man." He shrugged. "It looks like I'm going to have to check out."

"Go, go, go . . ."

Wayne pressed a button on his console. The correct answer was already flashing on the screen. Ben didn't move. Danny glanced up and saw a glass cylinder sliding down from above. It clicked into place, completely surrounding Ben, and a moment later there was a hiss as a cloud of poisonous gas belched out from the floor. Within seconds, Ben was invisible, lost in an ugly white fog that swirled around him. The audience was ecstatic, many of them on their feet, applauding. Wayne pressed a second button and powerful ventilators sucked the poison out. The cylinder rose. Ben was slumped forward. He could have been asleep, but Danny knew his eyes would never open again. He turned away as the platform disappeared beneath the stage.

Danny was sure he was finished. Ben Osmond might not have been a real friend, but somehow he had always seemed to be on Danny's side. Mary Robinson, on the other hand, was ice-cold and pitiless. She would never make a mistake. She would stand there and smile when

Danny finally stumbled and the ten million dollars would be hers.

When Danny's own question came, he could barely find the strength to work out the answer.

"Divide thirty by half and add ten. What do you get?"

The answer was obvious. Half of thirty was fifteen. Add ten. That makes twenty-five. The audience had gone silent. Danny could see the studio clock counting the seconds. Fifteen seconds! Fifteen plus ten equals twenty-five. He opened his mouth to give the answer. No. There had to be a trick. Think again!

Divide thirty by half.

Of course.

You had to think about the exact words. Divide thirty by the fraction—one half—and you got sixty. There were sixty halves in thirty. Add ten to that . . .

There was one second left.

"Seventy!" Danny blurted out.

"That is correct," Wayne said, and the audience applauded. Most of them had got it wrong. And Danny was clearly the underdog. During the course of the program, there had been a shift in sympathy. Most people in the studio now wanted the teenager to win.

Wayne turned to Mary Robinson. "How many animals of each species did Moses take into the ark?" he asked.

Mary smiled. Was she overconfident, or had the pressure finally gotten to her? The critics would be arguing about it for weeks to come. "Two," she replied.

Wayne blinked twice.

"Wait a minute!" Mary's face had suddenly changed. For the first time, her eyes were filled with fear. Her mouth had dropped. The little gold earrings trembled. It was an old chestnut and she had fallen for it! "Moses didn't take any animals into the ark," she corrected herself. "It was Noah. The answer is none!"

Wayne sighed. "That's absolutely correct, Mary. But I'm afraid I have to take your first answer. You said 'two' when the answer was 'none,' and I'm afraid that was wrong."

Before the audience could even begin its usual chant, he took out a handgun and shot her between the eyes.

The single shot was deafening. It seemed impossible that such a small gun could make so much noise. Mary was thrown backward, disappearing from sight. For a moment, nobody did anything. Then every spotlight in the studio swung around, focusing on Danny.

It wasn't quite over yet.

One question remained.

Wayne produced a golden envelope. Inside it was a

question that had been set by the prime minister himself. There were no lifelines, no help from the audience, no second chances. At this moment, it was all or nothing. Wayne took out a silver knife and cut open the envelope.

"Danny Webster," he said. "You are our last survivor. Answer this and you will be our undisputed champion. We're going to give you an extra five seconds to help you. How are you feeling?"

"Just ask me the question," Danny rasped. The lights were blinding him. He could feel them burning his brain.

"All right. Here it is." Wayne paused. "Can you tell me the name of the biggest library in the world?"

Total silence. It was as if the audience was no longer breathing. The clock had started ticking. In twenty seconds, Danny would either be very rich or very dead.

But he knew the answer! Danny wanted to be a librarian, and he knew that it wasn't the British Library. That was the second biggest, with over fourteen million books.

"It's the American Library of Congress," he said.

Another long silence.

"You're absolutely right!" Wayne said.

Everything went crazy. The audience left their seats once again, cheering and shouting. The security men closed ranks, forming a barrier in front of the stage. Fireworks exploded and brightly colored streamers rained down. Two floor managers ran forward and released Danny from his shackles. For the first time, he realized that he was soaked in perspiration. He found it hard to move. Bridget, the blonde in the bikini, came back with the attaché case. Wayne strode forward and took Danny's hand, at the same time thumping him on his back.

"This year's winner, just sixteen years of age, is Danny Webster. Ladies and gentlemen, I give you the youngest multimillionaire in the country!"

More cheering. Somehow Danny's parents had found their way onto the stage. His father was whooping with excitement while his mother smothered him in kisses.

"I knew you could do it, son!" Gary exclaimed. "You've made us! We're in the money!"

The next five minutes were totally chaotic for Danny. His head wasn't working. Nothing made sense anymore. He reached out as the attaché case was pressed into his hands and felt the diamonds rattling inside. Bridget kissed him. Wayne Howard embraced him. It seemed that everyone wanted to touch him, to congratulate him. His name was flashing on the screen in gold letters. The Wagner was playing again.

The security men had formed a protective tunnel and somehow he was bundled out of the studio and into the cold night air. But even here it wasn't over. There were two thousand people cheering in front of the giant plasma screen, which showed his own face, blinking, as he was led out. The world press was waiting for him. More than two hundred cameras were flashing in his face, blinding him, shattering the night sky. Reporters were shouting questions at him in a dozen languages. There was a stretch limo with a uniformed chauffeur holding the door for him, but there was no way he could move forward, not with so many people surrounding him. His father was laughing hysterically. His mother was posing and pirouetting for the cameras. The security men were still trying to clear the way. It was like the end of a war.

And then, out of nowhere, a helicopter appeared. It came down so fast that Danny thought it was going to crash. What was it doing? Were there more newsmen trying to break in on the scene? He saw a rope ladder snaking down.

Then something fell out of the sky. A grenade. Somebody screamed. A second later there was machine-gun fire. Danny saw several of the journalists being mown down. The grenade exploded. Yellow tear gas mushroomed out. Suddenly he couldn't breathe. Tears streamed down his cheeks.

Two men, dressed in black from head to foot, their faces covered by balaclavas, were climbing down the rope ladder. They weren't newsmen. One of them fired several shots into the crowd, killing the chauffeur and two of the security men. The other ran up to Danny and snatched the case. But Danny wouldn't let it go. He had won the competition. Over the past months, he had answered hundreds of questions. The prize was his!

The masked man pulled out a gun and shot him.

And at that moment he heard a voice, amplified, coming out of a speaker system that must have been concealed somewhere outside the studio, and somehow he knew that it was being broadcast all over the world.

"What a fantastic piece of planning by the Macdonald family from Sunderland, who must surely be the winners of *Steal a Million*, the reality program that turns ordinary people into master criminals. It looks like they've snatched the diamonds, and now nothing can stop them as they make the perfect getaway—"

Danny didn't hear any more. He saw his mother staring at him in horror and glanced down at his chest. Blood was pouring out. Then he was toppling forward. The attaché case was no longer in his hands. There was no pain.

A moment later everything went black and his one last thought was that, in a way, it was all very much like a television being turned off.

You Have
Arrived

Everyone knew who ruled at the Kenworth Estate: Harry Faulkner, Haz to his friends, and Jason Steel, barely fifteen but walking tall like someone ten years older. When a new obscenity appeared, sprayed over the side of somebody's house. When an old woman got her bag snatched at night. When a car, or the wheels or side mirrors of a car, went missing. When a window got smashed. . . . It had to be Haz and Jace. Everybody knew. But nobody liked to say.

The Kenworth Estate had been built in the sixties. It had probably looked fine when it was planned, but once translated to real life, it simply hadn't worked. There were three blocks of high-rise apartments with views, mainly of each other, and a whole series of individual houses that might look attractive from a distance but which soon lost their charm when you tried to negotiate your way along the maze of dark passageways that connected them. Crime Alley and Muggers' Mews . . . they all had names like that and the names told you everything you needed to know.

Even its location was against it. It was about a mile from Ipswich, just too far away from the nearest school or shopping center to make walking possible, especially when the east coast rain was sweeping in across the concrete. But nor was it quite in the countryside. It was surrounded by pylons and warehouses, with just one pub, the King's Arms, and one fish-and-chips shop close by. There was talk of the whole place being done up, the buildings painted and the lawns replanted, but talk was all it seemed to be.

Even so, life on the estate might not have been too bad for many of the residents, who were, by and large, a friendly bunch. People tried to help each other out. If one of the older residents got ill, neighbors would pop in for a visit. There were quiz nights at the pub. Now and then someone would organize a litter party and all the crumpled Coke cans and broken bottles would be carried off, only to reappear slowly over the months that followed.

But the one problem that wouldn't go away, even for a minute, was the local gang. It didn't have a name. It wasn't called the Sharks or the Razorboys or anything like that. Nor was it particularly organized. It was just there . . . half a dozen teenagers, maybe a couple more in their early twenties, prowling the estate, killing time, smoking, making life miserable for everyone else.

A boy named Bob Kirby had been gang leader for as long as anyone could remember. He was also known as Romeo because of the big red heart tattooed on his right arm, although nobody knew when he'd had it put there or why. Certainly, Kirby had very little love for anyone. He sneered at his father, beat his mother and terrorized anyone who got in his way. Bob had been a weight lifter, with muscles that wouldn't have looked out of place on a Hollywood star or, for that matter, a long-term convict. Once, in a fight, he had broken the jaw of a man twice his size. Aged just nineteen, he had been arrested twice and was well known to the local police, who were just waiting for him to make the one mistake that would put him into their care. But Bob had been careful. Either that or he was lucky. The Kenworth Estate was his and he ruled it in filthy jeans and his trademark hoodie, a concealed weapon in one pocket and ten Marlboro Lights in another, with a permanent scowl on his pockmarked face.

And then, one day, Bob Kirby disappeared. He was last seen driving east on the A14 in a stolen car and rumor had it that he had upped sticks and moved to London. This was strange, as he had no friends or relatives there.

Bob had no friends anywhere. Some people whispered that he had been stopped by the police on the way, beaten up and left in a ditch—but this was just wishful thinking. He had gone because he had decided to go. And the only thing that mattered was that, with a bit of luck, he wouldn't come back.

His place, however, had been quickly taken. Harry Faulkner had been Bob's lieutenant, his second in command and the first to do whatever Bob wanted. When old Mr. Rossiter's house was burgled and his war medals stolen, it was Harry who had put his elbow through the back window. He was pale and unhealthy looking, with tufts of greasy, fair hair cut short and a sty that had taken up permanent residence in the corner of his eye. His teeth were amazingly uneven and he had lost two of them in a fight ten years ago when he was barely eleven. He had been suspended from school more often than he had been in it and he too had been served with an arrest warrant. He appeared frequently on the lists passed between the police and social workers. He lived with his single mother, who drank, and a mongrel dog that limped around the wreck of the garden and cowered when Harry came home.

He had chosen Jason Steel to be his own right-hand man—something that had made Jason enormously proud, particularly as he was only fifteen and, despite his best efforts, still had no police record. As soon as Harry took him under his wing, Jason promptly gave up attending school, something his teachers couldn't understand because, despite appearances, he was actually fairly bright. Those appearances included a shaven head, hostile eyes and nicotine-stained fingers. Jason was scrawny and small for his age, hollowed out by the life he had chosen. He didn't sleep enough, eat enough or look after his personal hygiene in any meaningful way. He was just happy to be with Harry. That was his tragedy. He couldn't see how pathetic that made him.

The two of them spent their days doing very little. They seldom got up before ten or eleven o'clock in the morning. Once they were up, they ate large, unhealthy breakfasts and were outside the King's Arms by one. Here they would meet up with Den, Frankie, Jo-Jo, PK and Ashley—the other members of the gang. Of course, the barman wasn't supposed to serve them drinks. But Harry Faulkner was old enough to buy alcohol and the rest of them looked it, so why argue? Keep the boys happy and your windows might stay unbroken. That was the philosophy around here.

In the afternoon, the six of them might go shopping in Ipswich . . . or shoplifting, rather, for they seldom paid. Sometimes Harry and Jason would head off alone. They liked going to the cinema. One of them would buy a ticket and let the other in through the fire door. They took drugs, of course. So far they had stayed off the heavy stuff. Both of them were afraid, although neither of them would have admitted it. But they smoked grass and passed hours in a semiconscious state. For all seven gang members, this wasn't so very different from their normal state. They had found a way of making the day pass without noticing. If they were bored, they didn't know it. And if they knew it, they didn't admit it. They were happy being together. What else did they need?

But Harry and Jason were on their own the day they came upon the BMW.

It was parked just around the corner from the King's Arms, sitting in an empty street as if it had simply dropped out of the sky. What was an expensive car like this doing at the Kenworth Estate, anyway? It looked brand-new, although its license plate showed that it was actually three years old. A BMW X3, metallic silver with alloy wheels and sports trim, leather interior and electric sunroof, parked there as if it should be in some swanky showroom.

Incredible.

"Where do you think that came from?" Harry asked. He had a squeaky voice, the result of all his smoking, and he almost purposefully brutalized every word. "Whe' d'ya fink tha' caym frum?"

"I don't know, Haz," Jason replied. He was already

wondering what Harry would do. Run a key down the paintwork, certainly. And perhaps more.

"How much do you think it's worth?"

"I got no idea." In fact, Jason guessed its value would be around $25,000. The latest X3 went for about $40,000 new. He'd read that in a magazine. But it was always better to keep his mouth shut when he was with Harry. Being too clever with someone like that could be bad for your well-being.

"Who'd park something like that around here?" Harry looked across the surrounding wasteland, back toward the pub and across to the estate. There was nobody in sight. It was a cold day and drizzling. The winter months were drawing in.

"What you gonna do, Haz?"

Harry hadn't decided yet, but Jason could see all sorts of possibilities traveling across his eyes like prizes on a game show. The DVD player, the cuddly toy, the twenty-grand four-by-four . . .

"Let's get another drink," Jason went on. It was three o'clock in the afternoon and the pub would be closed by now, but there was something about the BMW that made him want to move on. It shouldn't have been there. It was weird. And there was something else. . . .

"Nah. Wait a minute." Harry was still deep in thought.

"That's a nice car," he said. "And it's here. And there's nobody about."

"Who'd leave a car like that out here?" Jason asked, almost exactly echoing what Harry had said a few moments before.

"Let's take a closer look."

"You think it's safe?" Jason wasn't sure why he'd said that.

"You think that little diddy car is going to get up and bite you?" Harry giggled. "It's safe!"

The two of them went up to the X3. It had tinted windows. The bodywork was gleaming. Inside, the brilliantly polished dashboard made Jason think of a sleeping tiger. He wanted to turn the key, to hear the growl of the engine, to feel the power that would come as the dials and gauges lit up.

The key.

It was in the ignition.

Harry had seen it too. "You see that?" he whispered.

"Yeah, Harry."

"They left the key in the car."

"Let's get out of here, Harry."

"What you talking about, Jace? They left the bloody key in the bloody car." Harry took another look around. "And there's no one here."

It was true. The drizzle was bouncing off the tarmac,

sweeping across the grim, uneven grass, hanging between the electricity pylons. It was keeping people indoors.

Harry opened the door of the BMW.

Even then, Jason thought that it must be a trick, that an alarm would go off and a dozen policemen would appear out of nowhere, pouncing on them and dragging them off to the nearest juvenile hall. But no policemen came. There was just the soft clunk of the lock disengaging and then they were looking inside a car that they couldn't have afforded if they'd both worked twenty-four hours a day for an entire year.

"Are you thinking what I'm thinking?" Harry whispered.

"You bet," Jason replied, although part of him wondered if Harry ever thought very much at all.

"Let's do it!"

They were inside the car before they knew it. And then came the wonderful moment when the doors closed and everything outside simply disappeared and the two of them were out of the drizzle, lost in the world of the car, surrounded by luxury and the latest technology. Harry had taken the driving seat, of course. Both of them knew how to drive, but Jason also knew his place. He was the passenger. Harry was the one who would be taking them for this ride.

"Wow!" Harry breathed the single word and giggled.

"Awesome!" Jason agreed.

Harry turned the key and the engine fired instantly. Jason heard the soft splutter and felt the vibrations. Never in his whole life had he sat in a car like this. He couldn't stop himself from smiling. Just a few hours before, he had been lying in his bed with its dirty, wrinkled sheets, wondering how he would spend the rest of the day. And now this!

"Let's get out of here, Harry," he said. He wanted to move. He wanted to leave the estate before the car's owner appeared and dragged them out. And there was still that something else nagging at the corner of his mind. A silver-gray BMW. It had a significance. But what was it?

The car had six gears. Harry whipped it into first, pressed on the accelerator, and at once they surged forward. Naught to sixty in eight seconds. That was what this car could do, and if Harry didn't quite manage it this time, they were halfway down the road before either of them had quite realized what had happened.

"This is unbelievable!" Jason shouted.

"This is cool!" Harry squealed.

The King's Arms had become a speck in the rearview mirror. A minute later, the estate had vanished from sight. Harry was clinging onto the steering wheel as if he were afraid of being left behind. To look at him, you would have thought it was the car that was driving him rather than the other way around. Jason drummed his hands against the dashboard. For the moment, sheer excitement had swept away all his doubts.

Second gear, third gear, fourth . . . the faster they went, the more confident Harry became. They raced down a series of lanes, and before they knew it, they had come to a T-junction and the A1071 stretched out in front of them, leading either to Sudbury in the east or Ipswich in the west. Suddenly there was more traffic. A police car whizzed across them without slowing down, and the sight of it reminded Jason that this was a serious business. They had just stolen a twenty-five-thousand-dollar car. This would be more than probation if they were caught. This could be jail.

"Where to, my man?" Harry asked. He sometimes talked in an American accent when he was really excited. He had picked it up from watching cop shows on TV.

"I don't care," Jason replied. The truth was, he couldn't think of anywhere he wanted to go.

"Norwich?"

"Yeah!"

"Or London . . ."

"How much gas we got?" It was the first sensible thing Jason had said. When the car ran out of gas, they would have to dump it. Neither of them had enough money to fill the tank, and anyway, it would be too risky driving into a gas station.

"We got a full tank," Harry replied. He sniggered. "Let's have a day at the seaside!"

"The seaside!" Jason crowed. It was his way of agreeing.

Harry slammed his foot down and they shot onto the main road, bringing a blare of protest from a VW that had to swerve to avoid them. They had turned left, heading for Ipswich and the Suffolk coast. Almost at once they were doing seventy miles per hour. Grinning, Harry edged the speed up to eighty. Jason knew that he was being stupid. They had already spotted one police car and speeding would only bring attention to them. But as usual, he kept his thoughts to himself.

And anyway, he had something else on his mind. It was the mention of London that had done it. He had remembered what it was about the BMW that had struck a chord. Of course. How could he have forgotten? Bob Kirby. Romeo. The gang leader who had disappeared. He had last been seen heading for London in a stolen car—and maybe it was just a rumor, but hadn't someone told him that the car was a BMW X3? It was a coincidence. It had to be. But even so, it was a little bit strange.

He turned his attention to the inside of the car. The

glove compartment was empty. There was a CD player but no CDs. There was also a slot for an iPod, but neither of them had brought one with them.

"Hey—that's cool!" Harry muttered.

The BMW had a satellite navigation system. Of course, it would be standard in a luxury car like this, but this one had risen out of the dashboard like something in a James Bond film, full color and high-definition screen. What was strange was that it seemed to have activated itself automatically. Neither of the boys had touched anything.

"Put in our destination," Harry commanded.

"I don't know our destination," Jason said.

"Well, think of one."

"How about Aldeburgh?" Jason remembered that it was a town on the Suffolk coast.

"Yeah. Aldeburgh." Harry frowned. "How d'you spell Aldeburgh?"

Jason typed in the letters and pressed the button to start the guidance. At once the screen lit up to show an arrow pointing toward a cartoon roundabout, which, according to the numbers floating below, they would reach in 100 yards. A moment later, a voice emerged from the speaker system.

"At—the—roundabout—take—the—second—exit."

Harry and Jason looked at each other, then burst out laughing. They had heard navigation systems plenty of times. But this car seemed to be equipped with the most extraordinary voice. It was like an old woman, shrill and high-pitched, not telling them where to go but almost nagging them. The system was surely faulty. It had to be. No BMW owner would want to drive with a voice like that.

The two of them were so amused that they almost drove straight into the roundabout even though the counter was clearly signaling its approach. 30 yards, 20 yards, 10 yards . . . at the last moment, Harry spun the wheel and they cut in front of an ambulance and veered from one lane to another. Then they had exited and they were following the A14 toward Felixstowe with two miles to go until the next turnoff. By now Jason was wondering if Harry would let him have a go behind the wheel. He had never been in a car as powerful as this. He would have liked to feel his own foot pressing down on the accelerator. But he doubted it. Harry was never very generous about anything and he liked to remind Jason of his place: number two. Jason stretched himself out in the comfortable passenger seat. Harry would probably slash the leather when they dumped the car. He might even decide to set it on fire.

"*Left—turn—ahead.*" The ridiculous old woman's voice cut in again.

"Left turn ahead!" Harry mimicked the sound with a high-pitched falsetto of his own and laughed.

"You think it's broken, Harry?" Jason asked.

"Turn—left—onto—the—A—12." It was almost as if the machine had heard him and wanted to contradict him. And sure enough, there was the signpost. The A12 to Lowestoft, the coastal road that would take them past Woodbridge and Orford and on to Aldeburgh.

Harry made the turn, then fished in his pocket and took out a packet of ten cigarettes. He offered one to Jason and they both lit up, using the BMW's lighter. Although Jason wouldn't have dared admit it, he didn't like smoking. He hated the smell and it gave him a sore throat. But generally, what Harry did, he did. Soon the inside of the car was filled with gray smoke. Jason turned on the air-conditioning and allowed the electronically chilled air to rush in.

"At—the—next—roundabout—take—the—third—exit."

"Let's turn this off, Haz," Jason said. Without waiting for an answer, he reached forward and pressed the button. The screen went black. They continued in silence.

It took them another forty minutes to reach Aldeburgh, a pretty coastal town with a shingle beach that stretched from one end to the other. Jason had chosen it because he had been here once when he was very young, before he met Bob Kirby or Harry or any of the other gang members. It had been a long time ago, but he still remembered the fishing boats moored on the beach, the brightly colored houses, wonderful fish-and-chips. It was a rich town now, full of Londoners with second homes. Maybe that was why Harry had agreed to come here. Loads of houses, empty from Monday to Friday. They had stolen a car. Why not break in somewhere while they were about it?

They parked the BMW in a parking lot at the far end of the town, next to an old windmill, then walked back down the main street, Harry tossing the keys in his hand as if he had owned the car all his life. After the excitement of the theft and the buzz of the ride, they were both thirsty—and Aldeburgh had plenty of pubs. Together, they set out to find one.

About halfway down the street, they passed a flower shop. Again, this was something that Jason wouldn't have dreamed of admitting, but he quite liked plants. There had been a time, before he dropped out of school, when he had thought about working in a garden center or even training to be a landscape gardener. His biology teacher had encouraged him and had fought on his behalf the first time he was suspended. Of course, she had given up on him in the end. Everyone had. But there were times when he felt a certain emptiness, a sense that things could have been different. Looking at the plants arranged on trestle tables in the street, he felt like that now.

There was an elderly man with white hair and spectacles, presumably the shop owner, packing away for the night. He was delicately loading plants onto a wooden tray and Jason recognized immediately what he had been selling. The plants were pale green with strange leaves shaped almost like mouths . . . for that indeed was what they were. Venus flytraps. Jason even remembered their Latin name. *Dionaea muscipula.* In a way, the plants were little miracles. There was nothing quite like them on the planet. They were carnivorous. The leaves were covered with tiny, sensitive hairs and when an insect flew in, they would spring shut, forming an airtight chamber. That would be it for the insect. There was no way out. Over the next five to twelve days, the creature would be dissolved and digested. That was how the plant fed. And even the most brilliant scientists weren't quite sure exactly how the trap worked.

"What you looking at?" Harry demanded.

"Nothing, Haz," Jason said, blushing slightly. He realized he had almost given himself away.

"Let's find a pub."

They moved on, and as they went, Jason noticed the old man glance at him almost sadly, as if he knew something that Jason didn't. Later on, he would remember that. But meanwhile, Harry had crossed the road and a few minutes later they were both drinking pints of Adnams—the local beer—and the tray of exotic plants was forgotten.

The rain had stopped and they spent two hours in Aldeburgh, drinking until their money had almost run out, then walking the High Street, sneering at the art galleries, playing soccer with a Coke can, testing the doors of parked cars in case any of them had something worth stealing inside. By six o'clock it was getting dark and suddenly they were on their own. They bought fish-and-chips and ate it on the seawall, looking out at the black, choppy water. It didn't taste as good as it had when Jason had come here as a boy.

"Well, this is a waste of time," Harry said at last.

"Let's go home," Jason suggested. It had already occurred to him that stealing a car lost much of its point when you didn't have anywhere to go.

"Yeah. We got our very own Beemer!"

"Right."

"We'll get it home and then we can trash it."

"The tires."

"The seats."

"The paintwork."

"We can drive it into someone's garden and set fire to it!" Harry whooped.

The car was still waiting for them where they had parked it. Harry pressed the remote on the ignition key and sniggered as the lights blinked and the locks sprang open. Once again he got into the driving seat. As Jason had thought, there was going to be no discussion about that. The BMW sprang into life at one turn of the key, that lovely, efficient growl of German engineering. And then they were away, knocking over an oil can as they left the parking lot and perhaps damaging the bodywork—but what did that matter? It was nothing compared with what they were going to do when they arrived home.

But it was a bit more difficult, getting back again. Night had fallen and a slight mist had rolled in from the sea. Neither of them had much sense of direction and it had been years since Jason had found himself in this part of the county.

"Turn the navigation back on," Harry said.

"Do we need it?" Jason asked. There was something about that old woman's voice that unnerved him, even though he had laughed about it at the time.

"Just do it," Harry snapped. He was focusing on the road ahead, watching the beams as they picked out the rushing tarmac. Jason wondered if he had ever driven in the dark before. He probably hadn't driven much at all. In fact, now that he thought about it, it was quite remarkable that Harry had even learned to drive.

Jason turned the navigation on and entered his own address—the Kenworth Estate, Sproughton, Ipswich—then punched the button to begin navigation. Almost at once, the voice began.

"At—the—next—junction—turn—right."

Which was strange because Jason was sure they had come the other way. And there, indeed, was the sign, IpsWICH 22 MILES, pointing to the left. But it was already too late. Harry had wrenched the wheel, doing what the voice had said. This was where the streetlamps of Aldeburgh ran out. As they completed the turn, they plunged into the darkness of a Suffolk night.

Jason thought about arguing but decided against it. They were both tired. Harry had downed four pints before they'd left the pub. And anyway, the navigation system would use lots of information before suggesting a route. Perhaps this was a shortcut. Perhaps there was a traffic jam on the A12. They seemed to be following a fairly narrow country lane and that, perhaps, was a good thing. The last thing they needed to see right now was another police car. It made sense to go back on quieter roads.

They drove in silence for about seven or eight miles. It really was very dark. The rain clouds had closed in, blocking any sight of the moon or stars, and suddenly there were no buildings around them. Instead, they seemed to be crossing open countryside with undulating fields and low gorse bushes dotted around like crouching soldiers.

"Take—the—second—turning—on—the—right."

The high-pitched voice broke the silence. Harry did as he was told.

Another couple of miles, this time through forest. They had to be on a back road. It was certainly narrower than the road they had just left, with trees jammed together on both sides, forming a tunnel over their heads.

"In—one–hundred—yards—turn—left."

The left turn was even narrower. Now there wouldn't be room for another car to pass them without pulling off to the side. Not that it looked as if many cars came this way. They had lost sight of any civilization. The woods were getting thicker and thicker.

"Fork—left—then—continue—straight—ahead."

The fork took them off the road and onto what was little more than a track. Jason could hear dead leaves squelching under the wheels. He wondered if they were even on tarmac.

"You sure this thing is working, Haz?" Jason asked.

"What thing?"

"You know . . . the navigation."

"Why wouldn't it be working, Jace?" Harry snapped. He knew they were lost and that was making him angry.

"We didn't come this way."

"Well, what do you suggest?"

Jason looked out of the window. All he could see was

leaves. The track they were on was so narrow that the branches of the trees were scraping the windshield. The BMW's headlights lit up a tiny world, perhaps five yards ahead of them. Outside the beams of light, there was nothing. "Maybe we should turn around and go back the way we came."

"There's nowhere to turn around."

"At—the—crossroads—continue—straight—over."

And that surely had to be a mistake. A fairly main road—at least it was definitely covered in tarmac with white lines dotted down the middle—crossed in front of them from left to right, promising perhaps a fast exit from the surrounding forest. Ahead of them was a rotting wooden gate hanging crookedly on one hinge. The gate was open and behind it there was a bumpy, muddy path—you couldn't call it a track or a lane—barely wide enough for the BMW to pass along. It was pitted with potholes, some of them full of water. A rusty barbed-wire fence, broken in places, followed it on one side.

"Take a right, Haz," Jason said—and this time Harry did as he suggested, but he had no sooner completed the turn than the voice cut back in.

"If—possible—make—a—U—turn."

"You want me to turn it off?" Jason asked.

"Nah." Harry shook his head. "We might as well leave it on. We don't have to do what it says."

"That's right." Jason nodded. They had picked up a little speed, following the better road. "It must go somewhere."

"If—possible—make—a—U—turn," the navigation system tried again. The screen was showing an arrow bent in the shape of a U. Harry ignored it.

The road led nowhere.

About half a mile farther down, Harry had to brake hard and they came to a sudden, sliding halt. A huge branch had somehow splintered and fallen down, blocking the way. Leaving the engine ticking over, the two of them got out of the car. It was very cold in the wood, far colder than it had been when they'd left. There was no breeze, but the air was thick and damp. The mist had followed them in from the coast. They could see it curling slowly between the trees.

"What now?" Jason asked. It was obvious that the branch was far too heavy to move.

"We keep driving," Harry said. His voice was sounding a little bleak.

"Have we got enough gas?"

"We got plenty of gas."

That at least was true. The BMW was still half full, and if they could only find their way out of the forest, they would have plenty enough fuel to get home. Almost reluctantly this time, they climbed back into the car. All the fun had gone out of their adventure. They just wanted to get out of this forest, to find themselves somewhere that they knew.

There was barely enough space to turn around. Spinning the wheel, Harry managed to reverse into the stump of a tree. Jason heard the metalwork crumple, and for a few seconds the engine screamed out of control. Harry swore and changed gear. In a way, Jason was almost glad that the car had been damaged. The BMW had gotten them into the mess. It deserved all the punishment it could take.

They had barely completed the turn before the navigation system began again.

"In—one—hundred—yards—turn—right."

And that was odd too, because neither of them had noticed a turnoff on that part of the road. But the machine was correct. In a hundred yards, they came to an opening between two trees and, beyond it, a track snaking its way through the forest. Harry took it, even though Jason's sense of direction told him they were going the wrong way. But what was the right way now? They were completely lost. He wished now that they had followed his instinct outside Aldeburgh, taking the turning marked IPSWICH, 22 MILES. By now they should have been safely back on the A12.

"Take—the—next—turning—on—the—right."

Harry seemed to have become enslaved by the ugly old woman's voice of the navigation system. Perhaps he didn't mind doing exactly what a machine told him, but Jason was less comfortable. He hated the idea of having to rely, one hundred percent, on a tangle of wires and software that might have been malfunctioning in the first place. Maybe that was why the BMW had been dumped at the Kenworth Estate. Nobody in their right mind would have actually wanted to drive there. Maybe the car's owner had gotten as lost as they were now and had gone off for help, accidentally forgetting the key. That made sense.

"At—the—crossroads—continue—straight—over."

Jason's heart lurched. He blinked several times, his mouth hanging open, and for a moment he really did look like a child and not like an adult at all. It wasn't possible! They were back exactly where they had been ten minutes before. Somehow, the various tracks had brought them back to the broken wooden gate and the track beyond. Jason swore. He could feel tears pricking against his eyes. This was getting nasty. He wanted to go home.

"Turn left," he said.

"It's saying straight ahead," Harry countered.

"The machine doesn't know what it's talking about. If we hadn't followed it in the first place, we wouldn't be in this mess."

And then a light blinked on in the woodland, straight ahead of them. It was about a quarter of a mile away, very tiny, almost concealed by the thick spread of the trees.

"There's something there," Harry said.

"What . . . ?" Jason squinted into the darkness.

"It must be a house or something. We can ask the way."

"*At—the—crossroads—continue—straight—over,*" the navigation urged them. The voice sounded almost cheerful. Why had it repeated itself, Jason wondered, when they weren't even moving?

But Harry needed no further prompting. He changed gears and the BMW moved forward again, through the gate and onto the track with the barbed wire along the side. As they rolled forward, the trees thinned out a little. Somehow the moon had finally broken through and they saw fields spreading out, what looked like rough farmland that was completely surrounded by the forest. Ahead of them, a cluster of buildings sprang up, made of red brick with weeds and ivy climbing up the guttering. They passed an abandoned tractor, a rusting coil—more barbed wire. The light seemed to have vanished and they wondered if they had really seen it. Whatever this place was, it looked abandoned.

They turned a corner and there, once again, was the light, coming from an open barn on the other side of a yard. A tall, uneven chimney had been built behind the barn, stretching high above it. And someone was burning something. Thick black smoke rose into the night, and even with the windows closed, Jason could smell meat that was being roasted and smoked at the same time. They drove through a second gate, this one made of steel and brand-new. There was a vehicle parked to one side, a refrigerated truck that looked old but in better repair, at least, than the tractor. Jason saw some words painted in red along one side.

AUNT MARIGOLD'S SMOKED MEAT AND BLACK PUDDING

100% organic. Made only from the freshest ingredients.

Somewhere, a dog barked. Behind them, Jason heard a clang as the steel gate closed and, just for a moment, he thought of *Dionaea muscipula.* The Venus flytraps that he had seen in Aldeburgh.

Harry pulled up in front of the barn. He didn't turn the key but the BMW stalled and they came to a halt. The two boys got out. The night air was very cold. They could feel it running through their hair, stroking the back of their necks.

This was a pork farm. It had to be. There was an oven burning at the back of the barn and the floor was covered with straw, which was splattered with blood that had dripped down from the carcasses hanging on hooks attached to wooden beams. But the carcasses didn't look as if they had come from pigs. They didn't look like any animal Jason had ever seen. He saw a leg severed just above the knee. What might have been a shoulder. And, on another hook, an arm. It might have been made of plastic, but Jason knew that it wasn't. It had been well smoked in the oven. The arm had had a bright red marking right on the shoulder.

A heart—and a name.

Romeo.

Jason felt his blood freeze. There was a rushing in his ears.

A woman appeared, coming out of the barn toward them. She had long silver hair, a yellow face and gray lips that were partly open, revealing teeth that could have come from the cemetery. She was wearing a dirty green apron that hung all the way to her feet. The apron was smeared with old blood. She lifted a hand to wipe her mouth with her sleeve and Jason saw a jagged knife, also bloodstained. Harry was standing dead still. He had gone white. Jason was surprised to see that Haz was crying. But

Jason was crying too. He knew what this was. He knew where they were.

The woman was not alone. A man—huge and bearded —had appeared behind the car, holding a length of filthy rope, the sort you might use to tie down animals. Jason caught sight of him in the side mirror. Then the woman reached them.

Her eyes blazed and she smiled at the two boys. Her voice was shrill and high-pitched. *"You—have—arrived,"* she said.

THE COBRA

The ancient taxi with its scratched paint and dusty windows rattled to a halt and the engine cut out. They had parked on a narrow street, next to a shop selling lanterns, chairs, boxes and chessboards, all of which were hanging off the front wall and spilling onto the pavement.

"Is this it?" Charles Atchley demanded.

"This is it," the driver agreed with a smile.

"But it's not a hotel!" Charles whined.

"It's a *riad*," his mother explained. "It's not quite the same thing."

The truth was that Charles Atchley had never wanted to go to Marrakesh. It might be a vacation abroad, but from what he had heard, the capital of Morocco would be hot and sweaty with no beaches, no McDonald's, no amusement parks and nothing much to do at the hotel except sit and read. And as he hated books, what was the point of that? Worse still, the food would be strange, the people would speak little or no English, there would be flies everywhere and he would have to spend hours either walking through ruins or struggling up the Atlas Mountains. All in all, he would much rather have stayed at home.

But as usual, of course, he was going to have no choice. Charles was fifteen years old, the only son of Rupert Atchley, a successful barrister. His mother, Noreen Atchley, produced illustrations for women's magazines. The three of them lived in a house in Wimbledon, south London, and Charles went to a local school where he did just enough work to stay out of trouble but not enough to make any real progress. That was the sort of boy he was. You could never point your finger at him and say that he was actually bad. But he was undoubtedly spoiled and really had no interests outside of fast food, computer games and Manchester United. Left to himself, he would have stayed in bed until twelve and then watched television all afternoon, perhaps with a plate of fried chicken and fries balanced on his knees.

It was hardly surprising that he was rather overweight. Again, he wasn't exactly fat. He just looked unhealthy, with ginger hair that he never brushed and a scattering of acne that moved—almost liked clock hands—around his face. He liked to wear tracksuit pants and baggy T-shirts, and he could even make his school uniform look shabby and out of shape. It must also be said that he was something of a bully. There had been one or two incidents with some of the younger boys at the school, but he had been clever enough to avoid responsibility, and although the teachers had their suspicions, so far they'd never had enough evidence to nail him down.

His mother and father adored him and turned a blind eye to most of his faults. Noreen had once waited in line all night to make sure he was the first boy on the street with a PlayStation 3, and Rupert was certainly overgenerous with the pocket money. Whatever Charles wanted, Charles usually got, even if he did have to stamp his feet a bit to get it.

It was only when it came to vacations, or any decision that affected the whole family, that his parents would insist on having their own way. After all, they would argue, they both worked hard—and they were the ones who were paying. So like it or not (and the answer was definitely not), Charles had been dragged to no fewer than six art galleries in Rome, to a whole selection of dreary chateaus in the Loire, to far too many shops in New York, and now it seemed he would just have to put up with whatever horrors Marrakesh had in store.

Even the airport seemed to confirm his worst fears. It consisted of a single, rather old-fashioned building that wouldn't have looked like an airport at all but for the runway outside. And it was hot. The breeze seemed to be blowing out of some enormous hand drier. It almost burned his skin and he was sweating and irritable long before the bags turned up—last, of course—on the single carousel.

His mood got no better in the taxi on the way to the city. His first impression of Marrakesh was of a vast cluster of low redbrick buildings all jammed together inside an ugly wall. Palm trees sprouted out of the rubble, but they somehow failed to make the place any more appealing. The traffic was terrible and it didn't help that the air-conditioning inside the taxi wasn't working. It was all the more annoying that both his parents were enchanted by what they saw.

"It's so exotic!" his mother exclaimed, peering out of the window. "And listen to that!"

From a high, slender tower—a minaret—the high-pitched voice of an imam was echoing across the city.

"Allahu Akbar. Allahu Akbar. . . . Ashhadu an la Ilah ila Allah. . . ."

"What's that racket?" Charles demanded.

His father, sitting in the front seat, twisted around. He had noticed the driver frowning next to him. "It's not a racket, Charlie," he explained. "You should be more respectful. It's the Muslim call to prayer."

"Well, I hope it doesn't go on too long," Charles muttered.

And now the hotel.

The Riad El Fenn was about halfway down the alley. A large wooden door opened into a dark, cool hallway with deep red walls and a chessboard floor. A bowl of white roses had been arranged in a vase on a low Arab-style table, and there were about fifty pairs of slippers—all of them different colors—spread out for guests who preferred not to wear shoes. From the hall, a passageway led to an inner courtyard with doors on all sides and four orange trees forming a tangled square in the middle.

Noreen had been right. The riad was more like a house than a hotel, with half a dozen different courtyards connected by a maze of stairs and corridors. Even after several days, Charles would still have difficulty finding his way around. There wasn't what he would have called a swimming pool here, although every courtyard had its own plunge pool, like something you might imagine in an Arabian palace, just big enough for five or six strokes from end to end. There were flowers everywhere, scenting the air and giving a sense of cool after the dust and heat of the city. And unlike a hotel, all the rooms were different. Some were modern. Some were old. All of them had a little surprise of their own.

Charles was sleeping next door to his parents in a turquoise room with a keyhole-shaped door and antique wooden latticework all around his bed. His bathroom was huge, with gray stone walls, a little like a cell in a monastery only with a shower at one end and, at the other, a bath almost big enough to swim in. There were more roses on a table and rose petals scattered over the bed. His parents had almost fainted with pleasure when they saw it. But the first thing that Charles had noticed was—no TV! No plasma screen. No flat screen. Not even a portable. He wondered how he was going to survive.

They had lunch together on the roof. That was another strange thing. The riad didn't seem to have a proper dining room. Everyone ate sitting on low cushions, at tables shielded from the sun by a canopy that stretched from one end of the roof to the other. Charles could barely recognize any of the food. There was some sort of bean salad and pieces of lamb cooked in a sauce, but there wasn't anything he actually wanted to eat.

His parents were in raptures.

"This is the most wonderful place!" Noreen exclaimed. "It's so beautiful. And so peaceful! I can't wait to get out my watercolors."

"The food is sensational," Rupert added, helping himself to a spoonful of couscous, which was a local specialty.

"Look at those flowers!" Noreen had a new digital camera and quickly focused it on a terra-cotta pot on the other side of the roof. She had taken at least a hundred pictures and they had only been there an hour.

"More wine!" Rupert lifted his glass and a waiter appeared almost at once, carrying a bottle fresh from the ice bucket.

What was even worse than all this was that, as Charles discovered, all the other guests were equally delighted by the Riad El Fenn. They swam in the pools, drank in the courtyards, took steam baths and massages in the warm, scented air of the hammam and chatted until midnight, sitting under the stars as if they had known each other all their lives. It didn't help that Charles was the youngest person there. One of the couples had two sixteen-year-olds, but the three of them didn't get along, so Charles was largely left on his own.

He spent the next twenty-four hours getting his revenge on the riad in all sorts of mean and spiteful ways. He jumbled up all the slippers and broke the leaves off the plants. He poured a glass of lemonade into one of the plunge pools. He even scribbled his name on a painting hanging up in one of the hallways. None of this helped the situation at all. In fact, nobody even mentioned what he'd done, which, in a way, made him even more annoyed.

And then, one evening, the Atchleys visited the *souq*.

This was the covered market that sprawled across the heart of the city with hundreds of little shops selling rugs, slippers, glasses, handbags, spices, plates and bowls, but nothing—as far as Charles could see—that anyone would actually want to buy. He was tired and footsore by the time they came out, Noreen now wearing a pair of ridiculous earrings that Rupert had bought for her at probably ten times the correct price.

"Aren't they lovely?" she asked, examining herself in the mirror.

"I think they're horrible," Charles replied.

"No need to be like that!" Rupert said. "Come on. Let's go to the main square. With a bit of luck we might see the cobras."

The main square—it was called the Djemaa el-Fna—was beyond the souq, in the old part of town, a huge open area surrounded by hotels and restaurants with long balconies and staircases leading up to crowded rooftops. It was just getting dark and the square was a fantastic sight with thousands of people milling around and food stalls with flames sparking and charcoal glowing and smoke climbing slowly into the sky. There were entertainers everywhere—magicians and acrobats, jugglers and storytellers—with fifty musicians competing with each other to make themselves heard above the din.

And there were the snake charmers. There were at

least half a dozen of them, each with their own basket, their own pipe, their own separate crowd, the sounds of their music fighting with each other in the open space. The Atchleys had moved toward the one nearest to them, on the very edge of the square, almost lost in the shadows. It was strange how set apart he was from the others, almost as if he didn't want anyone to watch him—or maybe it was the other snake charmers who didn't want him anywhere near them. Certainly, he had attracted fewer spectators than the rest of them. Only seven or eight people stood watching as the Atchleys approached.

Even so, the solitary snake charmer looked exactly like a snake charmer should, sitting cross-legged on a little mat in front of a round wicker basket. He was playing on a pipe, a dark, slender instrument that reminded Charles of the recorder that had once been forced upon him at school, although the sound it made was harder and more sinuous. He played for a moment and then Noreen gasped, her hand fluttering to her throat. A cobra suddenly appeared, silk-like and deadly, rising out of the basket and swaying just a few inches away from the pipe as the music continued.

The Atchleys pushed their way to the front so that Noreen could take another half a dozen photographs, the flashbulb briefly fighting against the approaching night. Rupert's mouth was hanging open. He had gotten a sunburn during the afternoon and his neck seemed to be glowing as much as the streetlamps. Charles couldn't help thinking how stupid they both looked. And as for the snake charmer . . .

He was a small man, at least sixty, with very dark skin, gray stubble on his cheeks and a hooked nose. He was wearing a long white robe with a waistcoat and loose-fitting cotton trousers. His feet were bare and his toes looked like pieces of old, gnarled wood. Charles only glanced at him briefly. He was much more interested in the snake, which certainly looked vicious enough with its flared hood, its spitting tongue, its tiny, evil eyes. It really did seem to be hypnotized, totally controlled by the music that wove an invisible pattern around its head.

"It's extraordinary!" Noreen whispered, afraid to raise her voice in case she broke the spell. "It's like something in a fairy tale!"

"That's one of the most venomous snakes in the world," Rupert told her. "It's got enough poison to kill a horse."

"Isn't it dangerous to be this close?" Noreen stepped back a pace, suddenly nervous.

"These people know what they're doing," Rupert replied. "It takes years of practice. But they know exactly the right tune to play. It's a bit like magic. But the snake will dance all night if they want it to."

"That's not true, Dad," Charles interrupted in a loud voice. "There's no magic and the snake isn't dancing. It's not dangerous. It's actually half asleep."

Both Rupert and Noreen turned to look at their son, who was standing with his arms crossed and a smug smile on his face. Some of the people in the crowd had also overheard him and were turning to hear what he had to say.

"I saw a program about it on TV," he went on. "The snake can't even hear the music. The only reason it's swaying is because it's following the movement of the pipe. And actually, cobras are very timid. They're not dangerous at all."

"But look at it, darling!" Noreen exclaimed. "It looks like it's about to attack!"

"Spreading its hood is just a way of defending itself," Charles explained. "It would much rather be back in its basket. And it probably doesn't have any poison in it anyway. The snake charmer will have made sure it was sucked out before he began."

"Young man, you are quite mistaken!"

Charles looked around to see who had spoken and was surprised to discover that it was the snake charmer himself. The old man had lowered the pipe from his lips and the cobra immediately disappeared back into the basket. The few spectators who remained drifted away without giving any money. Suddenly the Atchleys were on their own.

"The art of the snake charmer is an ancient one," the man continued. It was hard for the Atchleys to believe that such an old and Arab-looking man could not only speak English but speak it so well. He had a very culti-vated accent, which sounded completely unlikely coming from those yellowed teeth and cracked lips, but he spoke very slowly, as if remembering a lesson taught years ago. "My father was a snake charmer and his father too. I learned the skill when I was six years old. And sometimes I learned from my mistakes . . ." He held out his arm and as his sleeve fell back, the Atchleys saw an ugly crescent-shaped scar that could have been stamped into his flesh. "The bite would have killed me had my father not had a vial of antivenom," the old man continued. "Even so, I was ill for months and the mark of the cobra remains with me to this day."

"My son didn't mean to be rude," Rupert muttered.

"Your son displayed his ignorance and did not care if he was rude or not," the snake charmer replied. "He has spoiled my performance, and thanks to him I will have no money to take home."

"Let me pay you!" Rupert took out his wallet and produced a fifty-dirham note. He didn't seem to notice that this was hardly very generous. Fifty dirham was less than seven dollars.

"Say sorry to the man, Charles," Noreen suggested. She was rather hoping that the cobra would rise up and dance again. Her camera was still poised between her fingers.

"I won't say sorry, because it's true," Charles insisted. "I saw it on the Discovery Channel. It's all just a trick."

"You should be careful how you speak to me, child," the snake charmer muttered, and for the first time he looked angry. His eyes had narrowed and he was regarding Charles with the same quiet malice as the cobra itself. "You are a visitor to my country, so you should be respectful of its customs. And there are some things that even your television channels do not understand. Magic, for example, has a way of sneaking up on you and biting in ways that you may not expect."

"I don't believe in magic," Charles retorted. But some of the confidence had gone out of his voice.

"Let's get back to the riad," Noreen suggested. She gave the snake charmer a wobbly smile. "It was a pleasure meeting you," she wavered. "In fact, it was charming!"

The three of them turned and walked away, but Charles couldn't resist having the last word—or at least what passed as a word. Neither of his parents was watching. They were already searching for the passage that would lead them back to the riad. Charles dropped slightly behind, then twisted around and raised his middle finger, a universal symbol that he was sure the old man would understand. Sure enough, the snake charmer recoiled as if he had been slapped across the face. Then he composed himself and nodded slowly, twice. Once again, his jet-black eyes settled on the boy, and despite the heat of the evening, Charles couldn't avoid a small shiver of cold. But then his father called out to him. "Come on, Charles. It's this way." And a moment later they were out of the main square and making their way back through the souq.

By dinnertime, the whole incident had been forgotten.

The meal was served once again on the roof, and this time there were belly dancers performing to the wail and beat of a small band of musicians all dressed in brilliant white. The guests loved it and—to Charles's embarrassment—his parents insisted on joining in. His father was a large, well-built man, and the sight of him waving his arms in the air while shaking his stomach around was something that Charles felt would damage him for life. In the end he crept away and went to bed.

It was about eleven o'clock when he turned out the light. His parents were still upstairs, probably telling rude jokes by now—which is what they always did when they'd had too much to drink. Charles was fed up. The heat of Marrakesh wore him out and he was in dire need of a large plate of French fries. As far as he was concerned, the vacation couldn't end a day too soon. Five minutes later, he was asleep. His last, comforting thought was that at least when he woke up there would only be another three days to go.

But in fact, he was woken suddenly in the middle of the night. The room was not quite dark. Four windows looked out onto the courtyard and the moon was slanting in, washing everything a pale white. He turned his head and saw his watch, propped up against a lamp. It showed half past three. What was it that had disturbed him?

The sound came again, sliding underneath the door or through the window, and although Charles didn't understand why, it sent a shiver all the way down his spine. Music. The shimmering wail of a pipe. It was the snake charmer . . . it had to be. Charles recognized the sound from the main square. The old man must be somewhere outside the riad—although surely that wasn't possible, as he was fairly sure that his room didn't back onto the street. And yet he sounded so close! It was almost as if he were right inside the room.

Something moved.

Charles didn't see it, but he knew it was there. As the

hairs stood up, one after another, along the back of his neck, he heard its body, heavy and soft, sliding across the tiled floor. It was heading for the bed—but how had it gotten into the room? The door wasn't open. The windows were barred. His first thought was that it must be some sort of huge insect that had somehow slipped through a crack in the plasterwork, but he knew that wasn't true. The music told him exactly what it was, and sure enough, a moment later it rose up at the foot of the bed—inches from his feet—silhouetted dark green against the moonlight, its little eyes blinking malevolently, its tongue flickering, its hood stretched wide. Charles could imagine its body curled up beneath it.

The cobra.

It was there, with him, in the room.

For a few seconds it swayed from side to side as if unsure what to do. Then the music stopped. There was a sudden silence. It was the signal the snake had been waiting for. At once, it lunged toward him.

All the beds at the riad had duvets rather than sheets and blankets, and the snake had aimed for the gap between the soft material above and the mattress below. Charles knew at once that it had entered the bed with him and he tried to pull his legs back, tried to roll out of bed and hurl himself onto the floor. But his body wouldn't obey him. It was doing things it had never done before. His heart was heaving. His eyes were bulging. He seemed to have swallowed his own tongue. There were tears coursing down the sides of his face. He screamed for help, but only the tiniest of whispers came out.

Charles was lying on his back with his legs slightly apart. He was wearing pajama bottoms but no top, and he could feel the sweat sliding over his stomach. The music had begun again, so close now that the piper could have been sitting right next to the bed with the pipe beside his ear. Desperately, he looked down. He could just make out the bulge beneath the duvet as the cobra slithered first one way, then the other. It was climbing up between his legs, and he realized exactly where it was going to bite him.

Oh, God! He could imagine its fangs, perhaps as much as half an inch long. They were like hypodermic needles. He remembered that from the Discovery Channel too. When the cobra struck, it would inject him with a venom that would paralyze his nervous system. His muscles would dissolve. He would die slowly, unable to breathe, and when his parents came in the next morning, they would hardly recognize him. He would be a shriveled mummy, wrapped in pain.

The music stopped again. And in this second silence everything happened. The cobra struck. Charles felt its bite and screamed—and this time his voice came out loud and hopeless. At the same moment, his hands grasped the duvet and he threw it one way even as he threw himself the other, rolling off the bed and crashing onto the cold tiled floor. In the distance he heard voices, raised in alarm. Footsteps echoed across the courtyard. And then the door flew open, the lights went on and there were Rupert and Noreen, his father in pajamas, his mother in a nightgown with moisturizer all over her face.

"Charlie, darling? What is it?" she squealed.

"The s-s-s . . ." Charles was lying on the floor, trembling violently. He was almost hissing like a snake himself, but he couldn't get the word out.

"The what? What is it?"

"There's a snake!" The tears flowed more heavily. Charles knew that his parents had come too late. He had already been bitten. The agony would start soon.

"I don't see a snake," Noreen said.

"You've wet the bed," his father observed.

Charles looked down between his legs. Sure enough, there was a large damp patch on his pajamas, but there was no sign of any bite mark, no cut or tear in the fabric. As he began to recover, he had to admit that he wasn't feeling any pain after all. Meanwhile, his parents had moved into the room. His mother was picking up the duvet. His father was vaguely searching around the bed. Both of them looked embarrassed.

"There's nothing here," Rupert said.

"Come on, darling. Let me help you change out of those pajamas." Noreen took a fresh pair out of the cupboard and went over to her son. She was talking to him as if he were six years old.

"I heard music," Charles insisted. "It was the man from the square. He was outside the room."

"I didn't hear anything," Rupert muttered.

Noreen nodded. "You know what a light sleeper your father is," she said. "If there had been someone playing music, he'd have heard it." She sighed. "You must have had a bad dream."

"He was outside!" Charles insisted. "I heard him. And there was a snake. I saw it!"

"I'm going back to bed," Rupert growled.

He turned and walked out of the room, leaving Charles alone with his mother. By now Charles was beginning to accept that his parents must be right. The music had stopped. There was no sign of any snake. He hadn't, after all, been bitten. Now his face was bright red with embarrassment. He just wanted the night to be over so that he could forget all about it.

"Do you want me to run a bath?" his mother asked.

"No. I'll do it," Charles replied sulkily.

"Well, I'll stay until you're tucked up again." Noreen

had already taken off the bottom sheet. She was examining the mattress in dismay. "We'll have to turn this over," she said. "Maybe I'd better call room service."

"Just leave me alone."

"Are you sure, dear?"

"Go away."

She did. Charles went into the bathroom, showered and changed into clean pajamas. Then he went back to bed, laying himself down on the very edge and covering himself with a spare blanket that he had found in a cupboard. He still wasn't sure what had happened. A dream? It had been too real. He was old enough to know the difference between being awake and being asleep. And yet . . .

Somehow he nodded off once again. And the next time he opened his eyes, he was relieved to see daylight on the other side of the windows. Another day had begun.

He was a little sheepish when he joined his parents for breakfast on the roof, but for once they seemed to be behaving sensibly, for neither of them mentioned the events of the night before. Like everything at the Riad El Fenn, breakfast was an elaborate affair with croissants and coffee, pancakes dipped in honey, yogurt and fruit and delicious omelets for those who still had enough room. There were at least a dozen guests still at the table and Charles ignored them all as he plumped himself down on a cushion between Noreen and Rupert.

"We thought we'd visit the El-Badi Palace," his father said. He already had his guidebook open at the right place.

"And there's a wonderful garden," his mother added.

"I'm not staying here one minute longer," Charles replied. "I want to go home."

He had made the decision as he got dressed. All he wanted was to get out of Marrakesh. And his parents couldn't keep him here. He would scream if he had to. He would run away, grab a taxi and force them to put him on a plane. He should never have come here in the first place, and from now on he wasn't going to let anyone tell him what to do. If they wanted to go on vacation in the future, they could go without him. Otherwise it would be Disneyland and no argument! He had made up his mind.

"Well, I don't know . . . ," his father began.

Outside on the street, a pipe began to play.

It was the same music that they had heard in the main square—and this time there could be no doubt that it really existed. The other guests heard it and began to smile. Somehow the sound captured everything that was ancient and mysterious about a city that had been there for almost a thousand years.

Charles jerked upright in his seat.

"Charlie . . . ?" His mother quavered.

He was sweating. His eyes were distant and unfocused.

"What is it?" his father asked.

Charles got to his feet. He didn't want to but he couldn't stop himself. The music continued, louder, more insistent. "No . . ." He whispered the word and nobody heard it except him. His teeth were locked together. The other guests were watching. The music played.

And slowly, helplessly, Charles Atchley began to dance.

ROBO-NANNY

Later on, they would blame each other. It didn't matter which one of them you asked. They would both say that it had never been *their* idea to buy Robo-Nanny.

But it had seemed sensible enough at the time. After all, they were busy people—Sanjiv Mahal, international director of the world's second largest Internet bank, and his wife, Nicole, designer and photographer, in constant demand both on Earth and on the moon. Their days were crammed full of clients, meetings and reports. They were invited to dinner parties five times a week. They spent their entire lives traveling thousands of miles for meetings in Beijing, Tokyo, Moscow and Antarctica and seldom seemed to be on one continent—or even one planet—at the same time.

The Mahals had been married for fifteen years and had two children: Sebastian, age eleven, and Cameron, who was nine. And that was the problem. Everyone agreed that the boys were delightful—good-looking, intelligent and, for the most part, well-behaved. But like all boys they were noisy and demanded attention, whether it was Sebastian kicking a football around the house and playing his nano-guitar at full volume or Cameron drawing all over his bedroom wall or singing opera with a hologram of the complete London Symphony Orchestra while he was in the bath. Although there were two years between them, they could have been twins. Both were rather thin and small for their age, with brown hair that they never brushed, wide smiles and very dark eyes. Put them in the same soccer jersey (they both supported Chelski) and it would be hard to tell them apart.

The family lived in Kensington Fortress, which was one of the most exclusive areas of London and one with no drugs or knife crime . . . if only because it was surrounded by its own force field and nobody could get in or out without showing their ID cards to the local private police force. They had recently moved into a new home, which Nicole had designed herself. She had always wanted to live somewhere old-fashioned, with a sense of history, so she had modeled it on a twenty-first century mews house with shutters, window boxes and a proper staircase connecting the three floors. Of course, the red bricks and gray slate roof tiles concealed every luxury that the twenty-second century had to offer, including solar heating, a miniature hydroelectric generator in the kitchen, holo-TV in all the rooms and everything computer-controlled, right down to the bathwater. Even the staircase moved, at the touch of a button. The house was amazingly large. Anyone who walked in would know at once that the Mahals had to be seriously wealthy. They didn't have a garden—private gardens in London had long since disappeared—but they did have a small patio with a micro-BBQ and a vertical swimming fountain. They were a happy, successful family. All that was about to change.

Sanjiv Mahal was spending more and more time in China. Nicole Mahal had just accepted a commission to design sixteen holiday-pods in the Sahara Desert. The question was, who was going to look after Cam and Seb if the parents happened to be away at the same time? They would be at school every morning for three hours, but this didn't even involve getting out of bed as they both went to Hill House, an exclusive virtual school that they could plug into where they lay. And what would they do after that? There were local teen centers and exercise areas. Both children could dive into one of the thousands of Internet streams or turn on their PlayStation 207. But they still needed someone to cook and clean, to make sure they were washed and dressed, to stop them from fighting, to look after them if they became sick.

And one day, over breakfast, they found the answer. It was beamed down to them during a news scan.

"New—from Cyber-Life Industries," the voice announced. In the background, hypno-music was playing quietly to make the product seem even more fantastic. "Our new line of Robo-Nannys is now ready for immediate delivery. The model T-199 is our most advanced yet, with completely lifelike appearance and full range of face and voice types (our deluxe models include Australian, Eastern European and Welsh). The T-199 is programmed to deal with infants and children up to any age, and our new Emotional Self-Learning Software means that the nanny will quickly adapt to become a treasured part of your family. Kids giving you a hard time? Won't eat their genetically modified greens? Turn up the Severity Control™ and they'll quickly learn that nanny knows best! Firm friend or loving companion, the T-199 is the next step forward in modern child care."

"That's the answer!" Sanjiv exclaimed. He was a dark, handsome man, smartly dressed even at the breakfast table, the sort who made his decisions very quickly, although in this instance he would later swear that he was only responding to what his wife had suggested. "I don't know why we didn't think of it before. A Robo-Nanny!" He reached into his pocket and took out his Chinese Express credit card. "I'll call them now."

"I'm not so sure . . . ," Nicole began.

"What's the matter?"

"I just think we ought to talk about it, that's all," Nicole said. "I've always looked after the boys myself. I'm not sure I'm ready to hand them over to some machine that you've seen on a news scan."

"It's Cyber-Life Industries. They've got a terrific reputation."

"I'm sure they have." Nicole was uneasy without quite knowing why. "But it is very expensive," she blurted out. "Look at the price. Two million IY." The International Yen had been the world currency for half a century now. "Are you sure we can afford it?"

"Of course we can," her husband replied. "We've had a good year. I got my promotion. And your new contract in the Sahara will pay at least twice that amount."

"But I was going to take them with me."

"They'd hate it out there. Too hot and too many Martian wasps. Why did they ever import Martian wasps? The boys will be happier and safer here with their new T-199. I say we go ahead and order."

They discussed it a little more, and perhaps they might not have gone ahead with the purchase if Seb and Cam hadn't chosen that morning to get into a serious fist-fight. Nicole heard the screams and the crash of falling furniture coming from the upstairs bedroom and nodded at her husband. "I suppose it can't hurt to try," she said. "Maybe they'll let us have a three-month trial."

In fact, the salesman from Cyber-Life offered them more than that. He was a small bald-headed man with a round face and glasses; in his bright mauve suit, he looked a bit like a windup toy himself. He had introduced himself as Mr. O'Dowd.

"We offer a full no-questions-asked refund if you are not one hundred percent happy with your new purchase," he explained over a cup of soya tea that same evening. "But I can assure you, my dear Mahals, that we have never yet received a single complaint. I thought the T-170 was advanced. The T-199 is in a different league. It's the most reliable and human-looking robot we have yet constructed."

"When can we see it?" Nicole asked.

"You mean—when can you see *her,*" the salesman responded, casting a slight frown in Nicole's direction. "We encourage our clients to think of our nannies as real people rather than objects. Apart from anything, it helps the ESLS to kick in faster—"

"Emotional Self-Learning Software," Sanjiv muttered.

"That's right, sir. As a result, your nanny will bond much faster with your children—and they with her. And you can see her right away! I'll just unpack the container."

There was a large crate hovering on its antigravity

cushions in one corner of the room. Mr. O'Dowd pressed a remote control on the iBand he was wearing around his wrist and the crate slid silently across the room and opened. Nicole couldn't help feeling that it looked a bit like an old-fashioned coffin, even though it had been a hundred years since anyone was buried. These days bodies were all recycled.

But her fears were quickly swept aside by the young woman who now sat up and gently folded back the sheets of soft fabric in which she had been wrapped. If the nanny had been human, Nicole would have guessed that she would have been in her early thirties. She was neither fat nor thin but somewhere pleasantly in between, with an honest, open face, reddish hair and a scattering of freckles. She was dressed very simply in a V-neck shirt and jeans with her toes—brightly painted—poking through her sandals.

"Good afternoon, Mr. and Mrs. Mahal," she said. It was remarkable that she had already been data-fed with their name—or perhaps she had been listening to the conversation while she was lying in the crate. "It's a great pleasure to meet you." She spoke with a New Zealand accent. She had a very friendly voice.

"Hello," Sanjiv said. "And what's your name?"

"I'm Tamsin," Robo-Nanny said.

"All the T-models have names that begin with T," Mr. O'Dowd muttered. "Tracey, Tania, Tara, Toni, Tina, Terri and so on."

"I'm Nicole. And this is Sanjiv." It was clear that Nicole had quickly taken to the new arrival—but how could she have failed to? Tamsin was delightful. As she climbed out of the crate and brushed herself down, she moved like a ballet dancer. She was quite short, but that only made her more child friendly. She would be just a few inches taller than Sebastian. She also had the most wonderful blue eyes. Even though she had been delivered in a crate, it was already impossible to think of her as a robot. Everything about her—from her skin color to her smile—was totally human. Perfectly human, Nicole thought.

"Do you have an instruction book for her?" Sanjiv asked, and Nicole thought it was rather rude, talking in front of Tamsin like that.

But Tamsin didn't seem to mind. "I don't need an instruction book," she explained. "I've already been programmed with all my instructions and I'm quite able to look after myself."

"There are just a couple of things you need to know," Mr. O'Dowd added. "Could you show them your controls, please, Tamsin?"

"With pleasure, sir." Tamsin rolled up her sleeve to

show a small panel on her arm with a few flashing lights, switches and dials. It was the only evidence that she was in fact a machine.

"You can make adjustments here if you need to," Mr. O'Dowd continued. "For example, Tamsin speaks nine languages." He reached out and pressed one of the buttons.

"*Je suis ravi de faire votre connaissance,*" Tamsin said.

He switched her back to English. "You can also adjust her physical strength . . . useful if you want her to do any heavy lifting. And you'll find her Severity Control on her right shoulder. That's a very useful piece of kit."

"I believe it's unique to Cyber-Life," Sanjiv said.

"Absolutely." Mr. O'Dowd was pleased to be asked. "There are plenty of nannies on the market at the moment, but ours are the only ones that come with five different levels of severity. If your children are delightful and well-behaved, as I am sure yours are, my dear Mr. and Mrs. Mahal, then you only need to set Tamsin to level one. If they are a little unruly or disobedient, then you can turn the switch to level two or three. Tamsin will then make sure that they do their homework, brush their teeth or whatever—and she'll be a little less generous with sweets, stories and other treats."

"What about level five?" Nicole asked.

"I have never yet met a child that needed level-five severity," Mr. O'Dowd said, "and I would frankly recommend that you ignore it. Level-five nannies are mainly used on the outer islands . . ."

Nicole shuddered. The outer islands had once been oil rigs—at a time when there was still oil. Now they were used as floating prisons for juvenile delinquents. They were in the North Sea, a mile away from the Independent Kingdom of Scotland.

"What level do you think would be necessary?" Tamsin asked.

From upstairs came the sound of breaking glass as a thought-controlled hover ball smashed through a bedroom window.

"I'd say level two," Nicole muttered.

"Level two," her husband agreed.

"I'll just make the adjustment," Tamsin said. She reached farther up her sleeve and turned the dial. Nothing about her seemed to change. She smiled at the two parents. "Now," she said, "when can I meet your adorable boys?"

In fact, they waited until Mr. O'Dowd had left, taking the crate and a first payment of half a million IY with him. As Nicole said, it didn't seem right for the boys to see their new nanny being paid for and delivered in a box. Tamsin was sitting in a chair when they came into the room, but she rose up at once, obviously delighted to see them.

"Hello, boys!" she exclaimed. "You must be Sebastian. And you must be Cameron." She had gotten their names the right way around. It was a good start. "I'm Tamsin, your new Robo-Nanny."

She had told them at once that she was a robot, even though it would have been easy to pretend otherwise. The Law of Artificial Intelligence (2125) stated that no machine could pretend to be human when it was presented to its new owner. There had been some upsetting instances of robots pretending to be human in order to get jobs in McDonald's restaurants. The new law had made this a crime—and the penalty was instant demolition.

At first, the boys were unsure.

"Why do we have to have her?" Sebastian asked, turning to Nicole.

Some might have considered this to be a rude question, but Tamsin didn't seem offended. "Your parents need someone to help look after you," she explained. "They're going to be away on business a lot and they don't want to leave you on your own."

"Are you really a machine?" Cameron asked.

"I am. But you don't need to think of me that way, dear. I'd like to be your friend."

"What's your name?"

"I'm Tamsin."

"Tamsin? Tamsin?" Cameron played with the name for a moment. "If you're really made of metal, I'm going to call you Tin Sam," he announced.

And that was the name that stuck, even though the most state-of-the-art robots contained almost no metal at all and certainly not a trace of tin. But in the months that followed, Tin Sam proved herself to be worth every one of the two million International Yen she had cost. She was a great cook. She tidied and cleaned the house. She made sure the boys were properly dressed and gently scolded them if they forgot to vibro-clean their teeth or made too much noise. She loved playing games—whether it was hover ball (she didn't break any windows) or Space Monopoly.

She took the boys on trips around London. Tin Sam loved ancient buildings. She took them to the Gherkin, which had once been an office block but had been converted into a museum of extinct animals. She pointed out the tigers and the polar bears and seemed to know all about them. She took them walking in the maze of dark tunnels that had once housed an underground transport system and they went swimming in the crystal blue water of the Thames. Very soon the three of them became close friends, just as Tin Sam had hoped. She never lost her temper and—it seemed to Sanjiv and Nicole—the boys had never been happier. The whole house felt quiet and relaxed.

Finally the day came when the two parents had to be away at the same time . . . both of them on business trips. Nicole had farther to go. She had completed her work in the Sahara Desert and was now traveling to the moon— via the Jump Station in Florida. A whole new colony was being set up in the shadow of the Taurus Mountains and she was designing the interiors of the SLUMs, or Self-sufficient Life Utility Modules to give them their full name. Sanjiv was heading back to China. The children would be on their own with Tamsin for a whole week.

It was as the parents were leaving that the accident happened. At least, that was what they decided later, when they were trying to work it out. It was a Tuesday morning and Nicole and Sanjiv were sharing a magno-cab—which would ride the magnetic fields over London to the Heathrow Teleportation Center. From here, Nicole would be beamed over to America while Sanjiv—his body briefly turned into a billion separate molecules—traveled in the opposite direction to Shanghai. Tin Sam had baked a delicious zero-calorie cake to celebrate their departure. And she was there with the boys when they came down to wave good-bye. The two brothers weren't at all worried about being left behind. In fact, they were thinking of it as quite an adventure.

Sanjiv was carrying a heavy briefcase. Nobody bothered with luggage anymore, but he had a number of contracts which, for legal reasons, still had to be printed on old-fashioned paper. What happened really wasn't his fault. As he swung the case into the back of the magnocab, Tin Sam leaned forward to help him and the full weight of the case hit her on the shoulder. For a moment, she stood there as if frozen. Nicole glanced at her in alarm. She saw something flicker, quite literally, in Robo-Nanny's eyes . . . a tiny short circuit that flared up and then was gone.

"Are you all right, Tamsin?" she asked.

The nanny raised a hand to her forehead. "Yes, thank you, Mrs. Mahal."

"I'm terribly sorry," Sanjiv muttered. "I didn't mean to hit you."

"It's quite all right, sir. I'm not programmed to feel pain. And I don't think you've done any damage."

"Are you sure?"

"Absolutely."

"Well, that's a relief." Sanjiv glanced at his iBand. "It's time we were on our way," he said.

Mr. and Mrs. Mahal kissed the two boys good-bye and got into the magnocab. As they were swept into the air, Nicole looked out of the back window. The last thing she saw was Tamsin—or Tin Sam—standing between Sebastian and Cameron, holding each of their hands. The three of them couldn't have looked happier together. Even so, she was uneasy . . . without knowing why.

Things went wrong very quickly.

It began that same afternoon. To cheer the boys up after their parents had gone, Tin Sam had agreed to take them to the antigravity play center in what had once been the traffic interchange known as Piccadilly Circus. Seb and Cam had been looking forward to it all week. But when they came down to the hall, Tin Sam was frowning.

"Which one of you left the lights on in the bathroom?" she demanded.

Seb looked at Cam. Cam looked at Seb. It could have been either of them—but what did it matter anyway? All the lights in the house were nuclear powered. They could burn for a million years without even changing a bulb.

But obviously Tin Sam thought differently. "You should switch the lights off to save energy," she said. "So we'll stay at home this afternoon."

"But Sam . . . !" Seb began.

"Are you arguing with me, Sebastian?" Tin Sam demanded, and there was something in her voice that made both the boys tremble very slightly.

"He's not arguing," Cam muttered.

"And are you, by any chance, speaking with your mouth full?"

It was sadly true that Cameron was chewing a small piece of Astromint Gum, although it hardly counted as having his mouth full.

"What?" Cam asked.

"You don't mean 'what.' You mean 'pardon me.' "

"I don't understand," Cameron said.

"Well, you can go straight to your room and try to work it out," Tin Sam said. "I don't want to see either of you until tomorrow." There was something in her voice that convinced the boys it wouldn't be a good idea to argue. Rather grumpily, they both went up to bed. They just hoped she would be in a better mood in the morning.

But she wasn't. At breakfast the next day, things got even worse.

As usual, Seb and Cam came tumbling into the kitchen in their pajamas, the unpleasant events of the day before already forgotten. They were expecting Tin Sam to serve her delicious organic, free-range, non-chicken scrambled eggs and Beta-Fix breakfast cereal. But they were in for a surprise.

As they came in, she ran her eyes over them. "You haven't cleaned your teeth!" she announced, a frown of indignation spreading across her face. "My sensors can detect seven different bacteria. You also haven't brushed your hair or washed your hands."

"We can do that later," Sebastian said lazily.

"You'll do it now!"

"Oh come off it, Tin Sam—"

It was as far as he got. Tin Sam was holding a bowl of cereal and she suddenly upturned it all over Sebastian's head. Sebastian yelled out as ice-cold milk dripped down the back of his neck. Cameron laughed. That was a mistake. Picking up the wooden spoon that she had been using to stir the eggs, Tin Sam brought it cracking down, just above his left ear. Cameron howled.

"You really shouldn't laugh at your brother," Robo-Nanny explained. "It isn't kind. It isn't polite. Now, go away and wash, and then I'll serve breakfast."

The two boys did what they were told. Tin Sam had never behaved like this before and they were puzzled. At the same time, they had to agree that she had a point. Their mother was always telling them to wash their hands before they sat down to eat. In restaurants and other public places it was actually the law. Maybe, before she had left for her job on the moon, Mrs. Mahal had instructed the nanny to enforce the rules a little more strictly.

But their ordeal wasn't over yet. Indeed, it had barely begun.

When they returned to the kitchen, Tin Sam served the breakfast, but Sebastian had barely taken one mouthful before Tin Sam's hand slammed into the back of his head, almost knocking him off his seat.

"You were eating with your mouth open," Robo-Nanny explained.

"But if I don't open my mouth, how can I eat?" Sebastian demanded, not unreasonably.

Whack! Tin Sam hit him again—this time even harder. "Don't argue, Master Sebastian," she said. "You should never argue with grown-ups."

"But you're not a grown-up. You're a robot!"

Sebastian was going to wish he hadn't argued a second time. Without another word, Tin Sam seized hold of his jacket and jerked him out of his chair.

"What are you . . . ?" Sebastian began.

"You can stand here, Master Sebastian! That will teach you to make rude remarks."

She had dragged him across the room and forced him into a corner with his hands behind his back, and that was where she made him stand. All in all that might not have been such a terrible punishment, but seventeen hours later he was still there and she still wouldn't let him leave, even though his legs were aching and he was desperate for the toilet.

In the meantime, Cameron had gotten into trouble too. First, he was scolded for not making his bed, even though he'd never had to make it before. And when he did—grudgingly—do as he was told, Robo-Nanny took one look at his handiwork and flew into a rage.

"Sheets?" she shrilled.

They were crumpled.

"Duvet?"

It wasn't straight.

"Pillows?"

Cameron never found out what was wrong with the pillows. Seizing hold of them, Tin Sam tore them in half. A moment later the air was full of simulo-feathers, which fluttered around her head.

"You are a naughty, lazy, difficult child," she remarked, her normally cheerful face bright with anger.

"But—" Cameron began.

"No lunch. No sweets. No treats. No talking." The eight words came rattling out as if from a speak-your-weight machine rather than the world's most advanced robot, and she meant what she said. Cameron spent the rest of the day hungry and silent. It was only when it grew dark that he found the courage to ask if he could perhaps have a glass of water. It was a mistake. Tin Sam grabbed him, bent him over her knee and gave him six blows with the palm of her hand. It hurt. A week before she had used the same palm of the same hand to drive nails into wood.

The two boys went to bed in a state that was close to terror. They didn't understand what they had done wrong—or why everything had so suddenly changed.

How were they to know that, as he had left the house, their father had accidentally swung his briefcase into Robo-Nanny's Severity Control, moving it immediately from level two to level five? That would have been bad enough, but during the first night, the control had gone into meltdown. Robo-Nanny had a safety mechanism to stop her from becoming too severe, but sadly this had failed. By breakfast time on the second day, the Severity Control had reached the equivalent of level nine—and it was still rising.

Sebastian and Cameron cleaned their teeth several times, brushed their hair until it looked as if it had been painted on, and came down to breakfast as quietly as they could—but that still wasn't enough for Robo-Nanny.

"Aren't you going to say good morning to me?" she asked.

"Good morning, Tamsin," the boys chorused. They had decided to use her proper name.

"That's better. Now, sit down!"

The boys sat. They ate what they were given without saying anything and didn't even remark on the fact that the toast was a little burned and that the Bio-Rice Crispies were perhaps a little soggy. Their behavior was perfect right up to the last moment when Cameron set down his knife and fork. The two of them were about half an inch apart.

"When you finish your meal, you should put the knife and fork next to each other," Robo-Nanny said. Picking up the knife, she jammed it into Cameron's shoulder.

Cameron screamed.

"You should cover your mouth when you scream," Robo-Nanny said, and, picking up the fork, she plunged that into him too.

"Stop!" Sebastian yelled. As the older brother, he knew he had to protect Cameron, but he wasn't sure what to do.

"Shouting at the breakfast table?" Tamsin asked. She reached out for the saucepan, which was still hot, having just come off the stove, and swung it in a wide arc, catching Sebastian on the side of his head and throwing him off his feet.

"You wait until Mum and Dad get back," Cameron wailed. He was crawling across the carpet, trying to get away.

"I didn't hear you ask to leave the table," Robo-Nanny said. She leaned down and picked him up. Cameron suddenly looked smaller than ever. He seemed to weigh nothing in her hands. Holding him by the shoulders, she swung him around and hurled him at the wall. He crashed into it, plaster and brickwork cascading around him, then slid to the floor next to his brother.

"You're mad!" Sebastian shouted.

"What did you say?"

"You're . . ." The words died in Sebastian's throat.

Robo-Nanny's eyes seemed to have widened. There was a soft light pulsing behind them. A moment later, she lunged forward and seized him, holding him in a vice-like grip. "How dare you call me that!" she responded. "How dare you be so rude! Well, I'm afraid I'm going to have to teach you a lesson, Master Sebastian. I'm going to wash your mouth out with soap and water." And, dragging him over to the sink, she did exactly that, forcing half a tube of detergent down the struggling boy's throat and following it with a viciously rotating Pulsa-Brush that she had turned up to maximum strength. Sebastian tried to fight back—but he didn't have a chance. Lying on the floor, Cameron heard the terrible screams and gargling sounds. Then, fortunately, after just a minute or two, his brother slipped into unconsciousness.

Terrified and whimpering, Cameron crawled out of the kitchen. Moving as quickly as he could, trying to ignore his many injuries, he made it to his room and barricaded the door. It was just a shame that he had forgotten to take his homework with him. Ten seconds later, the door was blown off its hinges and there was Robo-Nanny with a Burglar Blaster automatic handgun in one hand and a dozen of his schoolbooks in the other. "What is seventeen times seven?" she demanded.

"I don't know!" Cameron wailed. Math had never been his best subject.

"Who was the first man on Mars?"

Cameron had forgotten the answer—but even if he'd remembered it, he wouldn't have had time to spit it out. Robo-Nanny fell on him. First she emptied the remaining bullets into him. Then she slammed all twelve of the books down on his skull. Finally, she tore out some of the pages and tried to stuff them into his ears. With the last of his strength, Cameron managed to lash out. His fist caught her on the jaw.

"Well, really!" Robo-Nanny exclaimed, and tore off his arm.

"Stop it!" Sebastian groaned. The older brother had recovered from his encounter with the Pulsa-Brush and had somehow arrived at what was left of the bedroom door. Cameron noticed that he was missing several teeth. "I've microtexted Mum and Dad. They're coming home."

"You naughty, naughty boy!" Tamsin shrilled, hitting him repeatedly with his brother's arm.

"They'll deal with you!" Cameron whimpered.

"But not before I've dealt with you!" Tamsin replied. She reached into her pocket and took out the laser carving knife that she had brought up from the kitchen. "Now, which one of you is going to be the first to be punished . . . ?"

Sanjiv and Nicole Mahal got back that same night.

They knew at once that something was terribly wrong. The house was shrouded in darkness. The central computer had been deactivated and all the alarms and voice-activation systems were turned off. Everything was much too quiet. Dreading what they might find, they tiptoed into the hallway. Sanjiv reached out and pressed the manual override on the lights.

Robo-Nanny was sitting, giggling quietly, surrounded by what was left of Sebastian and Cameron. She had cut the boys into about fifty pieces each, and the Mahals knew at once that they would never even be able to tell which child was which. There were cogs, wires and bits of circuit board everywhere. One of the boys' plastic hands was lying on the carpet, the fingers still twitching as the last beats of electricity flowed through it. A glass eyeball lay nearby. Sebastian's arm, with its own control panel, was sitting on the hall table. They knew it was Sebastian's because the serial number was still visible.

Fortunately, Cyber-Life agreed to provide Sanjiv and Nicole with two new robo-children, and a week later, the family was exactly as it had been when this all started. If anything, the two new boys were even more perfect than the old ones had been. They had been programmed with a slightly lower naughtiness level so that although they were occasionally mischievous and disobedient, nothing in the house ever got broken.

Tamsin herself was taken away, and the Mahals didn't ask what had happened to her. The two of them did argue occasionally about whose idea it had been to employ her, and they never came to any agreement. But then again, they were human . . . so what do you expect?

BAD DREAM

When Eric Simpson went to bed,
Silk pillows lay beneath his head.
The sheets, a perfect shade of white,
Were freshly laundered every night.
His quilt was utterly deluxe.
No fewer than two hundred ducks
Had met their maker to provide
The feathers that had gone inside.
The mattress was so very soft
It didn't lie so much as waft
Across the springs that held it up
Like froth above a coffee cup.
By now you will be well aware
That Eric was a millionaire—
At least his father was, for he
Had made a pile in property.
Show him a field and he would bawl,
"Why, that should be a shopping mall!"

An ancient woodland, in his mind,
Should be cut down and redesigned
And turned into a cul-de-sac
With fifty houses back to back.
In short, he took a real pride
In wiping out the countryside.
Young Eric really can't be blamed
For being similarly framed;
A herd of cows would make him shriek
And tremble for at least a week,
And even flowers had the trick
Of making him feel rather sick.
The city was his habitat.
His father had a penthouse flat
With views of concrete all around,
And that's where Eric would be found
Dreaming of the day when he
Might also work in property.
We join him now . . . it's half past ten.
He cleans his teeth (and flosses), then
He goes to bed, turns out the light
And settles down to spend the night
In total peace and comfort, which
Attend upon the super-rich.
But even as his eyelids close,
A sudden gust of something blows

Into his room. The curtains leap
But Eric's gone—he's fast asleep
And in that moment he is hurled
Straight into another world.
He's running through a moonlit wood.
The trees are close. This isn't good.
Why is he here? He stops to think,
And at that moment starts to sink
Into a bog. He feels it rise
Above his feet, his calves, his thighs,
And soon he finds—what rotten luck—
That he's become completely stuck.
He punches down. The wet mud splotches.
All around him, Nature watches:
It looks as if this boy from town
Will very soon begin to drown.
But Eric knows it's just a dream,
He wants to wake up, tries to scream,
But not a word escapes his lips
As inch by inch the cold mud grips.
He feels it clinging to his skin
And whimpers as it pulls him in.
He twists and turns. A single jerk
Might pull him free. It doesn't work.
Instead the movement's a disaster—
Now he's sinking even faster.

The swamp's already 'round his chest.
He has just minutes more at best.
A living thing, the horrid slime
Continues its relentless climb.
He puts his arms out, tries to float;
The mud has closed around his throat.
His lips draw back. His teeth are bare
As desperately he sucks the air
And strains his neck and lifts his chin
To stop the slime from rushing in.
His eyes are bulging, open wide,
As if he's been electrified.
Are things as dreadful as they seem?
They can't be. This is just a dream!
"A dream!" he manages to shout—
The words at last come bursting out.
At once the swamp climbs ever higher
As if to prove the boy a liar.
It fills his mouth and then his nose
As down and down and down he goes.
It's in his eyes. It's in his ears.
And finally he disappears,
Apart from one hand; in despair,
It stretches out to feel the air.
The fingers twitch just one more time
Then stop and sink into the slime.

The next day Eric slept in late.

The maid came in at ten past eight

With breakfast carried on a tray

And found to her intense dismay

The boy flat out upon the bed,

Facedown, hands out and stone-cold dead.

The maid (who had to be sedated)

Was told that he had suffocated.

"It can't be true!" she cried. "I fear

That something dreadful happened here."

And what was it that froze her blood?

Quite simply this: the smell of mud.

My Bloody French Exchange

I might as well say it straightaway. The French exchange was my dad's idea. As usual, he was thinking of what would be best for me without really wondering whether it would be something I would actually like. As far as I was concerned, the whole thing was unnecessary. Yes, my French wasn't up to much. But my SATs were still a whole year away and I was pretty sure that by then I'd be able to scrape through without spending two weeks being force-fed Camembert and French conversation.

But that's my dad for you. An overachiever. It isn't

enough that he's a farmer with about a million acres of land in the Cotswolds. He has a whole load of businesses too. So one day he's in Wellington boots, the next it's a pinstripe suit. And he expects everyone in the family to be the same. That's how I ended up with a twin sister who was top in just about every class in school and a cross-country champion too. A mum who was brilliant at everything. Even a dog that probably knew how to read.

And I hadn't done too badly myself. A's all the way down my school report. Captain of football. Captain of cricket. School leader. And in case by now you're thinking I must have been a complete jerk, I actually had friends too. We even got into trouble from time to time. I could tell you about the great Peeing-Out-of-the-Window incident, for example. But that's another story. And one that's a lot less horrible than this one.

My bloody French exchange.

I had just finished my second year at St. Edward's, a private school not far from Stratford. As the teachers kept on telling me, the third year was going to be tough because, of course, it finished with that delightful experience known as my SATs. My end-of-term report was pretty upbeat. Everyone agreed that I was going to have no trouble in math, history, geography, English and all the rest of it, but it was true that I was a little dodgy when it came to French. This was probably the result of having an extremely dodgy teacher. If you ask me, Mr. O'Reilly must have been the only language teacher in the entire private school system who spoke with a stammer. Not his fault, but it did make vocabulary tricky. We all assumed that every word was eighteen letters long.

My dad wasn't taking any chances. The summer break was nine weeks long, and before it had even started, he'd decided I'd devote two weeks of it to a stay in France. On my own.

"You've got to be kidding!" That was what I said when he told me. Or words like that, anyway.

"No, Jack. You'll have a great time. And it'll give you a real head start next term."

"But Dad . . . !"

"Let's not argue about it, old chap. I did a French exchange when I was your age and it did me a world of good. And you know perfectly well that the breaks are far too long. You usually end up being bored stiff."

This was true. But I didn't see why it would be any better being bored stiff in France. Not that it mattered. As usual, my arguments went nowhere. Or rather, they went to the Côte d'Azur, the south coast of France where some friends of friends knew a family who would love to have an English boy to stay with them for two weeks after which their own son, Adrien, would perhaps spend two weeks with the English family? Just what I needed! By the time Adrien was out of my life, almost half the break would be gone.

Normally, I like going abroad. But I felt gloomy as I packed my case, sneaking in a couple of paperbacks and my Nintendo DS so at least I would have something English in the days ahead. The Duclarcs lived just outside Nice. I had seen photographs of them, an ordinary-looking family sitting by the pool, and I had exchanged a couple of e-mails with Adrien. "I look much forward to meet with you." It seemed his English wasn't a lot better than my French. My dad drove me to the airport. It would be only the second time that I had flown alone, and at least this time I wasn't going to be made to wear a "junior traveler" label around my neck.

Nice was only about an hour and a half away, but it felt a lot longer. As I watched the gray ribbon of the English Channel slide behind me, it was almost as if I had somehow fallen off the edge of the world. Nothing was going to be the same on the other side. I had to remind myself that it was only two weeks, that I'd be able to telephone and e-mail every day, that hundreds of other kids did French exchanges and managed to survive. If the worse came to the worst, I'd just sit there and count the days. *Lundi. Mardi. Mercredi.* And whatever it was that came next . . .

Nathalie Duclarc was waiting for me at the airport

with Adrien. She was holding a sign with my name—JACK METCALFE—written in bold letters. Not that she needed it, as I was surely the only fifteen-year-old coming out of customs on his own. My first impression was of a small woman with very dark hair, rather pale skin and strangely colored eyes—somewhere between gray and green. It was easy to tell that Adrien was her son. He was the spitting image of her with the addition of a mustache, or at least the very beginnings of one. He was only fourteen, a few months younger than me, but it's something I've noticed about French kids. They like their facial hair and they try to grow it as early as they can, even if they can only manage a vague shadow along their upper lip.

"Hello, Jack. I hope you had a good flight," she said, folding the sign away. She spoke French. From now on, everything would be in French. But to be fair to her, she spoke slowly and clearly, and with a sense of relief, I realized that I could understand.

"I am Adrien. Welcome to my country." Her son nodded at me and smiled, and it occurred to me that he had probably been looking forward to meeting me as little as I had been looking forward to coming. Maybe this was going to be all right.

"Please, come this way. The car is not far."

Wheeling my suitcase behind me, I followed Nathalie to a parking lot on the other side of the airport, and of course we all had a good laugh when I tried to get into the driver's seat. It would take me a day or two before I remembered that the French drove on the right. It was eight o'clock in the evening and the sun had just set, but it was still baking hot, with no breeze in the night air. We drove for about twenty minutes, skirting the city and passing through a desolate industrial zone before finally turning off and climbing up a steep, narrow lane that was full of ruts and potholes, hemmed in on both sides by thick woodland. I was quite surprised. After all, we weren't far from the center of a major French city. And yet from the moment we left the main road, we could have been miles away, lost in the middle of the countryside. Somehow it felt darker than it had any right to be, though when I looked up, I was amazed to see the sky absolutely crammed with stars.

At last we slowed down and stopped. There was a solid metal gate blocking the way, but Nathalie pressed a remote control and it slid silently open. We swung around and up another steep path. There was just one building ahead of us. It was the house I was going to stay in.

It wasn't at all what I had expected. The Duclarcs' home was a low white building, very modern, with roofs that slanted at strange angles and windows the size of whole walls. These could slide back, opening the inside to the terrace, garden and the darkly inviting swimming

pool. The house stood on the side of a hill, entirely surrounded by trees, with Nice no more than a scattering of
bright lights far below. Madame Duclarc drove straight
toward a double garage built into the hillside under the
house. There must have been some sort of sensor. The
doors rolled open to let her in.

Inside, the house was even more unusual, with walls
of naked concrete, metal staircases and glass-bottomed
corridors giving me the impression of a sort of fortress—
though, again, a very modern one. The Duclarcs seemed
to like neon tubes so one room would glow red, another green, while the main living area, with its open-plan
kitchen, steel fireplace, spiral staircase and huge wooden
table reminded me of a theater stage.

Adrien's dad was named Patrick (pronounced Pat-
reek), and he greeted me in French that was rather more
difficult to understand, swallowing his words before
they had time to come out of his mouth. But he was still
friendly enough, a slim, athletic, curly-haired man—as
pale as his wife and son. Adrien was their only child, but
there was another member of the family at the table waiting to eat and, I have to say, I didn't like him from the start.

The Duclarc family had once lived in Eastern Europe,
and this was one of their distant relatives over on a visit.
He was Patrick's uncle or second cousin or something like
that . . . although it was explained to me, I didn't quite

manage to follow the French. My first thought was that he was ill. His hair was long and silver and looked as if it had never been brushed, hanging down just past his collar. He wasn't exactly thin. He had a sort of half-starved look, as if he hadn't eaten for a week. The way he sat, hunched over the table, you could imagine all the interlocking bones holding him together under his strange, old-fashioned clothes. I've already said it was boiling hot. Even so, the uncle was dressed in black trousers, boots, a white shirt and a loose-fitting black jacket that almost hung off him like a cape.

His name, I was told, was Vladimir Duclarc. I would have guessed he was about fifty years old, but I could have been wrong. His gray skin, his gnarled fingers and his hunched shoulders could have suggested someone much older. And yet, he had a certain energy. When he turned and looked at me, I saw something come alive in his eyes. It was there just for an instant, a sort of flame. He nodded at me but didn't speak. In fact, he spoke very little. French, I later learned, was his second language.

We sat down to dinner. I was feeling much more cheerful by now. For a start, the food was excellent. Smoked ham, fresh bread, three or four salads, a huge plate of cheese . . . all the food that the French do so well but which never quite tastes the same when you eat it at home. I noticed that Adrien drank wine, and although I was offered it, I stuck to Coke. The parents asked me a lot of questions about myself, my home in Burford, my family and all the rest of it. It would have been a nice evening.

Except there was something about Vladimir Duclarc that spoiled it. Every time I looked up, he seemed to be staring at me, as if he knew something I didn't. As if he were sizing me up. He ate very little. In fact, he didn't touch the salad, toying instead with a piece of raw ham that he chewed between small, sharp teeth, and even as he swallowed it with a little red wine, I could tell he would have much rather been eating something else. Me, perhaps. That was the impression he gave.

And there was one other thing that happened during that meal. Nathalie Duclarc had cooked some really delicious hot snacks. I'm not sure what you'd call them. They were slices of bread dipped in olive oil with tomato and mozzarella, baked in the oven. My mother made something very similar, and as I helped myself to a second portion, I managed to stretch my French vocabulary enough to say that she also used garlic in her recipe.

There was a sudden silence at the table. I wondered if I'd chosen the wrong word for garlic. But it was *l'ail*. I was sure of it.

"We never eat garlic in this family," Patrick said.

"Oh?" I wasn't sure what to say.

"My cousin Vladimir dislikes it."

"I hate garlic." Vladimir Duclarc spoke the words as if I had deliberately offended him.

"I'm very sorry . . ."

Next to me, Adrien was fidgeting. Then Patrick reached out and poured some more wine and everyone began talking again. The incident was forgotten—although I would remember it again in the days to come.

And the next few days were great. Patrick drove Adrien and me over to Monaco and we looked at all the million-dollar cars and ten-million-dollar yachts scattered around. We explored Nice—the markets, the cafés, the beach and so on. I went paragliding for the first time. We went to a couple of museums and an aquarium. I was beginning to think that maybe my dad had been right after all. I could actually feel my French getting better. I still found it hard to say anything very sensible, but I understood most of what Adrien and Nathalie said to me.

The only problem was that I wasn't sleeping very well. It was hard to say why not. It was hot and there was always a lone mosquito whining in my ear. Also, the bedroom was down a flight of stairs, underneath the main bulk of the house, and it never seemed to have enough air. But it was something more than that. I felt uneasy. I was having bad dreams. One night I was sure I heard wolves howling in the woods near the house. I mentioned this to Patrick and he smiled at me. Apparently, there *were* wolves in the area. The locals often heard them. There was absolutely nothing to worry about. But there was still something about them that kept me awake long into the night.

And then there was Vladimir Duclarc.

It must have been the third or fourth day of my visit that I realized something else that was rather strange about him. He never went out in the day. You'd think that with a huge swimming pool, local markets, the sea, there would be plenty of reasons for him to go outdoors, but in fact I never saw him until after eight o'clock, when the sun set. He spent long periods in his room and never talked about what he had been doing. Only when the darkness came would he walk out onto the terrace, craning his long neck and half closing his eyes as he took in the scented evening air.

One night he went out on his own. I actually saw him walking down the stairs, past the swimming pool and on toward the main gate, his footsteps so light that he almost seemed to be floating in the air. He didn't have a car and as far as I knew he couldn't drive. Nathalie was preparing the dinner and there was no sign of Adrien, so—on a whim—I followed him. I wasn't really doing anything. I mean, I was just playing a game, really. But it just seemed so odd for him to be disappearing into the darkness that

I couldn't help wondering where he was going and what he would do when he got there.

I reached the gate. There it was in front of me, a solid wall of sheet metal that had been stained by rust or rain. It hadn't opened, but suddenly there was no sign of Monsieur Duclarc. He had vanished. I knew it wasn't possible. He would have had to open the gate electronically to get out onto the main road, even if he was walking. But it hadn't moved. So where was he? I looked first one way, then another. Could he be hiding in the darkness? Was he watching me even now? No. That made no sense and, besides, I was certain he hadn't seen me. Something caught my eye and I glanced upward. A bat, almost invisible against the night sky, fluttered over my head like a piece of charred paper caught in a gust of wind. It was there and then it was gone.

And so was Vladimir Duclarc.

I didn't have much appetite that night. The empty chair on the opposite side of the table was somehow threatening. I could imagine an invisible man sitting there, his eyes fixed on me. For the first time, I felt homesick. I was even tempted to call my parents and ask them to let me return.

Perhaps I should have mentioned that I actually had a problem with the phones. It turned out that there was no mobile signal at the Duclarcs' home, and although they would have happily let me use their landline, it was right in the middle of the hallway where everyone would have heard, and I didn't like to ask. I'd brought my laptop with me, though, and I swapped e-mails every evening. Isabelle, my sister, had written a couple of times (assuring me that she wasn't missing me) and Mum and Dad had given me the latest news . . . a new tractor arriving, the wind turbine at the bottom of the garden breaking down, local gossip from the village. It all sounded so normal that once again I couldn't help feeling very far away. Not just another country but another planet.

It was on the sixth day of my visit that it all really went wrong. That was when I saw the mirror without the reflection.

Vladimir Duclarc had a bedroom at the end of the same corridor as mine. The house had a sort of guest annex, a lower floor that was built onto the side—and that was where the two of us were staying, slightly apart from the rest of the family. Most of the time (and certainly during the day) he kept the door shut. But I had seen inside a couple of times on my way to bed.

The room was as modern as the rest of the house, with an abstract painting—splodges of black and red—on one wall opposite the bed. The walls were gray concrete and the floor some sort of Scandinavian wood. Only the bed was antique, a four-poster that looked particularly un-comfortable and out of keeping with everything else. The room had one interesting feature. There was a full-sized mirror on one wall that actually swung open to reveal a walk-in closet behind. This was full of clothes that I as-sumed must belong to Nathalie and Patrick.

I'd actually been shown the room by Adrien when he had first taken me around the house and I had noticed the mirror as I walked past. Or rather, I'd noticed myself—the fair hair, the freckles and all the rest of it. Well, on the sixth day, just as I was on my way to dinner, I glanced down the corridor and saw Vladimir Duclarc standing next to the bed, fiddling with the cuff of the shirt he was wearing. He didn't notice me, which was just as well, because I stood there, wide-eyed, my whole body frozen as if a thousand volts of electricity had just been jammed through me.

Vladimir Duclarc had no reflection.

Now, I know what you're thinking. You're thinking that I'd gotten the angles wrong and that I simply couldn't see the reflection from where I was standing. But it wasn't like that. He was right in front of the mirror. Inches away from it. And there was no sign of him in the glass. Just vague shapes. He had no reflection!

And then the worst thing possible happened. I must have moved or made a sound because Vladimir glanced up and saw me staring at him. He was angry. I saw that strange fire in his eyes as his head turned toward me. He knew what I had seen. At once I muttered something that made no sense in French or English and hurried back to my room, closing the door behind me. But it was already too late. Why hadn't I moved away immediately, before he'd spotted me?

I stood there with my heart thumping, every one of my fingers prickling with fear. Perhaps I hadn't worked it out yet. Or perhaps I'd worked it out long before but had been trying to ignore it. All the evidence spread out in front of me, one piece after another. How could I have been so dumb?

Vladimir Duclarc never went out in the light.

He hated garlic.

He came from Eastern Europe.

He had somehow managed to vanish in front of the main gate seconds before I had seen a bat flickering away.

And he had no reflection.

And there was one last thing, one final piece of evidence that somehow entered my thoughts right then. Barely breathing, I went into the bathroom. I'd had a shower earlier that evening and the mirror was still steamed up. Slowly, I extended a finger and wrote a word in capital letters.

DUCLARC.

Then I began crossing out the letters. It wasn't an ana-
gram, but it was close enough. Take out a C and replace it
with an A. Then jumble it around and what did you get?

DRACULA.

So here's a question for you. Your starter for ten. Do
you believe in vampires? I didn't. Which is to say, I'd read
books and I'd seen films and I'd always comforted myself
with the thought that they were all made up. But that was
then. That was before I found myself hundreds of miles
from home in a house full of strangers in the middle of a
wood with wolves howling in the night and a man in the
next room with no reflection.

Now I remembered that vampires had been around
for hundreds of years, that thousands of stories had been
written about them. If vampires didn't exist, why had so
many writers taken an interest? And there was something
else. Dracula, the king of the vampires, had certainly been
a real person. We'd once talked about him at school, in
history. What was his first name? Oh, God! It was Vlad.
Vlad the Impaler, born in Transylvania (Eastern Europe)
in the fifteenth century. Historical fact!

Even then, standing on my own, I tried to convince
myself that I was wrong. There had to be a simple explanation. Lots of people don't like garlic. It could just be a
coincidence that Vladimir's surname was so close to Vlad
the Impaler's. I told myself that he didn't even look like

a vampire. But then I remembered the long hair, the pale skin, the clothes that were at least fifty years out of date, and I knew it wasn't true. If there had been a magazine devoted to vampires, he would have made the cover.

My first instinct was to run, to get away from the house and somehow find my way to a local police station. But I knew that was crazy. The police would never believe me. They'd think I was a stupid fifteen-year-old English boy and they would drive me straight back to the house, and if there was one sure way for me to end up with my throat torn out and my blood drained, that was it. Could I call my parents? The mobile wouldn't work, but there was still my computer. Yes. That was what I would do. I glanced at my watch. It was five past eight. I was already late for dinner. But the family could wait.

I grabbed my laptop and wrenched it open. My hands were trembling so much that I had to jab down three times before I hit the start button. And then the computer seemed to take an hour to boot up. But at last the screen was glowing in front of me. The house had no Wi-Fi, but I'd be able to connect over the telephone line. I'd already done so half a dozen times.

But this time it didn't work.

I double-clicked on the AOL icon and managed to get the home page on the screen. There was nothing wrong with the computer. But every time I tried to dial out, I got a busy signal. I must have tried twenty times before I suddenly heard Nathalie Duclarc's voice, calling me from upstairs.

"Jack. Dinner is ready!"

Once again, I froze. The computer bleeped uselessly in front of me. What was I to do? Join them and try to pretend nothing had happened? Or make a break for it? There was only one answer to that. It was dark. The gate was locked and, unlike Vladimir Duclarc, I couldn't turn myself into a bat and fly over the top. And even if I did manage to get out onto the lane, they'd catch up with me before I reached the main road. Right now it was night. The darkness was my enemy. If I could somehow hold myself together until sunrise, if I could survive, then I could take action. Maybe they'd take me into Nice. I could slip away and check in at the airport before they knew I'd gone. All I had to do was to pretend that nothing had happened. Vladimir Duclarc had seen me outside his room. But despite what I had thought earlier, there was always a chance that he believed his secret was safe. I just had to be very, very careful.

I left the room and climbed up the concrete stairs that led to the main living room, knowing exactly how a condemned man must feel on his way to the scaffold. The entire family was already around the table and nobody seemed to take much notice of me as I sat down. I noticed

Vladimir Duclarc was eating more hungrily than usual. Dinner that night was steak. My own meat had already been served. It was sitting in the middle of the plate with blood all around. Patrick said something and passed me the vegetables. I didn't understand his words. In fact, they echoed in my ears. I helped myself to a few pieces of broccoli and some potatoes. I had no idea how I would get through the next hour.

Fortunately, nobody seemed to notice that I was freaking out. Or maybe they were just pretending. Vladimir glanced at me a couple of times but said nothing. Nathalie asked me if I was feeling well and I told her that I might have had too much sun.

"You've hardly eaten anything, Jack," she said.

"I'm sorry." I'd barely had two mouthfuls of the steak. "I'm not very hungry."

"You don't like your meat *sanglant*?"

Sanglant. The French for "bloody."

"It's fine . . ."

But it wasn't. I've always liked meat, but right then I could have become a vegetarian in the blink of an eye. When I sliced a piece of the steak off with my knife, I didn't feel hungry. I felt like a surgeon in an operating room.

Patrick poured himself a glass of red wine. As I saw the liquid tumbling out of the bottle, I could only imagine something very similar pouring from my own neck. "You must get an early night, Jack," he said. "We need to look after you."

And this is what I was thinking. Were they all vampires or was it just cousin Vladimir? True, they were all very pale. They all had the same uncomfortable eyes. But surely they were normal? After all, Adrien and his parents had come out with me into the sunlight. Perhaps it was like this. Vladimir was the vampire and the rest of them were, as they had told me, distant relatives. They were similar to vampires but they weren't actually vampires themselves. That would make sense. But even if they weren't blood guzzlers, they still knew about their cousin. Their blood relative. They were protecting him. And that made them as bad as him, however you looked at it.

I had to fight my way to the end of the meal. But at last I was able to stand up and go to bed. There was one last thing I had to know.

"Is there a problem with the telephone?" I asked.

Patrick Duclarc glanced sharply in my direction.

"I tried to send an e-mail," I added. "I just wanted to tell my parents about the market that we visited today. My mother loves markets. It was a great market." I realized I was babbling and shut my mouth.

"Yes." Patrick nodded. "The telephone line is broken."

Nathalie smiled at me but her eyes were cold. "The repairmen will come tomorrow."

"You can telephone them then," Adrien added, although there was no need.

"Right." I forced a smile. "Good night, then."

"Good night, Jack."

They were still watching me as I went back downstairs to my room.

I went to sleep. It took me four hours and by the time I finally closed my eyes, the bed felt like a sack of potatoes that has been left out in the rain, but somehow I managed it. The next thing I knew, incredibly, it was ten o'clock and the sun was streaming in through the window. My clothes were scattered across the floor where I had left them. And there were no punctures in my neck, my wrists or anywhere else.

And here's the funny thing. With the coming of light, I began to doubt myself. My dad always had said that I had an overactive imagination and I really did wonder if I hadn't allowed my thoughts to run away with themselves the night before. The garlic, the hatred of light, the absent reflection, the name . . . it was true that they all pointed to only one conclusion. But vampires didn't really exist. Everyone knew that. What would my parents say if I asked them to take me home because I was scared? My sister, Isabelle, would never let me live it down.

When I went up for breakfast, Nathalie was in the

kitchen and she looked utterly normal, pleased to see me.

"Are you feeing better, Jack?" she asked me.

"Yes, thank you."

"Please. Help yourself!" There were croissants and honey on the table. Coffee and orange juice. I glanced out of the window and saw Adrien, already in the swimming pool. An ordinary family on an ordinary day.

"We thought we would go to Antibes this afternoon," Nathalie went on. "There is the Château Grimaldi, which may interest you. Also, there is a very beautiful cathedral that we can visit."

It was almost as if she had said it on purpose, to prove to me that I had imagined everything the night before.

"A cathedral?" I repeated. "Are you coming?"

"But of course. Adrien and I will come with you."

If she and Adrien were vampires, if they even had a drop of vampire blood in them, they wouldn't possibly be able to enter a holy place like a cathedral. That was when I decided that I wouldn't make a break for it after all. It was also when I made my single worst mistake. I also decided that I would put Vladimir Duclarc to the test. One small experiment and I would know exactly what he was. And if I was proved right, then I would contact my parents and nobody would be able to argue with me.

I spent the morning swimming and sunbathing with Adrien. We played Ping-Pong—there was a table in the garage—and chatted as if nothing had happened. Just after lunch we drove down the coast to Antibes, which was an impressive, densely packed town held back from the water by a huge seawall. The cathedral was a striking, strangely modern-looking building, all orange, white and yellow, next to the chateau that Nathalie had mentioned, but to be honest I don't remember much about it. Because this was where I was going to put my plan into action. And I had to do it without being seen.

Nathalie and Adrien had both entered the cathedral ahead of me—and I'd noticed that neither of them had so much as hesitated. I went in third and as I passed through the main door, my hand slid into my trouser pocket and cradled the empty shampoo bottle that I had stolen from the bathroom and hidden there earlier. I waited while the two of them walked ahead to the altar, which was surrounded by dozens of panels, each one showing a different biblical scene. Nathalie had told me that the altar itself was medieval. But I wasn't interested. I found what I was looking for almost at once. A font, close to the main door. And I was in luck. Just as I had hoped, it held a couple of inches of water.

Holy water. Do you get the idea? It was one thing that I knew a vampire couldn't stand. And there was no need to call my parents. If I was protected with a bottle of holy water, even a bottle that had once contained anti-dandruff shampoo, I would be safe. Making sure that nobody was watching, I managed to half fill it, then put the lid back on and slip it back into my pocket. I was feeling much more comfortable when, ten minutes later, we went back out into the cobbled courtyard and stood in the sun. The night could bring whatever it pleased. This time I was prepared.

In fact, the shadows were already stretching out by the time we got back to the house, and it was only then that I began to have second thoughts. Perhaps I should have legged it for the airport. Right now I could have been in the air, on my way home. But you have to put yourself in my shoes. This was a vampire I was talking about. A vampire in the south of France! If I'd run all the way home to England with an accusation like that and was then proved wrong, my parents would think I was crazy. I'd never live it down.

One way or another, I had to be sure.

Patrick was working late that night and we didn't eat until half past eight. When I came up to the living room, there was no sign of Adrien. Nathalie was in the kitchen, putting the finishing touches on a coq au vin. And Vladimir was sitting in an armchair with some sort of leather-bound book balanced on his lap. I've already mentioned that one feature of the living room was a spiral staircase. It stood to one side and twisted up to a gallery with bookshelves behind. Patrick had a desk up here and the gallery stretched the whole length of the room. It couldn't have been better. Making sure that nobody had seen me, I climbed quietly up and, keeping well back, continued along until I found myself directly above the reading man. The shampoo bottle was in my pocket.

Here, at last, was the final test. A tiny drop of holy water would mean nothing to an ordinary man. But to a vampire it would be like being stung by acid. It would burn his flesh—I'd seen it often enough in films. Being careful not to fumble, I took out the bottle and poured as little as I could into the cap. Then I reached out over the balcony. Vladimir Duclarc was directly below me. I turned my hand.

No more than two or three drops fell down, but they hit him directly on the head. And that was when I knew, without any doubt at all, that I was right. Vladimir screamed and leapt out of his chair. The book tumbled to the floor. As Nathalie rushed across from the kitchen, he stood there, one hand pressed against his face. It was as if he was being burned alive. I couldn't believe that a minuscule amount of water could have had such an effect. But of course, this wasn't ordinary water. This wasn't an ordinary man.

Vladimir looked up angrily. I threw myself back, pressing my shoulders against the bookshelves. He couldn't see me. He couldn't possibly have guessed I was there. Nathalie was next to him, dabbing at his skin with a tea towel. She was muttering to him—but even if she had been speaking in English I wouldn't have understood what she said. I stayed where I was, the bottle still in my hand. Eventually the two of them left the room, heading out into the garden, and I more or less tumbled back down the stairs. By way of an experiment, I dripped some of the holy water into my own hand. I felt nothing. It had no effect on me. But I wasn't a vampire. Not yet. Nor did I have any intention of becoming one.

I didn't go back to my room right then, although, as it turned out, everything would have been different if I had. I was feeling hot. The night was utterly still and seemed to be weighing down on me. I went out into the garden to get some air.

And that was when I heard them. Vladimir and Nathalie were kneeling close to the pool. He was splashing his face with non-sacred water. Neither of them heard me as I crept out behind them. But I heard them. And this time I understood at least part of what they said.

"Jack . . ." They were talking about me. "*Hier soir . . .*" Something about the night before. "*Le sang . . .*" That was definitely a word I knew. Vladimir had mentioned blood.

They talked for a couple of minutes. It was infuriating that I could only hear a few words of what they said and could only understand about half of that. But then came a sentence that rushed out of the darkness as if projected onto a screen.

"Il doit être tué . . ."

And that I did understand: "He must be killed."

Vladimir Duclarc spoke again.

"Ce soir." "Tonight."

What a fool I had been! I had managed to prove beyond any doubt that Vladimir Duclarc was indeed a vampire, but in doing so I had exposed myself and left myself a prisoner in the house at the very worst time, after sunset, with at least six hours of darkness ahead. As I stood there, it seemed to me that the heat of the night had been drained away, replaced by an Arctic chill. I was on my own with them. There was no way out. And by the morning I would be dead—or worse. Suppose they turned me into one of them? What would it be like to live for a thousand years, condemned to hide in the shadows, feasting on the blood of other human beings?

Why had my parents sent me here? What did my French exams matter anyway? How had I let this happen to me?

There was a storm that night, one of those fat, heavy,

spectacular storms that you only get in tropical climates when the heat of the summer becomes too much to bear. There was no wind but the thunder was deafening, the lightning so fierce that it seemed to rip the whole world in two. The rain held off for as long as it could. Then it all came down at once, smashing into the house and turning the dry earth into livid, splattering mud. The wolves were howling too—at least, I thought I heard them. But it was the thunder that I remember most, great fists of it, slamming into the side of the house as if it wanted to smash down the walls.

I was awake. Even without the storm I wouldn't have slept a wink. I watched the shadows leaping across the room, the intense white light blasting against the brickwork, lingering for a few seconds and then disappearing as fast as it had come. Where were Adrien and the others? I had no idea. Crouching, miserable, on the bed, still fully dressed, I cursed my own stupidity. I should have left when I had the chance. There was nothing natural about this weather. Vladimir Duclarc had somehow summoned it up.

"Il doit être tué . . . ce soir."

He must be killed. Tonight. Before he can tell anyone what he knows. We will make him one of us and he will serve us forever. Suddenly afraid, I reached out and turned on the lights. Nothing happened. The power supply had been cut. Of course. That would have been simple to arrange.

The door crashed open.

And there he was, on the other side. Vladimir Duclarc. He was wearing his black jacket. His long hair streamed behind him. His face, caught in another burst of lightning, had no color at all, a snapshot from a cemetery. His eyes blazed. His mouth was open, his teeth glistening white. I knew he had come for me. I had been expecting it. But this time I was ready for him.

"Go back to hell!" I screamed.

I had the shampoo bottle and I hurled the contents directly into his face, then followed it, hurling myself onto him. There was only one way to get rid of a vampire. I had known what I had to do and, horrible though it was to contemplate, I had prepared myself.

The wooden stake had come from the garden. I had found it in a flower bed and had sharpened it with a knife stolen from the dinner table. With all my strength, I rammed it into Vladimir Duclarc's chest, slanting down toward his heart. Another bolt of thunder struck at that precise moment. Vladimir screamed but I heard nothing. The sound was drowned out by the elements. I pulled the stake out and struck a second time. I felt the point tear through his soft flesh. Blood, warm and black, spurted out, splashing into my face. I felt nauseous. But I had to be sure. One last time I ripped it out and then stabbed down again. This time I found his heart. I saw the light go out in his eyes. Blood, pints of it, gushed out of his mouth. He fell to his knees and I stood over him, knowing that in seconds he would crumble into ash.

Except that he didn't.

He was dead. That much was certain. I was drenched in his blood. There was blood all over the walls and floor. Then the lights blazed on. The return of the electricity was so sudden and the lights so bright that I was startled. I looked around. Patrick and Nathalie Duclarc were standing in the corridor. Both of them were wearing dressing gowns. Patrick was staring at me, his face filled with horror. Then his wife began to scream.

There is not much more to tell.

It seems that I was wrong about Vladimir Duclarc. He wasn't a vampire after all.

First of all, he came from Slovakia, which is nowhere near Transylvania. He had a little house in a place called Kežmarok where he worked as an antiques dealer, specializing in traditional Slovakian clothes, which he himself liked to wear.

What else can I tell you about him? Well, he didn't like garlic, but you already knew that. But it also turned out that he suffered from a condition called photophobia, which meant that he was extremely sensitive to light. He couldn't go out in the day without giving himself severe headaches and permanently damaging his eyes. Not surprisingly, perhaps, he felt very embarrassed about his condition and the family preferred not to mention it, although, of course, all in all it would have been better if they had.

Apparently he had come to my room that night because he was worried about me. According to Patrick Duclarc, the entire family had been a little concerned about my behavior in the last few days. And they had thought I might be scared, on my own, in such a spectacular storm. Patrick and Nathalie had come downstairs a few seconds after Vladimir had opened the door. Both of them had witnessed the attack. Nathalie was now in bed, sedated. It was Patrick who had called the police.

After I had murdered Monsieur Duclarc, I was driven down to the police station at Nice, but I wasn't interviewed until the next day, when my parents arrived. Both of them looked completely shocked. They were accompanied by someone from the British embassy, a man called Mr. Asquith. They hadn't let me get changed yet. Apparently they still needed to take forensic evidence and I suppose I must have looked quite a sight, covered from head to toe in blood.

I told them about the way Vladimir had vanished over

the wall and I also described what I had seen in the mirror. My parents didn't say very much to me. Mum cried a lot and Dad just kept on staring at me and shaking his head. Anyway, Mr. Asquith went away for a few hours and when he came back to me, he explained that there was actually a small door in the wall—I'd never noticed it—and that far from turning himself into a bat, Vladimir Duclarc had simply let himself out that way.

As for the mirror, that was the stupidest thing of all. I've already told you that it was on a door leading into a walk-in closet. Well, what I hadn't realized was that door was covered in some sort of two-way glass. When the light was turned off inside the closet, the glass became a mirror. But when it was turned on, you could see right through it. When I'd seen Duclarc standing in front of the door on that sixth day, just before dinner, the light had been turned on. It was as simple as that. He had no reflection—and if I'd stood next to him, I wouldn't have had one either.

By now, I was feeling pretty sick, as I'm sure you can imagine. But there was still my last piece of evidence.

"What about the holy water?" I exclaimed. It was a relief to be able to express myself in English. "I dropped a tiny bit of it onto Mr. Duclarc and it burned him!"

But it seemed that the man from the embassy already had an answer to that.

"The water you dropped went straight into Monsieur

Duclarc's eye," he explained. "And it was in a shampoo bottle. It had mixed with the shampoo that was still inside. Monsieur Duclarc had sensitive eyes anyway . . . as a result of his medical condition. No wonder he cried out in pain. The shampoo stung him quite badly."

"But I heard them talking about me!" I protested. "He said quite clearly that he was going to kill me."

It took a little longer to work that out, but in the end we discovered that I was wrong about that too. Vladimir had been talking about me. He had been offering to give me a lesson in French and that was what I had heard. The French for "lesson" is *leçon* and not *le sang*, which sounds almost the same but means "blood." As for the rest of it, I had misheard that too. He had been complimenting me on my grasp of the language, and he hadn't said:

"Il doit être tué."

Which means "He must be killed."

But *"Il doit être doué."*

Which means "He must be intelligent."

It was all a terrible misunderstanding.

I had to stay with the French police for a whole week, but in the end I was allowed to return to England. But not home. My dad explained to me that, after what had happened, I wouldn't be able to come home for some time. Instead, I was sent to a sort of hospital called Fairfields. Actually, I might as well be honest. The sign outside read

East Suffolk Maximum Security Hospital for the Criminally Insane.

And that's where I'm writing this. I'm hoping they won't keep me here much longer, although it has already been one year. Mind you, my therapists tell me that I'm doing very well, and although they still give me lots of drugs, overall they're very pleased with my progress.

I also, incidentally, took my SATs while I was here. And I'm delighted to tell you that my visit to Nice must have helped. Because, despite the rather unfortunate things that happened during my stay, I got a 760 in French, so perhaps my father was right and the exchange was worthwhile after all.

SHEBAY

It was without doubt the most shocking thing she had ever heard.

"I'm sorry, Jenny, I really am." Her father was looking terrible. There were red rings around his eyes and he hadn't shaved. With his bald head, his round chin and his slightly protruding cheeks, he reminded her of one of those stocking stuffers she had once been given, the one where you use a magnet to drag iron filings onto a cartoon face. "You know things have been getting more and more difficult recently. This credit crunch. The business . . . all the problems we've been having."

"Your dad's done everything he could," her mother interjected. She had been crying. There was a tissue clamped in her right hand. Tears had turned it into a soggy mess.

"We've come to the end of the line," her father went on. "The banks won't cut me any more slack and, in a word, we're bankrupt. The house is going to have to go. And the car. I'm afraid the dog's going to have to be put down. And we can't keep you either. You're going to have to be sold."

And that was it.

At first, Jennifer Bailey couldn't believe what she was hearing. She thought that she must still be asleep and that she would wake up in a minute in her pink bed in her pink room and it would all have been a horrible dream. Of course she was aware that her parents were struggling. Her father had been working later and later every night, sometimes spending whole weekends at the office. There had been arguments and Jennifer had plugged herself into her iPod with the volume turned up high to block them out.

Businesses had been going bust all over the country. She'd seen it on the news. But she had never believed it could be as bad as this. Jeremy Bailey ran a garden or-nament business, selling fountains, furniture, bird tables, gnomes and exotic plants to customers all over the south of England. He had invented some of the products him-self. There was a birdbath, for example, that actually had a small bird shower attached. He had a radio-controlled gnome that sang highlights from Disney's *Snow White* and waved its arms in time to the music. And his range of garden furniture, manufactured from recycled wheelbarrows, couldn't have been more in tune with the times. What could possibly have gone wrong?

For twelve years, Jennifer had enjoyed an almost perfect life. She loved being an only child—it meant twice as much attention on birthdays and at Christmas—and she was never lonely. She adored her mother and she had a pet poodle—Boodle—who was allowed to sleep on her bed. She had a beautiful room in the family's three-story home in Watford and she had even been allowed to decorate it herself, painting and draping everything in her favorite color: pink. She went to an all-girls school just five minutes from the house, where she was popular and successful, adored by her teachers and admired by her friends. In a recent vote to choose the new student body president, she had come in first by almost a hundred votes.

And now this!

"Can't you borrow more money?" she asked with the wobble in her voice that usually meant she was about to burst into tears. But Jennifer forced herself not to cry. That would come later, when she was on her own.

Her father shook his head. "We're already up to our ears in debt. Credit cards, mortgage, bank loans . . . the lot." He sighed. "This is my fault—"

"Don't say that, Jeremy!" Jennifer's mother was a small, blond-haired woman (although the color now came out of a bottle). She was rather plump and always worried about her weight without ever actually doing anything about it. She also worked for the family business, doing the books. They had been married for seventeen years. "It wasn't your fault," she continued. "It's the market. They aren't interested in gardens anymore."

"They're cutting back," Jeremy agreed. He shook his head. "I should never have bought those Tibetan Prayer Bells."

"The bells were lovely!"

"But nobody bought them. And we ordered ten thousand of them."

"It's too late for regrets." Jane Bailey turned to Jennifer. "There's nothing we can do," she said. She dabbed at her eyes with the useless tissue. Her mascara was halfway down her cheeks. "You're going to have to be strong, darling. We all are. But we can't look after you anymore. Being sold is the best thing for you."

"But how are you going to sell me?" Jennifer asked, and this time there was a crack in her voice and she felt the tears pressing against her eyes.

"We've already put you on sheBay," Jeremy replied.

Of course, it was obvious really. Once there had only been eBay—for objects of every description. But recently two more sites had been added to the World Wide Web: heBay for boys. And sheBay for girls. Jennifer knew well that these were difficult times. The newspapers never stopped going on about it and anyway she'd seen it for herself. A dozen girls had been forced to leave school when their parents were no longer able to pay the tuition. And at least half of them had been sold on sheBay in a last attempt to make ends meet.

She just hadn't expected it to happen to her.

"I think I'm going to go upstairs, if you don't mind, Mummy," she sniffed.

"Of course, precious," Jane said, struggling to keep her emotions under control.

"I'm sorry, Jenny," her father muttered. There was nothing else he could say. I'm sorry. I'm sorry. I'm sorry. What difference did it make? She was still going to be sold.

She climbed up to the first floor and went into her room, closing the door behind her. Curiously, she still didn't cry, even when she noticed Boodle sitting on the bed waiting for her. The poodle was wearing a pink ribbon and as usual it was half asleep, but it wagged the short stump of its tail when it saw her. The dog had no idea that in a few days' time it would be taken away for a lethal injection and Jennifer didn't bother patting it. Right now she had other things to worry about.

She sat down in front of the computer at her desk, tapped a few keys and went into sheBay, navigating her way to the page for members' accounts. Over the past year, they'd sold plenty of items over the Internet, and although neither of her parents had said anything at the time, it was obvious now that they needed any money they could get. Jennifer knew their user name on eBay. It was their surname backward: YELIAB. Had they used the same word for sheBay? She typed in the six letters. The next page opened.

And there it was. Under ITEMS OFFERED her parents had pasted several photographs of Jennifer, taken at her last birthday party, at school and walking on Hampstead Heath. She remembered her father taking that last shot. He had been very careful about it, framing her between two trees with the sunlight pouring over her shoulders. Had he really been thinking of using it for this purpose at the time? Jennifer felt anger rising. He'd pretended that it was to go on his bedside table. How could he have been so mean?

Her name was written under the photograph. A description followed.

JENNIFER JUDITH BAILEY
Age: 12 years 1 month
Height: 5'1"
Weight: 101 pounds
Health: excellent
Jennifer is a delightful, intelligent girl with a friendly and

pleasant personality. She has done consistently well at school—
first in French and geography, second in math, physics and biol-
ogy. Her report cards (available for inspection) are outstanding.
In addition, she is a good cook and has kept a high level of fitness
by playing tennis and lacrosse.

She would make an excellent servant or companion. Al-
though a little shy, she has a reasonable grasp of world events
and is a good conversationalist. She is quick to learn and would
soon adapt to new work. She is our only daughter and we are
selling her with great reluctance. Offers starting at $1,000.
Further inquiries to jrbailey@btel.com.

The auction was to take place over the next forty-eight
hours. So far there were three bidders. SBEANSW3 had
opened the bidding at the $1,000 demanded. Someone
calling himself drMACNEILceh had raised it to $1,100.
Twenty minutes later, 666grimsby had gone to $1,300.
The bidding was now back with SBEANSW3, who had
jumped to $2,000, perhaps trying to scare the others off.
As far as finding out who these people might be, there
wasn't a great deal to go on, but Jennifer was a bright girl
and knew her way around the Internet. In the next few
hours she set to work, using a search engine—and common sense—to find out what she wanted.

SBEANSW3 was the first name she cracked. She
guessed, correctly, that *SW3* might be a London postcode,

and by entering *Bean* and *London* into Google, she eventually came across a restaurant in Chelsea. Why would they be interested in buying a young girl? Their website provided the answer—and unfortunately it wasn't for the washing up.

Welcome to Sawney Bean restaurant in Cloak Lane, just off London's famous King's Road, it read, beneath a photograph of an old-fashioned building made of white painted bricks. *Are you looking for the ultimate dining experience? Have you a special occasion that demands something very special indeed?*

We are London's only restaurant serving human flesh. Once a great delicacy in many parts of the world, "long pig" (as it was known) was only recently reintroduced to European haute cuisine. High in vitamins and low in saturated fats, the delicately poached thigh of a young boy or girl will provide you with . . .

Jennifer couldn't read any more. Her heart was in her throat and she wanted to scream or cry—or both! At the moment, SBEANSW3 was ahead in the bidding. If the restaurant bought her, she would be killed and butchered and then poached! She would end up as the ultimate dining experience! How could her parents do this to her? Surely they wouldn't let it happen. But, as wretched as it was, Jennifer knew that two thousand dollars was a lot of money and they needed every penny they could get.

She turned her attention to drMACNEILceh. In her mind she imagined an elderly family doctor who had been unable to have any children of her own. Dr. MacNeil would surely be a woman. Gray-haired and kindly. She was using her life savings to acquire a daughter.

But it turned out the truth was otherwise.

The initials *ceh* eventually led Jennifer to the Cambridge Experimental Hospital. Checking out their website, she found that Dr. Roderick MacNeil headed up its dissection unit. She had to look in a dictionary to find out what *dissection* meant.

The action of cutting up an organism. The practice of performing surgical experiments upon animals such as frogs, rats or small girls.

The hospital's website told her everything she needed to know—and more. The Cambridge Experimental Hospital was at the forefront of medical science, not only finding new cures for old diseases but new diseases with no cures at all. The policy of the hospital was not to experiment on animals. This was considered cruel and, at the end of the day, unhelpful. Instead, the hospital regularly advertised for children and, indeed, there was a link to a page where you could offer sons, daughters, nephews and nieces for sale. Preferably they should be sixteen years or under and in excellent health.

Jennifer blinked. Even as she had been sitting at the screen, the bidding on sheBay had changed—drMAC-NEILceh had just raised the sum being offered to $2,250, putting him clearly in the lead. Jennifer's head was spinning. Was being used for medical experiments any better than being eaten for dinner? Either way she ended up dead. What was going on? She was a pretty, clever, adorable girl. Her mother had often told her so. She baked delicious sponge cakes and she could play one or two pieces by Chopin on the piano. Surely there must be someone out there who wanted her for herself.

She was unable to track down 666grimsby. She knew that Grimsby was a town in the north and the three sixes did ring a faint and unpleasant bell in her head—but it was only the following morning, a Saturday, that she had a stroke of luck. By then, SBEANSW3 was back in the lead at an astonishing $3,000. Acting on impulse, Jennifer accessed her father's personal mailbox—and that was where she saw it. An email from 666.

```
> Can you let us have your daughter's
zodiac sign?
```

Fortunately, Jeremy Bailey hadn't seen it yet.
Jennifer typed back:

```
> Why do you want to know?
```

The answer came back almost at once.

> Blood sacrifice takes place on All
Hallow's Eve (October 31st). It helps
to incorporate the child's star sign
into the ritual. Sincerely, Ethan
Kyte.

Jennifer thought she was going to be sick. First a restaurant for cannibals, then a hospital that wanted to cut her open for experiments, and now a coven of witches! For that was what 666grimsby undoubtedly was. The slightly unusual name—Ethan Kyte—led her to a website that only gave her more horrible details about what she already knew. Yorkshire had a long history of witchcraft and it seemed that the descendants of certain fifteenth-century witches had regrouped and were using blood sacrifice and black magic spells to raise powerful demons. 666 was, of course, the number of the devil. Their next "sabbat"—or secret meeting—was going to be in October. On his blog, Ethan Kyte wrote that he was actively looking for a young girl or boy to provide the necessary blood sacrifice.

But there was absolutely nothing she could do. The sale was due to end on Sunday night and there were only the three bidders interested in her. That was when Jennifer did finally cry. Tears, hot and heavy, flowed down her cheeks and dripped off her chin. On the bed, Boodle began to whine.

"Oh, shut up!" she exclaimed. What did the dog know? It had an easy option compared to her.

Outside, the weather had turned gloomy, as if reflecting her mood. The clouds had rolled in over Dandelion Close and the color had drained out of the neat, square garden that her mother lovingly maintained. A single gnome stood near the gate, jerking its arms and humming "Heigh ho, heigh ho." She had always thought it was adorable, but now she hated it. Why had her father ever dreamed up the stupid thing? Why couldn't he have started a business that actually worked?

During the course of the day, the bids climbed rapidly. By teatime, Jennifer was worth $4,500—which is what Ethan Kyte and his witches were prepared to pay to summon up the devil. Nobody else was interested. Jennifer was thinking of packing her bags and running away. She had nowhere to go and the police would probably find her and bring her back, but she had to do something! Maybe she could make it to the south coast. She could stow away on a ferry bound for France . . .

And then, just after six o'clock, a fourth bidder appeared.

The bid was $4,600 and the customer profile read

talltreesEastcott. With a sense of excitement, Jennifer returned to Google. This one wasn't hard to track down. Eastcott was a village in Wiltshire and Tall Trees had its own website.

Her heart leapt. An image had appeared on the screen of a beautiful country house on its own grounds. There were two people standing in front of it. They could have been anybody's grandparents, white-haired and smiling. Underneath them a caption had been written on a yellow ribbon in flowing letters: *An orphanage in the English countryside.*

There was just one paragraph of text, but it told Jennifer everything she wanted to know.

After traveling around the world, Gerald and Samantha Pettigrew founded the Tall Trees Orphanage in 2001 with funds raised from private charities. Their aim is to provide a healthy, natural environment for orphans who might otherwise be exploited or even killed, taking in babies and young adults and caring for them on their extensive estate. Gerald and Samantha were both awarded the OBE in 2003 and have written extensively on matters relating to their work.

Jennifer felt a flood of relief. She wasn't an orphan—at least, not in the strictest sense of the word—but she was certainly being exploited and killed. Quickly, she pulled up some pictures of Eastcott. Although it wasn't the prettiest of villages, it was situated in glorious countryside, right on the edge of Salisbury Plain. It had a village green and a handful of shops. Jennifer could already imagine herself growing up here. There would be other orphans. She would make new friends. And in time she would forget all about Watford and her parents.

But would the Pettigrews bid enough to save her? The auction was due to end on Sunday night at ten o'clock. It was now almost seven o'clock on Saturday and they were only one hundred dollars ahead of the competition. The bidding didn't change again, and at nine o'clock Jennifer was sent to bed. Her mother, still clutching a tissue, read her a bedtime story, but her eyes never left the book and when she kissed her daughter, she avoided her eyes. Jane Bailey was ashamed of herself. And, Jennifer thought, she had every right to be.

Jennifer hardly slept at all that night. Once, at one in the morning, she got up and rebooted the computer, but it only confirmed her worst fears. Dr. MacNeil, the man who wanted to cut her up for medical experiments, was back in the lead with $5,000. The Pettigrews hadn't returned to the auction and Jennifer was certain they had forgotten her.

The next morning, at first light, she returned to the screen, but nothing had changed. It was a Sunday and as usual her parents went to church, but Jennifer stayed behind, pretending she had the flu. All day, she sat at her computer and watched as Dr. MacNeil, Ethan Kyte and Sawney Bean fought over her. By the evening, it looked as if her future lay in haute cuisine . . . the London restaurant had raised the bidding to $7,500. At least the coven of witches had dropped out. After their $4,500 bid had been beaten, they hadn't bothered to come back. Presumably they would just have to find someone cheaper for their blood sacrifice.

At eight o'clock she was on the operating table.

At nine o'clock, with a price tag of $9,000, she was the main course.

Still nothing from the orphanage.

The restaurant had one last try at half past nine. With thirty minutes until the end of bidding, it went to $9,500.

Dr. MacNeil didn't respond.

Five minutes to ten. Jennifer had cried so much she thought she was empty, but even so, the tears came from somewhere. She could imagine herself tied up in an oven. Maybe they would put an apple in her mouth. She just hoped she would give whoever ate her food poisoning.

And then, with one minute to spare, the miracle happened. The Pettigrews returned with an offer of $10,000. Jennifer could imagine her father gloating at that sum of money. She had reached five figures! But she didn't care. Surely this had to be the last word. The orphanage was taking her. Somehow they had found the necessary funds and she was going to be saved.

The minute hand on her Barbie alarm clock ticked to ten o'clock. The sheBay screen flashed red. The sale had closed. Gerald and Samantha Pettigrew of the Tall Trees orphanage in Wiltshire had won.

Things happened very quickly after that. Jeremy Bailey received a check in the mail and went straight to the bank to cash it while Jane Bailey packed her daughter's bags and bought her a single rail ticket to Pewsey. Apparently Eastcott was too small to have a station of its own. A few days later—once the check had cleared—a taxi came to the house to take her to Paddington, where she would catch the train.

Her parents stood awkwardly by the front door.

"Well, good-bye, my dear," her father said. "Don't think too badly of us. We did try to be good parents."

"We did everything we could," Jane sobbed.

"Maybe things will go a bit better for us and one day we'll be able to buy you back."

"I don't want to come back!" Jennifer cut in—and her voice was cold. "I don't ever want to see you again and I'll never forgive you for what you've done."

Her father went pale. Her mother began to cry all the harder.

"I'll have a much happier life without you, if you want the honest truth," Jennifer went on. "I always thought your garden business was stupid. And I hated living here. I'm really glad this has happened. I'd much rather be with the orphans than with you. I'm an orphan now myself. Good-bye!"

She got into the taxi and was swept away.

The journey to Pewsey took a little over an hour. Jennifer had brought a book with her, but she spent most of the time looking out of the window, watching as the grayness and graffiti of London was replaced by the lush green of the English countryside. She wondered if there might be any other orphans on the train, but although she went up and down the corridor a couple of times, she seemed to be the only child traveling alone.

Pewsey station was delightful with its two long platforms, a single footbridge and neatly arranged tubs of flowers. Gerald and Samantha Pettigrew were waiting for her outside the ticket office, and she liked them immediately. He was a short, round-shouldered man with a thick crop of untidy white hair, dressed in an old pinstripe suit missing some of its buttons. Samantha was taller than her husband, wearing a loose dress and Wellington boots. She had a rather long nose with a thin pair of spectacles balanced halfway down. They were both smiling, with a twinkle in their eyes, and they looked even sweeter and kinder than they had in their photograph. Jennifer was bursting with questions as they put her suitcases in the back of their car—a rather muddy Land Rover—and drove her through Pewsey and on toward Devizes.

"Is it far?"

"Not far now."

"Is there a swing in the garden?"

"Under the chestnut tree!"

"Do the orphans know I'm coming?"

"Oh yes. They're very excited."

They reached Salisbury Plain, which sloped up, huge and empty, on their left. Ahead of them lay the village of Urchfont with its pretty duck pond and thatched cottages. The road twisted through open fields and centuries-old woodland with Eastcott ahead of them until at last they turned into the driveway of Tall Trees. And there it was, an old black-and-white manor house with oak beams and roses climbing up between the windows. The car pulled up. The Pettigrews got out.

"Shall I bring my luggage?" Jennifer asked.

"No. Come inside, dear," Mrs. Pettigrew trilled. "We can see to all that later."

Jennifer hurried through the front door. Several things

struck her at the same time. The house had very little fur-niture inside. The walls and the floor were bare. There was a strange smell in the air. And she could hear some-thing, a sort of deep grumbling, coming from somewhere farther inside.

"This way!" Mr. Pettigrew exclaimed. He threw open a set of double doors. The grumbling became louder. In fact, it was more like growling.

"What is . . . ?" Jennifer began.

But she had already seen what lay on the other side of the doors. There was a deep pit and, far below, a dozen animals were pacing back and forth, their vicious claws scratching against the straw-covered concrete, their eyes glowing hungrily, their bones rippling beneath their orange-and-black fur.

"Here they are!" Mrs. Pettigrew waved a hand over the pit. "Our family of orphans."

"Orphans?" Jennifer quavered.

"Orphaned Bengal tigers," Mr. Pettigrew explained. "Babies and young adults. It's terrible how they've been neglected. They would die if they were left on their own. But we look after them, Samantha and me. We let them roam on the grounds. We watch over them. And some-times, as a special treat, we even get them fresh meat."

"But . . . but . . . but . . . ," Jennifer began.

The Pettigrews grabbed hold of her. They were surprisingly strong. She felt herself being lifted off the ground.

"Feeding time!" Mrs. Pettigrew exclaimed.

A moment later, Jennifer was hurtling through the air, diving headfirst toward the waiting pack below.

Are You Sitting Comfortably?

I never liked Dennis Taylor, not from the start. I didn't like the way he dressed with his blue blazer and silk cravat. I didn't like his mustache. I didn't like the way he laughed at his own jokes. But the very worst thing about him, the thing that made me squirm and wonder how I was going to survive the next ten years, was the fact that he was about to become my stepdad. How could Mum do this to me? Had she gone completely mad?

I had never known my father. He'd left home when I was very young and I didn't find out why. I'm sure my mum would have told me if I'd asked, but I never did. You may think that strange, but the truth is that the two of us were happy together. The life I had was the only one I knew. So why go digging up the past when all it will give you is dust in the eye?

We lived in a small house in Orford, which is right on the coast in Suffolk. There were only two bedrooms, but we didn't need any more as I didn't have any brothers or sisters—just a load of cats that came and went as they pleased. Mum worked part-time in a local hotel. She'd been left quite a bit of money by an eccentric aunt years ago and she'd put it all in the bank for when she needed it. So although we weren't exactly rich, we weren't hard up either.

Mum was actually working at the hotel when she met Dennis. He was looking for a house in Orford . . . he planned to move up from London. Well, one drink led to a chat, a chat led to lunch and soon they were seeing each other on a regular basis.

They got married at St. Bartholemew's Church, which was much too big and drafty for the little congregation that turned up. I was there with my best friend, Matt, and a handful of villagers. Mum's parents were still alive, but they lived in Scotland and she didn't invite them because she was afraid that the journey would be too much for them. Dennis hadn't been married before. He produced a sister who was plain and sulky and a best man who apparently sold shares in the city. That was what Dennis did, by the way. Stocks and shares. He described himself as an entrepreneur. He liked sprinkling his language with French words.

After the service, they flew to Barbados for their honeymoon. Mum would have been happy just going to Cornwall or the Lake District. But Dennis convinced her that they should do something more special. He also persuaded her—he was short of cash—to pay. I watched them leave, their car almost crashing into a white van that turned the corner, coming the other way. At the time, I wondered if there was an omen in that. And in a way, as you will see, I was right.

I stayed with Matt and his parents while they were away, and when they got back I was a little ashamed of myself for being so mean about it all. I was against Dennis. I didn't want Mum to get married. I hadn't wanted them to go to Barbados. But here was Mum, suntanned and as happy as I'd ever remembered her. She'd bought me lots of presents, including earrings, a straw hat, a wrap, a carved wooden tortoise and all sorts of other stuff. She'd also taken hundreds of photos on a camera that Dennis had bought her at duty-free. Seeing her like that, I made a resolution. I wasn't going to complain. I was going to adapt. I had a stepfather now. I was going to make him feel welcome.

It wasn't easy. Dennis didn't buy a house as he had planned. He simply moved into ours, which made sense because selling and buying would have been so expensive, and anyway the market was pretty dead. I didn't say anything. It wasn't as if I was going to have to move out of my room or anything like that. But from that moment, everything changed.

You see, a house has a rhythm. The way people move around in it . . . it's a bit like the workings of a clock. Suddenly, when I wanted to take a shower, Dennis would be there ahead of me. I couldn't wander around the kitchen in my underwear and T-shirt anymore—I had to get dressed for breakfast. I felt uncomfortable watching TV in the evening. If Dennis and Mum were together in the living room, I felt almost like an intruder. And then there were the unfamiliar smells and sounds. Dennis's aftershave. Classic FM blaring out of the radio every morning and Jeremy Paxman, religiously, every night. The dirty clothes that he never put in the laundry bin. Curled-up cigarette ends (yes—he smoked) in the ashtrays.

I'll get used to it, I told myself. I tried to get used to it. Over the next few months I never complained. Christmas came and we had a pleasant enough time together.

I had my finals to think about. Mum still seemed happy, although I noticed she was working longer hours at the hotel. Apart from that, Dennis seemed to be looking after her okay.

I forget exactly when I began to realize that things were going wrong. I suppose money was the start of the slide downhill. Isn't it always? Dennis had sold his house in London, but after he'd paid off the mortgage he hardly got anything out of it. Also, his business wasn't going very well. I know that Mum had lent him money from her savings—she'd mentioned it to me—but of course the stock market had taken a dive and all of it was gone. I noticed that bills weren't being paid. There was a pile of them stuck in a corner of the kitchen. Some of them were printed in red ink. Final demands.

At the same time, Dennis was spending more and more. He'd bought himself a new car, a BMW, which was parked on the street outside. There had also been other brief vacations—weekend breaks in Paris and Rome, staying in five-star hotels. I'm not saying my mum hadn't enjoyed these trips. But there was always the question of who was going to pay, and it followed her around like a cloud.

The biggest expense of all was Dennis's study. He needed somewhere to work, he said, so he had an ugly conservatory constructed at the back of the house and used it as an office. It completely spoiled the garden, it cost thousands, and worse still, there was a problem with the construction (he'd used builders who had been recommended by one of his friends), and so we had to spend thousands more putting it right.

My mum was paying for everything. She'd never even been paid back for Barbados. I knew because one morning they had an argument over the breakfast table. It came as quite a shock to hear their voices raised, and it made me wonder if there hadn't been other arguments when I was at school or, in whispers, when I was asleep.

Mum had just opened a bill from a company that supplied fine wine. That was another of Dennis's extravagances. He loved expensive clarets. Some of the bottles cost thirty or forty dollars.

"We can't pay this!" my mother exclaimed. She was staring at the bill, completely shocked.

"How much is it?" Dennis glanced at the total and raised an eyebrow.

"I really don't think you should have bought so much, Dennis. Not in the current climate. We'll have to send the wine back."

"We can't send it back."

"Why not?"

"It would make me look ridiculous. Anyway, I've already opened some of the bottles."

"But we can't afford it!"

Dennis scowled. "You really have no understanding of money, do you, Helen," he said. "It's true we're going through a bad patch. But I'm chasing one or two very interesting deals and everything will sort itself out in time. We just have to keep our nerve, that's all."

"But we've got dozens of bills . . ."

"Don't you trust me?" Dennis looked offended, but at the same time there was something else in his face, something I hadn't seen before. He looked threatening. "I've told you about this share opportunity in London. If it works out—"

"But what if it doesn't?" My mother sat down and for a moment she looked close to tears. "We've gone through nearly all my savings in less than a year! I'm working extra hours."

"I'm working too!"

"I know, dear. But sometimes I wish you'd work a little less. Your work is actually bankrupting us."

That evening, Dennis took us all out to dinner at the Golden Keys to cheer us up. This was a smart pub in Snape, about five miles away. He ordered champagne and a nine-inch cigar. But when the bill came, I noticed he slid it over to my mum.

"Left my credit card behind," he explained. "You get this, Helen. I'll pay you back."

He had to smoke the cigar outside on the terrace, and while he was gone, I asked my mum if things really were as bad as they seemed.

"I don't know, Lucy," she said with a sigh.

"Has he really used all your savings?"

"I'm afraid so. He says you have to spend money to make money, but I don't think . . ." She broke off. "Don't worry about this," she continued. She sounded completely worn-out. "I'm sure it'll work out in the end."

"Are you still glad you married him?" I hadn't meant to be so direct, but the words just slipped out.

"Of course!" she replied instantly, but I wasn't convinced.

"You could always divorce him," I said.

Mum's eyes widened. I turned around. Dennis had come back into the dining room. He was standing right behind me and he must have heard what I had just said.

"Where's the cigar?" Mum asked. She looked really frightened. She was wondering if he had heard what we were saying.

"It made me feel sick," Dennis said. He reached for the car keys, which were lying on the table. "Let's go home."

None of us spoke on the way back. As soon as Dennis had parked his BMW, I hurried into the house and up to my room. I just wanted the evening to be over. But it wasn't yet. Not by a long shot.

I'd just gotten into my pajamas when my door opened and Dennis came in. I was quite startled to see him. He never usually came into my bedroom. He must have seen the expression on my face, because he smiled at me in that lazy way of his and said, "I just came in to say good night."

"Good night, Dennis," I said. I'd never called him Dad.

But he didn't leave. He sat down on the bed. "You know, I couldn't help overhearing what you said to your mum back in the restaurant," he drawled. "I'd hate to think you were turning her against me."

"I'm not," I replied.

"That's not how it sounded to me." He looked me straight in the eye. "In fact, young lady, I'd say you were more or less against me from the start."

It's funny how things can change in an instant, like the wind blowing out a candle or a door swinging open to show something horrible on the other side. That was how it was for me then. Dennis hadn't done anything or said anything unpleasant. He was still sitting there in his smart blazer and gray trousers with one leg over his knee. But he was suddenly a completely different man, and I realized two things at the same moment. I was scared of him. And he knew I was scared . . . it was what he wanted.

"I have to say . . . ," he went on, reasonably. "It would

make life very difficult if you were my enemy. I'd have to think about separating you . . . sending you away to a boarding school."

"You can't afford boarding school," I said. I regretted the words as soon as I'd spoken them.

"We can sell this house. Get something smaller in Woodbridge or Leiston. Just your mother and me. Helen does what I tell her. You may have noticed that. You talk to her about me, she'll tell me—and you'll suffer the consequences."

He stood up. I flinched. For a moment I thought he was going to hit me. That was the power he had, a sort of animal quality. He had the upper hand and he knew it. He took one last look at me, then walked out of the room. I stayed where I was. I was trembling. That was the effect he'd had on me. And that was when I began to wonder. Was Mum afraid of him too?

In the next few weeks, Dennis's business affairs didn't get any better, but he didn't seem to care. By now we had mortgaged the house again. A home in Orford, even a tiny one like ours, was worth a lot of money. But the question was—how would we ever pay it back? As far as he was concerned, Mum was a virtually bottomless well and he could continue drawing on her until she was sucked dry. And then, just when I thought he couldn't be any greedier or any more demanding, up came the massage chair.

Dennis had seen it advertised in a magazine: the Silver City ProElite Massage System Deluxe. In the picture, it looked like something you might find at an upmarket dentist—a series of padded leather cushions on a swiveling steel frame with headphones for the built-in MP3 player and two remote controls, one for massages, one for music. According to the advertisement, the SCPMSD came with state-of-the-art roller and air bag technology, a powerful (but silent) tri-point hydraulic system, a choice of fifteen different programs as well as a unique Body Memory feature that automatically took your weight and measurements and selected the massage to suit your needs. Other bonuses included a super-strong air pressure option, a full-color LCD, economy standby mode and automatic shutoff. The SCPMSD was being offered at a special once-only price of $3,950 plus tax.

"We're simply not getting this," Mum said, pushing away the advertisement, which Dennis had thrust under her nose.

"But it's my birthday!" Dennis scowled. In fact, his birthday was still a month away.

"I'd love to get it for you. But I simply can't. There's no money in the bank and my credit cards are all over their limit."

"We can get another credit card."

"Why do you need a massage chair?" Mum asked.

Dennis rubbed his neck. "Living with the two of you, always criticizing me all the time! You have no idea how stressed I am. If I was more relaxed, I'd be able to concentrate on my business a little more."

"I'm sorry, Dennis. I'm sure it would be a lovely thing to have. But I'm afraid this time it really is out of the question."

The massage chair turned up a few days later. It was a monstrous thing that took four men to carry in, and by the time it had been installed in the living room, there was hardly any space for anything else. Dennis wasn't there when it arrived. He was at the pub, somewhere he'd been spending more and more time recently. After the deliverymen had finished their work and gone, I found Mum in the kitchen. I could tell that she'd been crying.

"Mum!" I went over to her and this time I wasn't going to hold back. "Why are you putting up with this?" I demanded. "It's stupid. You should get rid of him. You should kick him out."

"Shh!" She turned around and for a moment she looked terrified. "You don't understand, Lucy. I can't . . ."

"Has he threatened you?"

"No. It's not like that."

"Then why?"

I heard the front door open and my heart sank.

"He's not so bad," my mum whispered. "And maybe he'll be happy . . . now that he's got his chair."

In fact, Dennis was delighted. He sat in it at once and began to experiment with the programs, trying to find the one that suited him best.

Have you ever seen a massage chair? For something that was meant to be a luxury item, this one was really hideous. The leather was black and highly polished, and even if it was packed with the latest technology, it still looked awkward and old-fashioned. It was also very big, completely enclosing Dennis when he sank into it . . . a bit like a mummy in its sarcophagus. The chair sat on a metal plinth. There were supports for his arms and legs, and when the program started, these gently pressed on both sides of his wrists and ankles, massaging them and at the same time keeping him in the correct position. Cushions also inflated behind his head and around his neck, and hidden rollers moved up and down his spine, under his hips and thighs and even behind his calves. Every inch of his body had been catered for and, just as the advertisement had stated, the massage chair was practically silent with only a faint humming as it went about its work.

I hated that chair. You have to remember that we lived in a small, pretty house, and the chair—with its pistons and rollers and air bags and leg traction—completely spoiled it for me. I could always tell when it was on. I couldn't hear it, but the walls of my bedroom vibrated. I thought of it as a monster in a cave. If any of our friends had seen it, they would have said it was completely out of place, better suited to an airport lounge or health club. But not many friends visited us anymore. (They didn't much like Dennis either.)

Dennis had the chair for less than a week before it broke down. He'd used it every evening. He had a set pattern. After dinner, he'd pour himself a glass of expensive wine, light one of his expensive cigars and sit there in his black leather beast with a vague smile on his face, watching TV. Meanwhile, Mum would do the laundry and maybe the ironing before she went to bed and I'd stay in my room, doing my homework, almost afraid to go out.

Well, one evening, just before I went upstairs, he got himself all set up, reached for the remote control, pressed down with his thumb and . . .

Nothing happened.

"Helen? Have you been tampering with this?" he demanded.

"No." My mum stopped, a pile of clothes in her arms.

He tried again. "It's not working."

"Is it plugged in?" Mum asked.

"Of course it's plugged in, you stupid woman. You can see for yourself. The green light is on."

"Well, it's not working."

"I know it's not working. I just said that."

"Maybe it's blown a fuse," I suggested, secretly hoping it was something more serious.

"We need to call someone in," Dennis said.

"I'll find someone," my mum said. She was really upset. I don't suppose she cared about the stupid chair but she didn't want Dennis to be in a bad mood.

She rang the chair company the following morning, but that was the next crisis. The Silver City ProElite Massage System Deluxe was still under guarantee, but Dennis had lost the paperwork and they said they wouldn't come to the house without it.

"We can get someone local," I said. "I bet it's something simple. Maybe one of those stupid pistons has fallen off or something."

"Lucy!" My mother rolled her eyes nervously, even though Dennis wasn't in the house.

"I'll find a number," I said.

I went into the kitchen. The Yellow Pages telephone book was lying open on the windowsill next to the sink, and here's the strange thing. As I walked over to it, there must have been some sort of breeze in the room, because the pages fluttered and turned as if the telephone book were opening itself. Stranger still, by the time I reached it, it had settled in exactly the right place, because an advertisement in a black box in the top corner drew my eye immediately.

THE MECHANIC
**General household repairs. Electrical,
plumbing, computer hardware, domestic.
Tel: 00010 005 500
We fix everything.**

I showed the advertisement to Mum and she rang the number, although she was a little puzzled by all those zeroes. What sort of phone had a number like that? I'm not sure she was even expecting to get an answer, but she was connected after the first ring. She spoke briefly to someone at the other end of the line, then put the phone down.

"They're coming on Saturday," she said.

"Are they expensive?" I asked. I was always worrying about money these days even if it was the one subject we never talked about.

"They didn't say." Mum saw the look in my eyes. "However much it is, it'll be worth it," she said. "Dennis loves that chair. And it does help keep him calm."

The mechanic turned up at ten o'clock the following Saturday, exactly when he'd said he would. He came in a white van that reminded me of something. Had I seen it before, the day of the wedding? If so, it was a strange coincidence. At any event, he entered the house carrying a neat metal toolbox. He was a very short man, barely taller than me, dressed in blue overalls with a Biro behind his ear. At first sight, I thought he might not be British. He was dark-skinned, bald, with a mustache that was a little too big for his face. His teeth were a dazzling white. All in all, he didn't look like a mechanic. He looked like someone who had dressed up as a mechanic.

Dennis had just finished breakfast and followed the mechanic into the living room. The little man was already crouching in front of the chair.

"What a beauty!" he was saying. "The Silver City ProElite Deluxe! Multi air bag system. Twin twenty-six-point shiatsu rollers! I congratulate you, sir, on your good taste. Only the best for you. I can see that!" He straightened up. "I bet you must love sitting on this."

"It doesn't work," Dennis said.

"That's the trouble with Silver City," the mechanic agreed. "They're unreliable. It's Japanese engineering. Not that I've got anything against the Japanese. Great cars. Great TVs. But when it comes to massage chairs, they can be a bit shoddy, a bit slapdash . . ."

"Can you fix it?" Dennis asked.

"I can fix anything. It might take an hour. It might

take all day. We won't know that until we've got the back panel off and I've had a quick scout around inside."

"How much will it cost?" Mum asked.

"Fifty dollars plus tax, or forty dollars cash."

I could see Mum was relieved. We'd had plumbers and electricians come to the house and they'd charged double that just to walk through the door.

"Mind you," the mechanic went on. "Let's hope the vertical sensors or the spine rotation systems haven't blown. That could be more expensive. And I might have to take out the motherboard. This Japanese circuitry . . . it can play all sorts of tricks."

"Just mend it," Dennis said. "I'm going out."

Dennis had recently taken up golf. Mum had used her connections at the hotel to get him a cut-price membership at a local club. As soon as he had gone, the mechanic set to work. He opened his toolbox to reveal a gleaming array of spanners on the top shelf with a dozen screwdrivers, pliers, wrenches and tweezers neatly lined up below.

"Would you like some tea?" Mum asked.

"No, thank you, Helen," the mechanic replied. "But I wouldn't mind a glass of water. Tap, not mineral. And maybe a slice of lemon?"

"Right . . ." My mum sounded bewildered.

And there was something that puzzled me. I had been

there when she had made the telephone call and I was there when the mechanic arrived. Mum had never told him her name. He couldn't possibly have known it.

But he had called her Helen.

The next time I looked into the living room, the massage chair had been turned inside out. The mechanic had taken off the leather cushions to reveal a metal panel, which he had unscrewed. Now there were about a thousand wires spilling onto the carpet and I could see metal pistons, cogs, wheels and circuit boards packed together inside. The mechanic was whistling cheerfully, but my heart sank. I'd decided that he was a complete fraud. I didn't believe for a minute that he had the faintest idea what he was doing.

I was wrong. He worked for three hours, occasionally stopping to sip the lemon-flavored tap water that he had requested. When I went back into the room, the chair had been put back together again and looked as good as new. He was just screwing the panel back into place.

"Is it fixed?" I asked. It was the first time I had spoken to him.

"As right as rain, Lucy. Fixed and fastened."

"How do you know my name?"

"Your stepfather told me." He slipped another screw into place and began to turn it.

"Do you live in Suffolk?" I asked him.

"No, no, no. Not me."

"So where do you live?"

"I get around."

At that moment, my mum came into the room. She took one look at the chair and I could see the relief in her face.

"It was the auxiliary sprocket," the mechanic told her. "Would you believe that someone had put it in upside down! It short-circuited the main drive. And without the main drive the whole thing was a nonstarter." He picked up the remote control and pressed a button. The massage chair began to vibrate the way it always had. Music played in the headphones. The back rollers gently pulsated. Everything seemed to be working.

"How much do I owe you?" my mother asked.

"Forty dollars if you don't mind paying cash," the mechanic replied.

"But you've been here for hours," Mum said.

"Yes. It took a little longer than expected. But the price I quote is the price you pay. And forty dollars it is!"

"Well . . . thank you very much."

Mum reached for her handbag and took out two twenty-dollar bills. The mechanic rolled them up like a cigarette and slipped them into his top pocket. "It's been a pleasure meeting you," he said. "And a pleasure working on the Silver City ProElite. What a chair! What a great investment! I wish you hours of pleasure. Good day!"

He had already packed up his toolbox. He picked it up and left.

Dennis was in a bad mood when he got back from the golf club, which meant that he had lost. But he brightened up a bit when he saw the massage chair.

"Is it mended?" he asked.

"Yes, Dennis," my mum said.

"Did that man demonstrate it before he left?"

"He turned it on."

"Did he run through all the programs?"

"Well, not all of them—"

"You shouldn't have let him leave without going through all the programs," Dennis said. "If he's damaged it . . ."

"It seemed to be working all right."

"We'll see!"

Dennis didn't actually try the chair until after dinner. As Mum and I cleared the table, he lit a cigar, poured himself a glass of wine and ambled into the living room. I heard the squeak of the cushions as he sat down. Then came the faint *tish-tish-tish* of the music being played through the headphones. A moment later, the chair—and much of the house—began to vibrate.

"Well, that seems to be all right," my mum said.

"Let me make you a coffee," I said. Mum was looking exhausted.

"Thank you, Lucy. That would be nice."

How long did it take for everything to go wrong? I can't tell you. Even now I find it hard to remember exactly what happened. Maybe I don't want to. My therapist told me that sometimes, without even trying, we block out things too horrible to recall. Not that I'm seeing a therapist anymore. But she might have been right.

"Helen!" It was Dennis calling my mum. But already there was something in his voice. He didn't just want another glass of wine or an ashtray for his cigar. It wasn't just that he'd forgotten his reading glasses. Something had gone wrong.

My mum put down the pan she'd been drying.

"Helen!" His voice was louder, more high-pitched. And there was something else. The sound of the chair had intensified. The walls of the kitchen were vibrating more violently. A plate trembled its way to the edge of the counter, fell to the floor and smashed.

Together, we ran into the living room.

At first, it looked as if Dennis was clutching the massage chair with all his strength, but at once we saw that he was actually trying to escape from it. But he couldn't. The wrist and ankle pads that were meant to hold him gently in position had overinflated, effectively pinning him down. His fingers were writhing but he couldn't release his arms. At the same time, his entire body was convulsing as it was pummeled by pistons and rollers that were hopelessly out of control. They were battering him! I couldn't believe what I was seeing. It was as if the massage chair had become an electric chair in an American jail and we were witnessing a horribly botched-up execution.

"Let me . . . aaaaagh!" Dennis screamed, but we could barely hear him. The headphones were still sitting lopsidedly on his head, but the volume control must have broken because we could actually hear the bass and the drumbeat filling the room, impossibly loud. TISH-TISH-TISH. What it must have been like for Dennis with the speakers clamped over his ears was impossible to imagine—and I didn't need to imagine it, because a second later one of his eyes exploded like a wet balloon.

My mum screamed, then ran forward and snatched up the remote control. Dennis had dropped it on the carpet. I saw her thumb stab down on the stop button, again and again. But the chair didn't stop. It hadn't even begun. Dennis was jerking about like a mad thing, his wrists and ankles still pinned down and his chest and thighs heaving. Blood was pouring out of his nose. His fingers were writhing. And he was still screaming, the words incoherent now. The chair was stretching his face in every direction so that I hardly recognized him.

I had to do something. But what? I was terrified. I didn't want to go near the massage chair. But I couldn't just stand there and let it kill him. Suddenly I had an idea. I ran over to the wall and ripped out the plug.

The massage chair picked up speed.

How could that be? Did it have a secondary power source? Or had it somehow stored up enough energy to continue its hideous destruction? The twenty-six-point shiatsu rollers underneath Dennis's legs surged forward and I heard his bones break. All of them. They were unable to withstand the pressure. Then it was his ribs, snapping one at a time as the tri-point hydraulic system slammed into him again and again.

"Unplug it!" Mum screamed at me.

"I have!" I screamed back.

It was already too late for Dennis. I'm not even sure he was still conscious. The massage chair was shuddering and shaking as if it were trying to leave the room, and he was being thrown from side to side with all sorts of disgusting fluids splattering across the furniture. And then, finally, it had to happen. The quadruple rollers behind his head, the ones that promised the best spine massage ever, locked together with ferocious strength. Dennis's neck broke with a snapping sound like a branch of a tree. The machine stopped.

Silence filled the room.

Gently, the air bags deflated, allowing Dennis to slump forward so that now he looked asleep . . . if you could ignore his twisted frame and all the blood oozing out of him. The music had stopped. Smoke was trickling out of his ears. The chair itself looked worn-out, ready for the scrap heap. Somewhere inside it a final spring snapped with a faint twang.

I thought my mum would be in hysterics, but she was surprisingly calm.

"Lucy," she said. "Leave the room."

"Yes, Mum."

"We'll call an ambulance from the kitchen."

"Yes, Mum."

"And the police."

There's not very much more to tell.

The police investigated, of course. They were particularly keen to speak to the mechanic, the man who had supposedly fixed the massage chair. It was still unclear how the machinery could have malfunctioned in quite such a remarkable way. The chair was taken apart by forensic scientists. The software and electronics were minutely examined. But no one was left any the wiser.

And the mechanic had disappeared. There was still the number in the telephone book, but when the police tried it, they got no reply. It wasn't that the number had been disconnected. According to the telephone company, it had never existed in the first place, and for a short while the finger of suspicion pointed at my mum. Could she have deliberately sabotaged the massage chair to murder Dennis? Even the police had to admit the idea was ridiculous. She had no engineering knowledge. And as far as the outside world was concerned, she had no reason to want to kill her husband.

Even so, the complete disappearance of the mechanic was a mystery, particularly as he could most certainly have helped the police with their inquiries.

In the weeks that followed, there were a couple of pleasant surprises. First of all, Dennis had a small life insurance policy that paid out following his death. But much more significantly, Silver City, the manufacturers of the ProElite massage chair, got in touch with my mum. They had heard what had happened and they were very anxious that they were going to get the blame. Dennis's horrible death could have ruined their business if it had been made public . . . and Mum could easily have sued them. So some lawyers came to see her, and in the end, to apologize for her distress—and to keep her quiet—they wrote her a check. I was there when she opened it. It was a six-figure sum.

I saw the mechanic one more time.

A year had passed. Mum and I were still living in the

same house in Orford, although we'd now had the conservatory removed. Mum had gone back to working just three days a week and I was in the middle of my finals. It was a beautiful day with a huge summer sun high in the cloudless sky. We'd just been shopping in Woodbridge and were on our way back to the car. We'd swapped the BMW for a new car, something smaller and less fancy that better suited our needs.

And that was when I saw a white van tearing down the street, perhaps on its way to someone else's house. I even got a glimpse of the mechanic behind the steering wheel, with his bald head and mustache. And although I may have imagined it, I could have sworn he turned toward me and winked.

A moment later, he had turned the corner and gone, and the last thing I saw were the words written on the side of his van. THE MECHANIC. And just below that: WE FIX EVERYTHING.

And I had to admit that, in his own way, he had.

PLUGGED IN

He was such a nice boy. Everyone in his family agreed. He was the sort of boy you could be proud of, who would get a dozen A pluses and go to the best university, who would have a wonderful career and who would look after his parents when they were old. An only son, of course. There's no one more devoted than an only child . . . maybe it helps that there are no brothers or sisters to fight with. Not that Jeremy would ever have fought with anyone. Every evening he helped wash the dishes without being asked. He walked the dog without complaining. Other parents might sit worrying about drugs and cigarettes and nightclubs full of predatory girls. But Jeremy Browne seemed untouched by the modern world. He was impervious to it. He was the sort of boy that Enid Blyton might have written about—the famous five, the sensational six or maybe just the wonderful one.

He lived in Finchley, in north London . . . a large Victorian house on Elmsworth Avenue that had once been rather grand but, like many of the houses around it, had been converted into apartments. The Browne family had the bottom floor with a bright and airy basement and a garden. Jeremy liked to help with the gardening too. His father was the local manager of a well-known building society. His mother taught at a primary school just behind Finchley Central subway station. Mike and Irene Browne had arrived at parenthood fairly late in life—indeed, Jeremy had come as a complete surprise . . . though a wonderful one, of course. The three of them were often seen shopping together, at church or strolling on Hampstead Heath with their dog, Scampi—a mongrel that had once been rescued by the RSPCA—racing ahead of them.

Jeremy was unusual in that he was academically gifted, physically remarkable and athletically an all-around sportsman. He was a very handsome boy with long, fair hair, blue eyes and the sort of smile you'd notice across a room. By the time he was fifteen, he had begun to fill out. He was already taller than his mother, and with his broad shoulders, thick neck and general air of confidence he could easily have been mistaken for an American football player. He loved sports. He played for his school football team, did rugby training most weekends and had even considered professional ice-skating . . . there was a rink over at Alexandra Palace, not far away.

There were, it has to be said, a few people who thought that Jeremy was just too good to be true. He was not the most popular boy in the school. Many of the other children mistrusted him and some threw hurtful insults his way. Even some of the teachers had their doubts. To be passionate about the poetry of William Blake was fine . . . but at the age of twelve? And then there was that tricky moment when he tried to convert his math teacher to Christianity. JEREMY BROWNE IS GAY read the graffiti on the side of the nearest bus shelter, and sadly this was one of the kinder things that had been written about him.

And it would have been no surprise either that it was Jeremy who volunteered to drop in on the new neighbor who had just moved onto Elmsworth Avenue. The very last house on the street was also the smallest and the shabbiest and had for some time been a concern to the other residents. The square of grass that was the front garden had become overgrown. The trash cans were overfilled with bottles, old newspapers and plastic supermarket bags filled with garbage. No recycling here! The windows were dusty and the roof was in disrepair. But fortunately the last occupant had left and now the house had been rented out again.

It was often said that this area of London was a particularly friendly one and more like a village, really, than a
major suburb. Everyone looked out for each other, whether
it was via the Neighborhood Watch or just a quick gossip over the garden fence. And so it was that word began
to spread about the new arrival. He was an elderly man,
single and a foreigner—from Poland or perhaps Hungary.
There were some who said he had been a hero of the Second World War, although that would make him at least
ninety. Another report suggested that he was actually a
retired nobleman—a grand prince or a duke. His name?
The postman, who chatted to everyone on his round,
quickly revealed that it was Jákob Demszky. This was
the one certainty. Everything else was rumor. He was
a widower. He had come to England for his health. He
might even have been born here and had come home to
die.

The moving van had come and gone very quickly. It
was obvious that Mr. Demszky did not have much in the
way of furniture or personal possessions. Since his arrival, he had been spotted a couple of times, once making
his way home with a shopping basket in one hand and a
walking stick in the other, once pottering about outside
the house, trying to clear a drain.

He was a tiny man in a dark, old-fashioned suit with
a coat hanging off his shoulders so that he was a bit like

bat man . . . not the comic hero but a sad, dusty creature that might be found in an abandoned castle or church. He walked slowly and with difficulty. Indeed, any movement seemed to give him pain. His shoes were well-polished and he wore two gold rings on his left fingers. One of them contained a jewel that sparkled, bloodred, in the north London sun. His walking stick was topped by a silver ram's head, the horns curling into the palm of his hand.

"You know, I think I ought to go and see him," Jeremy announced one Saturday at breakfast.

"That's very thoughtful of you, Jeremy," his father said over a spoonful of organic muesli.

"He must be finding it very strange," Jeremy continued. "Apparently he doesn't speak much English. And there's tons of work to do at that house."

"Why don't you take him a slice of my homemade treacle tart?" Jeremy's mother suggested. "I could wrap it in foil."

Very soon after this conversation, Jeremy found himself clutching a large wedge of tart and knocking on the door of 66 Elmsworth Avenue (the bell seemed to be out of order). It took Mr. Demszky a long time to answer it, and Jeremy could imagine him lifting himself painfully out of his chair and shuffling along the corridor—but eventually the door swung open and there he was, staring out with eyes that were both politely inquiring and a little nervous.

"Yes?"

"Hello. My name is Jeremy Browne. I live at number fifty. I was wondering if there was anything I could do to help you." Jeremy lifted his package. "And my mother thought you might like a slice of her homemade treacle tart."

Mr. Demszky considered all this as if trying to make sense of it. Then, a soft, happy smile spread across his face. "How very kind! Please, come in."

Jeremy followed the old man through a darkened hallway and into the kitchen, which seemed bare and empty with just a few food supplies and a couple of chipped mugs on the Formica surface. Jeremy had already realized that Mr. Demszky spoke better English than he had been told, though with a heavy accent. The man really was very small indeed, as if he had shrunk into himself over the years. His skin was completely gray with dark liver spots on his neck and the side of his head. His hair was white, curling limply down over the collar of his jacket. His fingers were long and misshapen with yellowy nails that were somehow more animal than human. But most unnerving of all were his eyes. They were colorless and bulged slightly out of his face, like two plastic sachets filled with water. He grunted as he sat down. There were gaps in his teeth and Jeremy could see his tongue, as gray as the rest of him, flickering behind them.

"Would you like some tea?" Mr. Demszky asked.

"Let me make it for you," Jeremy said. That was his way. He had come here to help and he certainly wouldn't let the old man make any effort for him.

"No, no. I already had." When Mr. Demszky spoke, his voice was partly trapped in his chest. He had to force the words with difficulty and they came out in a wheeze. "What did you say was your name?"

"It's Jeremy Browne."

"How old are you, Jeremy Browne?"

"I'm fifteen."

"That is a good age. That is a very lovely age."

Despite himself, Jeremy was feeling a little uncomfortable. The old man was staring at him in a most peculiar way, as if he had never seen a boy before, and he was trembling as if the journey to the door had almost been too much for him. "Is there anything I can do here to help you?" he asked.

"You are so very kind!" Mr. Demszky nodded so vigorously that Jeremy heard the bones in his neck creak. "I expected you to come. Yes. But so soon? So soon?" He paused for breath. "You could perhaps do a little gardening?" He spread his hands. "There are dead leaves. Dead plants. So much that is dead. Have you the time to help me in the garden? I will pay you."

"I don't need paying," Jeremy said. "Just show me what you want me to do."

Jeremy worked for three hours that day. He also returned the following Wednesday and did three hours more. This time, his mother came with him, and after meeting Mr. Demszky, she took the opportunity to spring clean much of the house and even invited the old man to join them for dinner the following week. Although Jeremy wouldn't have admitted it, he was a little uneasy inside number 66. The house was dark and musty and smelled of something he couldn't quite place. He hadn't wanted to pry, but he couldn't help noticing that many of the doors were locked. He had been unable to enter the study, for example, and the curtains in that room were also drawn so he couldn't look in from outside. At any event, he felt more comfortable out in the fresh air, so he had set to work clearing out the garden shed, which was full of rubbish, some of it quite possibly hazardous. His father had already volunteered to drive it down to the local dump.

Jákob Demszky did come to dinner—and he brought gifts for the entire family. Hungarian wine for Mike and flowers for Irene. But for Jeremy, he had something rather special. He took out a black cardboard box tied with a black ribbon and slid it across the table. Lying there, it reminded Jeremy of a miniature coffin, and for a moment he was unsure whether to open it.

"What is it?" he asked.

"Unwrap it," Mr. Demszky said.

"Go on, Jeremy." His father laughed. "It won't bite you."

Jeremy picked up the box, slid off the ribbon and opened it. From the weight, he had been expecting a pen or perhaps a multipurpose knife and was surprised to find himself holding an MP3 player . . . although it wasn't like any MP3 player he had ever seen before. It wasn't an iPod or anything modern. In fact, it wasn't branded at all. It was just a rectangular block of plastic, flat and chunky, with a glass window and a few controls.

"It is for you," Mr. Demszky said. "To thank you for your help."

The MP3 player was obviously a Hungarian model, for when Jeremy switched it on, a series of strange words floated across the screen. TÉPŐFARKAS . . . GONOSZUL . . . AKTÍV.

"What does that mean?" Jeremy asked.

"It's warming up," Mr. Demszky explained.

"Why don't you give it a try?" Irene said.

Jeremy picked up the machine. The earbuds looked

too big for him, with wires as thick as spaghetti, and he wondered if it would even work and—if it did—what it would play. But when he plugged it in, he was surprised to discover that Mr. Demszky had already downloaded several tracks by his favorite bands: Coldplay and the Killers. More than that, the quality of the MP3 player was amazing. The music poured into his head in a torrent, sweeping away the dining room, the tick of the grandfather clock, the entire world. Every lyric, every note was crystal clear. It was as if he had been transported to the front row of the O2 Center. He was actually sorry when his mother served the first course and he had to switch it off again.

The evening was a huge success. Mrs. Browne had cooked lasagne, her signature dish, and although Mr. Demszky hardly ate anything, he talked at length about his life in Hungary . . . it turned out that he had once owned a castle near Budapest and for fifty years had been one of the country's most celebrated scholars. He had lectured in astrology, psychiatry and medieval history. He had actually been the head of a society that had been formed in the Middle Ages and which still met on certain days of the year to discuss philosophical issues. There had to be a full moon, Mr. Demszky explained. Otherwise, the members—the Boszorkánys, as he called them—would not come out.

"And what are you doing in England?" Mrs. Browne asked.

Mr. Demszky paused for a moment. He looked from his plate to Mrs. Browne and then from her to her son. "I came to meet people like you," he said.

In the weeks that followed, the Brownes saw a lot of their new neighbor, helping him in small ways or just popping in to see that he was all right. And Jeremy never walked up the road without his new MP3 player plugged into his ears. It was incredible. Not only did it have his two favorite bands, but all the other music that he loved had somehow found its way into the machine, as if arriving there overnight. Three days before Take That released their new single, it magically appeared on his playlist. It seemed he only had to think of a tune and he would find it . . . without even having to pay. And there was something else rather strange. The MP3 player didn't seem to have a battery compartment. In fact, there were no plastic panels or visible screws at all. It was molded together with just the single socket for the jack at the end of the earplugs and the switches to start the whole thing up. He vaguely wondered if it might not be solar-powered, but that was ridiculous. Solar-powered MP3 players didn't exist.

But it never slowed down or stopped. For the first time in his life, Jeremy got into trouble at school. MP3 players weren't allowed, but Jeremy couldn't resist plugging himself in between lessons, out in the yard, and he found himself dreaming about the music during lessons, ignoring whatever the teachers said. He wore it to and from school and kept it on in his room when he was doing his homework. He still went around to Mr. Demszky's from time to time—the garden was beginning to look delightful—and he worked all the harder with the music enveloping him, transporting him into its own world. Beyoncé, Oasis, Kings of Leon, the new tracks kept arriving and Jeremy kept on listening. At night, in bed, he still read books, but he did so to the rhythms of Leona Lewis or Estelle, and his parents became familiar with the *tish-tata-tish-tata-tish* sounds that came from their son every morning at the breakfast table.

They became a little concerned. Like many other teenagers, Jeremy had begun to communicate less and less . . . but until now he never had been like other teenagers. He had been special. What had happened? All he did was listen to that wretched music. Irene Browne was the first to mention it. They didn't talk to each other as a family anymore, she said. She even began to think that meeting their neighbor might not have been such a good thing after all. He seemed to have snatched something of her son away, and she suggested to her husband that maybe it would be a good idea to remove the MP3 player, to give Jeremy a rest. But before either of the Brownes could act, something else happened that completely took their minds off modern music and earbuds. Jeremy became ill.

It was hard to tell when it began. Maybe it had been about two weeks after Mr. Demszky had moved in, but on the other hand it could have actually started before he arrived. It appeared, first, to be a sort of virus. Jeremy was tired all the time. He was finding it hard to get up and, in the evening, he went back to bed as soon as he could. He still had an appetite but he didn't enjoy his food, eating it mechanically, without any sense of taste. His eyes seemed to have lost some of their color. He moved more slowly and gave up his rugby training, saying that he didn't feel like it. A strange rash appeared on the side of his neck. He began to wheeze.

At first, the Brownes weren't too worried. All teenagers, after all, like to stay in bed. But as his movements became increasingly listless, as he became quieter and more withdrawn, they decided to take him down to see Dr. Sheila McAllister at the local clinic for a quick checkup. Jeremy didn't argue. He had to wait at the clinic for an hour and a half before he was seen, but the time passed quickly enough, listening to music through his MP3 player, nodding his head in time to the track.

Finally, he was examined. Dr. McAllister asked him if he was sleeping. Yes, certainly. Jeremy had no trouble getting to sleep. It was waking up that was the problem.

Was he eating properly? His mother assured the doctor that Jeremy ate three proper meals, including breakfast, and that he always had plenty of fruits and vegetables, five portions a day, just as the government recommended. The doctor took a blood sample. It did seem possible that Jeremy was anemic. Or maybe there was something wrong with his thyroid gland. It was all very strange, but she was sure there was nothing serious to worry about. Generally speaking, Jeremy was in very good shape. This could all be down to a bout of flu. She told the Brownes to come back in two weeks if there was no change.

Jeremy thanked her and slipped his earbuds back in. Robbie Williams took him out of the clinic and back onto the street.

His situation did get worse . . . much worse. Over the next few days, Jeremy became more and more listless. He took several days off school. Physically, he seemed to be shriveling up. His cheeks, once so healthy and full of color, were now sunken and pale. His eyes had lost their focus. Both his parents had stopped work to be with him, but he barely talked to them. Sometimes it was as if he was far away. He lay in his room for hours at a time, listening to the MP3 player, staring at the ceiling while he got thinner and thinner. He was still eating, but the food had no effect. His lips had begun to shrivel. His hair was turning gray.

More doctors and specialists began to appear. Blood and urine samples were taken. It was thought he might have a serious viral infection. The Brownes were asked if he had been offered drugs. Jeremy was taken to the hospital, where he was scanned from head to foot. Various illnesses—diabetes, thyrotoxicosis, tuberculosis and brucellosis—were all suggested. Jeremy was tested for all of them. He was found to have none. For the first time, the dreadful word *progeria* was uttered. Progeria, a genetic disorder, was also known as the aging disease. It was very rare. There was no known cure. But Jeremy didn't hear any of it. He had gone rather deaf and he didn't care anyway. Long after his parents had gone, he lay in his bed in the children's ward, only partly aware of his surroundings, listening to his MP3 player, which lay on the pillow beside him, the thick white wires snaking up to earbuds that seemed to be burrowing farther and farther into his head. *Tish-tata-tish-tata-tish-tata-tish* . . . the soft beat of the percussion whispered across the ward as the duty nurse walked quietly by.

Briefly, he was sent back home again. There was nothing the hospital could do for him, and so it had been decided to send him to a special neurological clinic on the South Coast. Scampi the dog had already been taken away to live with relatives in Yorkshire. On Jeremy's last night on Elmsworth Avenue, Mr. Demszky came to visit, bringing with him a box of Hungarian chocolates with pictures of folk dancers on the lid. It was only October and not yet cold, but he was wearing a black cashmere overcoat that reached all the way to the ground. His face was partially hidden by an old-fashioned floppy hat.

"How is Jeremy?" he asked, still standing on the doorstep. For once, Mrs. Browne had not invited him in.

"He's not well," she said. The worry of the last weeks had changed her. She was short-tempered. She didn't want to see her neighbor and she didn't care if he knew it.

"There is no improvement?"

"No, Mr. Demszky—and if you don't mind, I'd like to get back to him. We're leaving for Brighton tomorrow."

"I brought these . . ." He lifted the box.

"Jeremy isn't eating chocolates, thank you very much. We'll let you know if there's any news."

She closed the door in his face.

Mothers can be irrational sometimes. It was only then that Mrs. Browne remembered that Jeremy had fallen ill shortly after he had met Mr. Demszky. And at the same moment, she found herself thinking about the MP3 player. Jeremy had always liked music, but since he had been given that machine, he had become obsessed with it, listening to it twenty hours a day—at school, doing his homework, in the bath. Once, she'd actually torn it away to stop him from listening to it during meals. Jeremy had screamed at her. She had never seen him like that before. She thought of the ugly slab of glass and plastic that was probably playing even now. It was almost as if . . .

It was almost as if it was sucking the life out of him.

A private ambulance came for Jeremy the next morning. He was able to walk out to it—but only just. His parents had to support him, one on each side. He was mumbling to himself, his eyes barely focused. He had lost a lot of his hair and his skin was gray and wrinkled. Some of his teeth had come loose. If any of the other residents of Elmsworth Avenue had been watching, they would have been shocked. He looked like a very old man.

He did not have the MP3 player with him. At the last moment, acting on a whim, Mrs. Browne had pried it out of his hand and she had left it in his room, on the table beside his bed. Jeremy had tried to complain, but the words barely came. He allowed himself to be led downstairs. Minutes later they were on their way to the North Circular Road, which would take them around London on their way to the south.

Half an hour later, Jákob Demszky entered the house.

By now he knew that the Brownes kept a spare key in the pot beside the front door, but even if it hadn't been there, he would have found it simple to break in. He opened the door and went straight over to the stairs. He had only been in the house a few times but he had no trouble finding his way to Jeremy's room, as if he was being guided there by something inside. And indeed there it was, sitting where Mrs. Browne had left it. Mr. Demszky chuckled to himself, a strangely unpleasant sound. He reached out with a trembling hand and for a moment his fingers hovered over the MP3 player like a large bird about to land. Then he snatched it up and left.

He walked back to number 66 and went straight to his study, one of the rooms that Jeremy had never visited. Had the boy gone in there, he might have been surprised by some of the ornaments on display: the human skull on its pedestal; the black candles, squat and half melted; the golden cross that stood upside down on the mantelpiece. It might then have occurred to him to go onto the Internet and look up the English for *boszorkánys*—or indeed for *tépőfarkas* or *gonoszul*. But alas, it was far too late. Jeremy's eyesight had gone. It had failed him long ago.

Mr. Demszky set down the MP3 player and put on a pair of spectacles that were actually inch-thick magnifying glasses. They would have turned even a period at the end of a sentence into the size of a button. Squinting through them with his round, watery eyes, he produced a tiny screwdriver and ran it over the MP3 player until he found four equally tiny screws in the base. Taking enormous care, he unscrewed them and the secret panel that Jeremy had never noticed fell off in his hands. The inside of the MP3 player was exposed. There were no batter-ies . . . just a mass of circuits and a single switch turned to the left. Using the screwdriver, Mr. Demszky slid the switch over to the right, into reverse, then screwed the panel back into place.

With a contented smile, he picked up the earbuds and pressed them in. It gave him extra pleasure knowing that, until very recently, they had been in Jeremy's ears. Somehow it helped to connect the two of them. Mr. Dem-szky did not like modern music. He turned on the MP3 player, rested his white hair against the back of his chair and began to listen to a symphonic poem by the Austrian composer Antonin Dvořák. The music was dark and ma-jestic. It flowed into him like a moonlit river and grate-fully he absorbed it.

Maybe it was a trick of the light. Perhaps not. A few minutes later, his skin had regained some of its color and his hair was a little less white.

POWER

Arthur and Elizabeth Reed had never expected to have children. It was something they had decided, almost from the moment they had gotten married, and thirty years later they had no regrets. It wasn't that they disliked children. It was just that they preferred a quiet life, spending what little money they had on themselves or their friends.

When they met, Arthur was running the village post office, which also sold sweets, stationery and other useful items to the inhabitants of Instow in Devonshire. He was a small, round-faced man who always seemed to be smiling and who knew all of his customers by name. He lived in a very ordinary house at the end of a terrace, but with wonderful views of the sand dunes that rose up and down in yellow waves with a flat blue sea on the other side.

One of his customers was Elizabeth Williams, a cheerful, attractive woman who worked in the local bakery just a few yards down the road. Nobody was really surprised when the two of them announced their engagement. It seemed that the whole of Instow turned out for their wedding. The bakers gave them a cake with pink and white icing, three tiers high. They took a week off for their honeymoon, which they spent in Greece, and when they came back, Mrs. Reed, as she was now, sold her apartment and moved into her husband's house.

Thirty years is a very long time to describe in a few sentences, but for the Reeds, time seemed to slip past without even being noticed. They had been in their late twenties when they met, but suddenly they were in their late fifties. Arthur's black hair had turned gray. He had to wear glasses to read. He found that he was forgetting where he had put things. And Elizabeth, after a series of minor illnesses, had become rather frail. When she went out walking, she carried a stick and could be seen waving it vengefully, as if determined that the miles would not defeat her.

In a strange way, age suited them. In fact, newcomers to the village could hardly imagine that they had ever been young. And they were still completely happy in each other's company, laughing at each other's jokes or enjoying long silences. They had just about enough money. Their house was cozy and just the right size. All in all, they had no complaints about the cards that life had dealt them. They were looking forward to a long and comfortable retirement.

But, as it happened, Elizabeth Reed had a younger sister named Janice. The two of them hadn't seen each other for many years, mainly because Janice lived in Manchester, which was a long way away, and since her marriage they had become increasingly uncommunicative. From a note scribbled in a Christmas card, Elizabeth learned that Janice had a son. Another brief letter informed her that Janice had divorced. After that . . . nothing. Elizabeth wrote several times but got no reply. She even wondered if her sister was still alive.

So she was very surprised to receive, one day, a telephone call from a man called Mr. Norris who explained that he was an attorney representing Janice. He wondered if the two of them could possibly meet. Elizabeth didn't want to travel up to Manchester, but Mr. Norris assured her that he could easily come to Instow, and so it was arranged.

The attorney came down the following Wednesday afternoon. He was a thin, tired-looking man in a suit that seemed to have gotten quite badly crumpled on the train—or perhaps it had been like that when he put it on. He carried a battered leather briefcase that hung open to reveal a handful of legal documents, a newspaper and a half-eaten Kit Kat.

"It's very kind of you to see me, Mrs. Reed," he began. He spoke slowly and without very much emotion. "You too, Mr. Reed."

Arthur Reed had of course stayed in with his wife. The two of them were sitting side by side on the sofa, holding hands.

"May I begin by offering my condolences with regard to your sister."

Elizabeth had been fearing the worst, but even so, the statement took her by surprise. "I didn't even know she was dead," she said.

"Then I must apologize for breaking the news to you in this manner. Yes. I'm afraid to say that Janice Carter passed away two weeks ago."

"Carter?"

"Her husband's name. She married a man named Kevin Carter in 1995. You never met him?" Elizabeth said nothing, so he went on. "They were married for ten years, but I'm afraid after that he left her."

"How did she die?" Elizabeth asked.

"She had a nervous breakdown." The attorney took a breath. "She hadn't been well for a long time. And I'm sorry to have to tell you this, but in the end she took her own life. She jumped off a bridge into the River Irwell."

"Why would she do a thing like that?"

"She didn't leave a note."

Both Arthur and Elizabeth blinked in surprise.

"It's clear that you had little connection with your sister," Mr. Norris went on. "Were you aware of her situation? I mean . . . her state of mind?"

Elizabeth shook her head, dumbfounded. "I feel very bad about it now," she said. "But Janice led her own life. She didn't even give me her telephone number and she hardly ever wrote."

"We have been trying to contact her ex-husband," Mr. Norris went on. "But so far there's been no trace of him. We believe he emigrated to New Zealand after the divorce. It's possible he changed his name—"

"Why would he do that?" Arthur asked.

"I can't imagine."

"He didn't keep in contact with his son?"

"No. And I'm glad you asked that, Mr. Reed, as that's very much the point of this visit. Craig is thirteen years old. He'd just started middle school in Manchester when his mother did what she did. Right now he is being looked after by the local authorities. There are no relatives on his father's side of the family. And the only relatives we've managed to find on his mother's side . . ."

"Are Arthur and me." Elizabeth completed the sentence.

"So what will happen to him?" Arthur Reed asked.

He could see the way this was going and there was a certain dread in his voice.

"Well, under normal circumstances, Craig would have to go into an orphanage," the attorney replied. "But you are his uncle and his aunt. So we wondered if you might be interested in taking him in."

There was a long silence. Both the Reeds were thinking of many things, but mainly they were thinking of each other. They had lived together for a very long time and they had become used to being alone.

"Do you have a picture of Craig?" Elizabeth asked at last.

"As a matter of fact I do," Mr. Norris replied.

He opened his briefcase and took out a color photograph about the size of a postcard. It showed a dark-haired boy in a school uniform with a round face. He was rather plump and he had a crooked tie. Craig Carter wasn't smiling. In fact, he wasn't even looking at the camera. Something seemed to have caught his attention at the edge of the frame and he seemed almost annoyed to be having his photograph taken.

"I won't pretend that Craig is an easy boy," Mr. Norris said. "He hasn't done very well at school and his report cards don't make entirely pleasant reading. But that said, he is only a boy. He has lost his mother in the most terrible circumstances and I feel certain that a complete change of scene is exactly what he needs. I'm sure you'd agree that anything would be better than an orphanage. On the other hand, the decision is entirely up to you. You've obviously never met him and he doesn't know you exist. Everybody would understand if you chose to walk away."

But the truth was that Elizabeth and Arthur already knew what they had to do. How could they possibly walk away? It didn't matter that they knew nothing about this boy. He was family. He needed their help. There was really nothing more to be said.

That evening they discussed the entire business over a supper of cheese on toast and hot chocolate, which Elizabeth Reed carried in on a tray. Arthur noticed that she sat down a little more heavily than usual, resting her walking stick against her chair. He could see that she was unhappy and guessed what she was going to say.

"Arthur," she said. "You and I have been together for many years and we never had children of our own. I suppose we didn't really want any. We were happy the way things were. And now, suddenly, this boy—this teenager—is being offered to us. If you don't want to take him in, I'll quite understand. . . ."

"Of course we must take him in, old girl," Arthur replied. He had called her "old girl" even when Elizabeth had been young. "Flesh and blood and all that."

Elizabeth sighed. "He may not find it easy to adapt to our way of life," she said. "We're very quiet down here. This house is very small. You're too old to kick a soccer ball around and I'm too tired. He'll probably think we're a couple of old fossils."

"Still better than an orphanage," Arthur said. "And Instow is a lovely place. Maybe he'll enjoy it. Make friends. A new start."

"Poor Janice." Elizabeth shook her head. "What a terrible thing."

She telephoned Mr. Norris the next day, and a week later the postman brought a stack of documents that they had to sign and return to the council offices. The next three weeks were spent preparing the house. Fortunately, there was a spare bedroom on the second floor, and Arthur Reed got a local man in to redecorate. He had no real idea what a teenager would like but guessed that it wouldn't be floral wallpaper and antique furniture. The room was painted white. A high sleeper bed was brought in with a desk underneath. The curtains were replaced by blinds. At the end of it, the room looked very modern and new.

Craig Carter arrived a week later with a scowling social worker who introduced herself as Ms. Naseby. Apparently, she hadn't enjoyed the train journey down from Manchester and needed two Anadin tablets with her cup of tea. Craig himself sat there with a blank expression on his face. Elizabeth and Arthur hadn't had a chance to say anything to each other, but their first impressions were not entirely favorable. It seemed unfair to judge the new arrival too quickly, and yet . . .

Craig wasn't fat, exactly, but he was certainly out of shape. It was obvious that he had never taken much exercise and had eaten all the wrong food. He had poor skin and his hair, unbrushed, looked dank and lifeless. There was a triangular scar under one of his eyes, and Ms. Naseby explained that one of the other boys at his school had hit him with a brick. Craig shrugged when he heard this but didn't speak. He was wearing jeans and a T-shirt, both of which needed either washing or (Elizabeth thought) burning, as they were dirty and full of holes. He didn't seem to have much interest in his new home or the people in it. His eyes, a muddy shade of brown, were utterly lifeless.

Ms. Naseby was in a hurry to get back home. She gave the Reeds two telephone numbers—her own mobile and a general help line—and left as soon as she could. She had come by taxi from the station and had asked the driver to wait outside. She ate two sandwiches, drank half a cup of tea and left, the Reeds noticed, without saying good-bye to Craig.

The Reeds may have been old and old-fashioned,

but they were not stupid people. They hadn't expected things to be easy and nor had they fooled themselves that Craig would accept them as his new foster parents just like that. But they were both pleasantly surprised by the way things went in the following weeks. Craig appeared to like his new room with its view over the sand dunes. He had never actually been to the seaside and soon his room was full of shells and oddly shaped pieces of shingle that he had found on the beach. He was introduced to a new school in nearby Barnstaple, and although the teachers reported that he was way behind with his studies, they had every expectation that he would catch up. He enjoyed Elizabeth's cooking—she had, after all, spent years working in a bakery—and to begin with he even helped wash up.

Arthur Reed watched the new arrival warily. In fact, for the first time in their marriage there was a certain tension between him and Elizabeth. But it was a tension they both shared, a bit like sailors sensing a coming storm. The sun might still be shining, but they both knew that what had begun as a pleasant cruise might at any time become a howling nightmare with both of them forced to abandon ship.

Things went wrong one step at a time. It was as if Craig had been testing the ground, checking out the opposition before he showed himself in his true colors. And once he had the measure of the Reeds, the school, the neighborhood . . . then it could begin.

He stopped making his bed. That was the first thing. Elizabeth had asked him to make his bed because she had a bad back and found it difficult to lift the mattress. But after two weeks, the bed remained unmade, the sheets crumpled, the pillows on the floor. Indeed, the whole room became increasingly untidy, with a strange sour smell and clothes everywhere. Soon it no longer seemed to belong to the rest of the house.

Arthur and Elizabeth said nothing. After all, Craig was a teenager and all teenage bedrooms are a mess. Arthur had borrowed a copy of *Proper Parenting* from the library, and the author advised him not to make an issue of it. "Young people need their own space," the book explained. "If they wish to live in conditions close to squalor, then they must be allowed to make that choice."

Then it was a question of food. Meals became increasingly difficult as there were all sorts of things that Craig suddenly refused to eat—mainly vegetables and fruit. Elizabeth had thought he liked her home cooking, but at dinnertime he would push his plate away and slouch with his elbows on the table and a sullen look on his face. As a result, he began to lose weight. He didn't get thin. He just looked sick and lopsided, and once again Arthur sought advice in *Proper Parenting*. "Many teenagers shy away from fresh food," it explained. "And the more you try to force it on them, the more they will resist. In extreme cases, it may be necessary to seek medical advice."

But this wasn't needed in Craig's case because quite soon he began putting on weight again. Even a place like Barnstaple had fast-food restaurants and he had taken to visiting them after school, stocking up on fish-and-chips and kebabs, burgers and takeout Chinese. The house was soon strewn with wrappers from chocolate cookies, chips and ice cream.

And how had he gotten the money to pay for them? That was another worry. Arthur had given Craig a small allowance from the day he had arrived, but one Friday afternoon, he and Elizabeth were shocked to get a telephone call from the principal at St. Edmund's in Barnstaple. It seemed that Craig had been bullying several of the smaller children, forcing them to give him their loose change or, even worse, to steal money from their parents and bring it to him at school.

That weekend, Arthur and Elizabeth sat Craig down in the living room and talked to him seriously about their life in Instow and how they had hoped he would make the effort to fit in. It was a mistake. For that was the weekend that war was declared.

"I know life hasn't been easy for you," Arthur was

saying. "But your aunt and I were really hoping that this would be a new start—"

"I hate it here!" Craig cut in, and the awful emphasis that he put on the word *hate*, the way he almost spat it out, shattered any remaining illusions the elderly couple might have had. "This is a poxy little house in a poxy little place and I wish I was back in Manchester."

"But if you were in Manchester, you'd be in an orphanage," Elizabeth faltered.

"At least I wouldn't be living with two wrinklies. There's nobody here my age. There's nobody to hang out with or have fun."

This wasn't actually true. There were plenty of teenagers in Instow, which, apart from anything else, had a fine sailing club. But by now they had decided to give Craig a wide berth.

"I'm doing the best I can," Elizabeth explained.

"I don't like you," Craig replied. "And you smell."

"I really don't think you should talk to your aunt like that," Arthur muttered. Two pinpricks of deep red had appeared in his cheeks.

"I'll talk to her any way I like. What are you going to do about it?"

What Arthur Reed did was to call Ms. Naseby that same afternoon. And again the following Monday. In fact he called her, and her help line, several times before his call was finally answered. He was then passed from department to department, from social worker to social worker, but it seemed the bottom line was this. He and his wife had agreed to take Craig. It had been made perfectly clear to them that the child might take a while to adapt. But so far he hadn't set fire to the house or committed any serious criminal act. So like it or not, they were stuck with him. The council had taken Craig off their books and they didn't want him back.

Arthur and Elizabeth had been happily married for more than thirty years. But now, for the first time, they found themselves torn apart.

Elizabeth felt dreadfully guilty. It was she who had opened their door to Craig Carter. She was the one who was related to him. And so all this worry and unhappiness had to be her fault. When Craig was arrested and cautioned for shoplifting, she blamed herself. When he was faced with expulsion from St. Edmund's for threatening a teacher, she actually fell ill. She hadn't been exactly young when Craig arrived, but soon she was looking positively old. One night she slipped on a sneaker that Craig had left on the stairs, fell down and fractured her hip. The neighbors wondered if she would even survive.

Meanwhile, Arthur Reed retreated into himself. Once or twice he tried to have it out with his adopted nephew, but Craig simply sneered at him and walked out of the room without speaking. Arthur had noticed that a great many of his personal possessions had begun to vanish. In particular there was a handsome pair of silver cuff links that Elizabeth had bought him for his fortieth birthday. One day, walking in Barnstaple, he noticed them in the window of a secondhand jewelry shop. A few days before, Craig had bought himself a new leather jacket. It didn't take very much to put two and two together. But there was nothing very much Arthur could do. A week later, thirty dollars disappeared from his wallet. Then his wallet went too. By this time, Craig had taken up smoking, and the smell of burning tobacco wafted down from his bedroom, filling the entire house.

Not many people came to visit Arthur and Elizabeth anymore. Once, they had been surrounded by friends, often giving lunches and tea parties. But there had been several incidents. The sandwiches that had been found to contain a whole bottle of diarrhea tablets. The dog poo in the pockets of coats left hanging in the hall. The cars with nails resting against their front tires. The lady who had brought her pet poodle and had gone into the kitchen only to find it shaved bald.

What were the Reeds to do?

They couldn't get rid of Craig. The authorities didn't want to know. Nor could they reason with him, for any attempt at discussion now ended with a barrage of foul language. Elizabeth was back from the hospital, but her limp was worse than ever and Arthur could only sit in pained silence, angry with himself, angry that he had so little control over his own life.

So they tried a new tactic. They couldn't fight with Craig, but perhaps they could win him over. If they tried to understand him, if they gave him what he wanted, he might even now turn a corner and accept his place as part of their family.

For his fourteenth birthday, they bought him designer jeans, a skateboard, an iPod and two new games for his laptop computer. In fact, they got him everything he had asked for, and for just a couple of days he seemed genuinely happy. But that all ended when Elizabeth made the mistake of serving cauliflower cheese for dinner. Craig hated cauliflower cheese and by the end of the evening he was back to the scowling, swearing, bullying hulk that they had so unfortunately inherited.

The next day was a Sunday. As usual, Arthur and Elizabeth went to church and then, because the weather was nice, for a walk along the beach. As they approached the house, they were surprised to see Craig sitting on a sand dune. His fingers were very stained and they could smell the smoke on his breath, so they guessed that he must have just stubbed out a cigarette. Even so, it was rare to find him out in the fresh air.

"Is everything all right?" Elizabeth asked. Whenever she spoke to Craig, she flinched, wondering what the answer would be.

"I want one of those," Craig replied.

Elizabeth turned and saw what he was looking at. There was a man in his early twenties out on the sand with a power kite. The kite itself was huge, a brightly colored curving strip of silk or nylon, like a parachute cut in half, connected to two handles by a series of cables. The man wasn't just flying the kite. The kite was flying him. He was running across the beach and leaping into the air, rising ten or twenty yards above the sand like a superhero. Elizabeth could see the muscles on his bare arms bulging as he fought to keep the kite under control. One moment he would be on the sand, the next his legs would be pedaling high above. When he came back down, he had to dig his heels in to stop himself from being pulled away. He was fighting with the wind. His hair was streaming around him. He reminded Elizabeth of a cowboy trying to bring a rearing horse under control.

"It looks fun," Craig said.

"It certainly looks exciting," Elizabeth agreed. "But you've just had your birthday, Craig. And we got you everything you asked for."

"But I want a power kite," Craig whined.

"When I was a boy, 'I want' never got anything," Arthur remarked.

"When you were a boy, there were still dinosaurs," Craig responded. He looked at Elizabeth and there was a gleam of menace in his eyes, and not for the first time Elizabeth thought about the death of her sister and began to understand perhaps why she had thrown herself off a bridge. "I want a kite," Craig said. "And if you don't get me one, you'll be sorry."

Elizabeth ignored the threat. She had been to the local toy shop and had discovered that even a small power kite would cost more than a hundred dollars. More to the point, she had no doubt that even if she went out and bought the wretched kite, Craig would fly it a couple of times and then lose interest. After all, he hadn't even unwrapped the skateboard they had given him, even though he had nagged them just as much to buy one.

So she was very surprised when, lying next to her in bed that evening, Arthur disagreed with her.

"I think, all in all, it's a good idea," he said.

For a moment, Elizabeth didn't reply. Arthur didn't speak much these days. Since Craig had arrived he seemed to have shrunk into himself to the extent that often she had no idea what he was thinking.

"The boy wants a kite. Let's get him one."

"But the money . . . ," Elizabeth muttered.

"It might be worth it. Get him out in the fresh air."

"It seems very wrong," Elizabeth countered. "We bought him all those presents for his birthday and he didn't so much as even thank us."

"We have to do the best we can for him," Arthur said. "After all, we said we'd look after him. I'll look into it tomorrow."

Elizabeth looked at her husband, lying in his pajamas with his soft blue-gray eyes and his white hair. There were hollows in his cheeks that she hadn't noticed before and she realized that it had been a long time since she had seen him smile. She thought he was wrong about the power kite but decided not to argue. After all, power was what this was all about. Craig had been living with them for only nine months, but he had usurped all the power in the house. He was the one in control. Somehow, Arthur had been knocked off his perch. Arguing with him now would only make him feel all the worse.

Sadly, the decision to buy a kite only led to further argument. Craig had already found a website that sold boards, kites and all sorts of accessories. It was as if he had known that Arthur and Elizabeth would cave in. But, as they soon discovered, power kites came in many shapes and sizes with prices that rose steeply to many hundreds of dollars. Craig had settled on a brand called Laserblade.

But the question was whether to go for the Laserblade 1.8 ("an ideal moderate to strong wind buggy kite, perfect for those new to the sport") or the Laserblade 6.0 ("awesome power and brilliant rate of turn . . . for experienced kite flyers only").

Elizabeth remembered the man she had seen on the beach. A less demanding kite made obvious sense. Craig was small for his age . . . the amount of cigarettes he smoked had seen to that. He really had no muscles at all. She could see him being pulled flat on his face by the first strong gust of wind, and after that the kite would be consigned to the garbage bin. Anyway, there was the question of cost. The Laserblade 6.0 came in at an eye-watering $400.

This, of course, was the kite that Craig had set his heart on. And once again Elizabeth was completely astonished by Arthur's response. The price didn't seem to bother him at all.

"I'm not sure, Craig," he muttered, examining the picture on the computer screen. "I do wonder if it might not be a bit too big for you to handle."

"It's not too big. It's perfect."

"But suppose it pulls you over? You could get hurt."

Craig scowled. "If the wind is too strong, I'll let go." He shook his head as if he was having to explain himself to an idiot. "I'm not stupid, you know," he said. "I know how to fly these things."

"Well, you'll have to promise me you'll be careful. We don't want you in bed with a broken leg."

Craig said nothing and two days later the new kite arrived in the mail. By this time, Elizabeth was a little angry. She didn't say anything but she hated seeing her husband give in to the spoiled, heartless brat that she now knew her nephew to be. Nor did she think that indulging Craig would help. She could already see that Craig would get as much out of them as he could and would still go on to demand more. She wished now that she had never opened her door to him. She wished the Manchester authorities had never found her.

"We'll take it up to Millbrook Common," Arthur said over breakfast. "There's plenty of room there and we can see if Craig can get it to fly."

"What about school?" Elizabeth asked.

"I wasn't at school yesterday or the day before," Craig reminded her. This was something new. Craig had begun to play truant with increasing frequency. So far, nobody had complained. It was possible that the school simply preferred not having him there.

"There's a good, stiff breeze today," Arthur muttered. "Good kite-flying weather . . ."

Millbrook Common was an open space between Instow and Barnstaple with farmland all around. It was certainly a good place to choose for a first flight. There would have been too many people on the beach and anyway, with Craig skipping school, it was probably better to go somewhere more out of sight. The common was also high up, which meant that it was more open to the breeze. Arthur, Elizabeth and Craig took a bus up there after breakfast. Craig was carrying the kite. Elizabeth had the assembly instructions. Arthur sat with one hand in his pocket, lost in his own thoughts.

Eventually they found themselves on the edge of a wide, bumpy field with wild-looking grass that somehow looked hundreds of years old. The sea was far away and below them. Elizabeth drew her coat around her. It was the end of the summer and the leaves were already beginning to turn. She could feel a certain chill in the air and it seemed to her that there was much more of the breeze up here than there had been below.

"I'm not so sure we should fly the kite here," she said. "Maybe the beach would be better after all."

"But we've come all the way up here now!" Craig complained.

"The boy's right," Arthur muttered. "We're here now, so we might as well give it a try."

"But Arthur, there's a lot of wind—"

"Craig has already said. If he feels he's losing control,

all he has to do is let go." Arthur still had his hand in his pocket. "Come on!" he exclaimed. "Let's see if we can work out how to put this thing together."

It took them a long time. There were lots of different cables, struts to fit into place and knots to tie. Eventually, they managed to construct the Laserblade, and Craig and Elizabeth held it down while Arthur unrolled the twenty-five-meter flying line. There were two handles at the end, one for each hand. He knelt down and examined them, running a finger along the tightly woven material ("sleeved Dyneema, specially designed for a better grip"). When he was sure that everything was ready, he looked up.

"All right!" he shouted. He had to raise his voice to make it heard above the wind. "Let's see if we can get flying."

Arthur and Craig swapped ends, passing each other in the middle of the field, and for a moment, if anyone had been watching, they could have been duelists, meeting at the appointed time. Craig reached the handles and picked them up, gripping them tightly in the palms of his hands. Elizabeth was trying to keep the kite steady, pressing it against the ground. The Laserblade was a brilliant red, blue and green and it was already trembling like a trapped butterfly. Arthur joined her.

"Are you all right?" he asked.

Elizabeth glanced at her husband. For the first time in

thirty years, she realized that she had no idea what he was thinking. "I suppose so," she said.

"Don't be cross with me, old girl. I'm just trying to do what's best for Craig."

The two of them leaned down and picked up the kite. Twenty-five meters of cord hung across the jagged grass to the two handles and the boy at the other end. Suddenly he looked very small, compared to the enormous kite.

"Ready?" Arthur shouted.

"Let it go!" The boy's voice barely reached them. He could have been a mile away.

"Good luck!"

Arthur and Elizabeth pushed upward at the same moment. In fact, they didn't need to do anything very much. The wind seized hold of the Laserblade and almost ripped it out of their hands. The kite flew up as if it had exploded out of the ground. It was a quite beautiful sight, the brand-new colors standing out against the gray, stormy sky. The two cables soared up with it. Elizabeth gazed anxiously at the boy clinging on to the other end.

"It's too strong for him," she muttered.

"He'll be fine," Arthur replied.

And for a few seconds, he was right. Craig dug his heels in and struggled to keep the kite under control, pulling first one cable, then the other. He was leaning backward, shouting with pleasure, his fists pounding left and right as if he were fighting an invisible enemy. The kite was now high above him, dancing around his head. All Craig had to do was harness its power. Then he would be able to run forward and jump. Briefly, he would fly—just like the man he had seen at the beach.

There was only one problem. The man on the beach had been flying power kites for many years and his model had an aspect ratio of only 4.7 meters. In other words, it was one size smaller than Craig's and—more to the point—the wind hadn't been so strong that day. He had known what he was doing. Craig did not. He had barely read the instructions that came with the kite. Certainly, he had ignored the many warnings.

The first indication that something was wrong came when Craig's happy cries became a wail of dismay. He seemed to be punching harder and harder, his entire body jerking, like a puppet in the grip of a mad puppeteer. He was slamming his heels into the soft ground, trying to anchor himself, leaning ever farther back, his arms stretched out high over his head.

"He's losing control!" Elizabeth said.

"No. He's having a high old time," Arthur retorted.

"We should do something!"

"If he's not happy, he can let go!"

In truth, there wasn't much they could have done anyway. Craig was twenty-five meters away from them, the same distance as the kite above his head. He seemed to be swearing—at them or at the kite, they couldn't say. And suddenly his feet left the ground. Craig had wanted to fly. He had been given his wish.

But only for a few moments. He must have risen three or four meters into the air, jerked off the ground by the kite. Unfortunately, he had no control. He slammed down again.

"Bravo!" Arthur shouted.

Elizabeth turned to him. "Arthur, you don't understand!" she cried. "He's not having fun. He's completely out of control!"

"Nonsense!" Arthur waved a cheerful hand in Craig's direction. "It reminds me of when I was young. I always loved kites."

"But Craig isn't loving this one . . ." Elizabeth broke off as Craig was jerked into the air again. This time he hung there a little longer and landed even harder.

"Wonderful!" Arthur shouted.

"I think he's broken his ankle," Elizabeth exclaimed.

It was true. Craig was howling. There had been a definite snap as he hit the ground and his left foot seemed to be pointing the wrong way. He was trying to hold himself up on just one leg. He was screaming now but his words were incoherent, swept away by the wind, which, if anything, seemed to have gotten stronger.

"You're right," Arthur muttered. "He's hurt himself." He put his hands up to his mouth, forming a sort of funnel. "Let go of the kite!" he shouted. "It doesn't matter if we lose it. Just let go!"

But Craig seemed grimly determined to hang on, despite his injury. Still screaming, he was suddenly thrown forward and then, before anyone could do anything, he was being dragged at about twenty miles per hour, facedown, across the field.

"Let go!" Elizabeth called out. "Let go! Let go!"

It was as if Craig hadn't heard her. He was like a prisoner being tortured on the rack, his arms stretching out in front of him, his legs—with one foot dangling horribly—behind. The two old people could only watch as he was dragged diagonally across the field, thistles and stinging nettles whipping into his face.

"Where is he going?" Elizabeth wailed.

"He won't get far," Arthur observed. "There's a fence ahead."

In fact, there were two barbed-wire fences running parallel between the common land and the field below. Elizabeth was sure that Craig would get tangled up in the first of them and come to an abrupt, if painful, halt. But it seemed that the wind was playing tricks with him. At the last moment, it lifted the kite, which in turn yanked Craig off the ground. For a couple of seconds he was standing on his own two feet. Then he ran straight into the first barbed-wire fence.

Elizabeth and Arthur heard him scream as at least a dozen cruel metal spikes dug into Craig's chest, belly and thighs. But at least he seemed to be pinned there. His ordeal was surely over.

"Let go of the kite!" Arthur yelled again.

But still Craig didn't listen. He stood there, clinging to the handles, looking both ridiculous and hideous, his white shirt covered with grass stains, his arms and face already covered in stings and blisters. One of his eyes was closed. There was blood trickling from a gash on his head.

"We'd better go and help him," Elizabeth said.

She was too late. A fresh blast of wind hit the kite and Craig was dragged over the first barbed-wire fence and then the second. The Reeds could only watch, horrified, as his clothes were torn off him. It was impossible to imagine what the wretched boy must be feeling, but his screams echoed all the way down to the coast and several people, out walking their dogs, stopped and looked around them, wondering what could be making such a horrible noise.

Somehow, incredibly, Craig cleared the second fence. But he had left most of his clothes behind him. His jeans, in twenty pieces, hung in tatters on the spikes. His shirt was just a bundle of rags. Even his boxers had been dragged off as he was carried forward. Wearing only baggy under-pants, he was dragged across the second field. And worse things were to come.

"Watch out for the cattle!" Arthur shouted.

Craig was in no state to watch out for anything. There were about half a dozen cows and a single bull in the field, and he only became aware of them as he was thrown once more onto his face, landing slap in the middle of a freshly laid cow patty. Somehow he managed to stagger back to his feet. Now his entire body—his face, his chest, his thighs—was dripping with brown slime. And still the kite urged him on.

"Drop it!" Elizabeth screamed.

A couple of dog walkers had reached the edge of the field and were watching with undisguised horror.

Craig still refused to save himself.

He was running, stumbling with his broken foot, straight toward the herd. The bull saw him coming and lowered its head, two huge horns twisting toward him. Almost gleefully, the kite dragged Craig toward it. Eliza-beth closed her eyes. She heard Craig scream as he was gored. The animal twisted its head. Craig continued past. His underpants were now hanging off one of the bull's horns.

"Why won't he let go of the kite?" she whimpered.

"It means too much to him," Arthur replied. "He must be afraid of losing it."

Craig was in the far distance now. He was getting smaller by the minute. All they could see were his back, his legs—now motionless—being dragged through the grass and his outstretched arms still clinging to the handles.

"I don't like the look of those electricity pylons," Arthur murmured.

Elizabeth looked up just in time to see Craig leave the ground completely, rising ten or even twenty meters into the air. And, sure enough, there was a pylon directly in front of him, carrying high-voltage electricity down toward Instow. The boy was flying right into it. There was no way he could avoid it.

Craig was little more than a speck in the distance when he hit the wire. At once there was a tremendous fizz and the boy was burned to a frazzle. For perhaps five seconds, all that was left of him was a black silhouette, a sort of statue made of ash. Then that fell apart and finally the kite came free, leaping cheerfully to one side and disappearing off beyond the trees. A shower of black dust tumbled back to the ground.

Of course there was an inquest. Arthur Reed was seriously reprimanded for buying a fourteen-year-old boy a kite which he couldn't possibly have controlled. But he was able to argue in court that he had suggested a smaller kite and that Craig had refused to listen. His schoolteachers and some of the local shopkeepers also testified, and the coroner had to agree that Craig had really brought his terrible end upon himself.

Most significantly, the dog walkers and several other people who had been out on the common that day appeared as witnesses. They had all heard the Reeds urging the boy to let go of the kite. For some reason, he had refused to listen to them. His death, as prolonged and as painful as it had been, was entirely his own fault.

Or so they all thought.

But perhaps it was just as well that none of them had been with Arthur Reed when he got home that day. He had been quite alone when he had gone upstairs to his bedroom so nobody had seen him glance over his shoulder to make sure that Elizabeth was out of sight. And nobody knew anything about the tube of superglue that had been in his pocket when he took Craig out to fly the kite and that had come out only once, when he had leaned down to examine the handles.

The tube of glue was still there, but it was almost empty now.

Arthur dropped it into the drawer beside his bed, then went back downstairs to the kitchen, where Elizabeth was waiting and made them both a nice cup of tea.

THE X TRAIN

The Johnsons had never been to New York. They didn't want to go there—and why should they? Anything they wanted to buy they could find in Dallas or Houston, and if they needed a vacation, there was always Hawaii. Five days in New York in the middle of the summer would mean humidity and traffic, expensive food and even more expensive hotel rooms that would probably be far too small. Then there were the New Yorkers themselves . . . fast and unfriendly, if not downright rude. And too many of them! How could so many people live in so little space?

But the vacation was a gift and it was a difficult one to refuse. Herb Johnson was a lawyer, a senior partner in a medium-sized firm that specialized in corporate litigation. One of his clients, a company called TexChem based in San Antonio, was being prosecuted by the EPA after it had been caught dumping twenty thousand gallons of toxic waste in a local river. A guilty verdict would have destroyed them. The publicity alone would have been as lethal as the chemical cocktail that had poisoned every fish for five miles in both directions.

Herb had gotten them off. He and his team had worked around the clock for three months, but it was his own performance in the courtroom that had finally won the day. He had ridiculed the prosecution, intimidated the witnesses, undermined the evidence and enchanted the jury. His closing argument was a masterpiece: a mixture of straight-talking, sarcasm and persuasiveness, with just a little venom thrown in. By the time he had finished talking, a guilty verdict was about as likely as a UFO crash-landing onto the courthouse roof.

The CEO of TexChem was delighted. As it happened, he knew Herb Johnson personally. The two men played golf together. And a couple of days after the verdict, he arrived at Herb's office.

"Herb, you did a great job!" he announced. "And I want to find a way to thank you personally."

"There's no need for that, Hank . . . ," Herb began.

"No. I know how much work you put into this, burning the candle at both ends. You need a rest, and I'm going to pay for it. How would you and your family like a long weekend in New York City?"

"Well . . ."

"I'm going to fly the three of you out. You, Tammy and that sweet girl of yours. What's her name?"

"Madison."

"I have shares in a hotel—the Wilmott on Sixth Avenue. I'm going to tell them to give you the executive suite. And you should see a show while you're there. Just pick one and I'll arrange the tickets."

"Honestly, Hank . . ."

"Don't thank me. Don't mention it. It's nothing less than you deserve!"

The trouble was that Herb Johnson didn't dare argue with the CEO of TexChem, who was the sort of man who, once he had made his mind up about something, wouldn't budge an inch. He remembered a time, after a game of golf, when Hank had offered to buy a round of beers for his best friend—a man named Joe. Joe had protested in a friendly sort of way and as a result the two men hadn't spoken again for seventeen years. Hank had a violent temper. Even as a witness during the trial, he had scowled at the judge to such an extent that Herb had been nervous the entire case might actually be lost.

And so when Herb returned home that evening, he knew that there was no way out of the weekend trip.

"I'm home!" he shouted as he entered the house in Plano, a suburb just outside of Dallas.

"Dinner in five!" his wife called back from the kitchen.

And that night, over grilled ribs, curly fries, coleslaw and oven-baked beans, Herb told his family the news. He already had the dates of the trip. They would be flying in just three weeks. The hotel was booked, the tickets to *Mamma Mia!* already purchased.

"Honestly, honey. I'm not sure we need to go to New York," his wife protested. She was a small, round woman with horn-rimmed glasses that hung on a loop around her neck and hair that changed color every few months, none of which looked even remotely natural.

His daughter was more vocal. "I'm not going!" she exclaimed.

"Madison . . . ," Herb began.

"Daddy, I've got a party that weekend. Everyone's going to be there."

Parties were important to Madison. She was in her second year at the Margaret P. Rutherford School for Girls, one of the most expensive and exclusive educational establishments in the state. If you didn't have a steady boyfriend by the time you were sixteen, you might as well admit that you were . . . well, a freak. And of course, parties were where you met them. Madison had set her eyes on Charlie Meyer, a jock who lived a few streets away. Charlie was the quarterback for his high school football team and he was a dead ringer for the actor Robert Pattinson, though without the vampire teeth. He would be there. It was out of the question that she could miss it.

"Why can't Hank just send us a case of champagne or something?" Tammy suggested. She glanced nervously at her daughter, who was on the edge of tears.

"It's all been arranged," Herb insisted. "I know it's not something we particularly want to do as a family. But there was no way out of it. This is my job. I can't afford to offend Hank. This is my career we're talking about! We're just going to have to go. And let's look on the bright side. It's all free. It's only five days. Maybe we'll have a good time."

But none of them were smiling as, three weeks later, they disembarked from the plane at JFK. Even the first-class seats hadn't lifted their spirits. Tammy was tight-lipped. Madison was plugged into her iPod, her eyes focused on her feet. Even Herb looked crumpled and defeated after the long flight. He was wearing a white suit with two gold buckles, one fastening his tie and the other his belt. Like Tammy, he was very short and he was a little overweight. In fact, Madison was the only slim one in the family, towering over her parents, which somehow gave the impression that, although she was only fifteen, she was the one in charge.

There was a chauffeur waiting for them at the arrivals hall and a limousine parked outside, but still the family refused to cheer up. They trooped out as if they were heading for prison rather than a long weekend in one of the most exciting cities in the world.

The Wilmott Hotel was at the very southern end of Sixth Avenue, next to the neighborhood known as SoHo—and this disappointed them too. They would have much rather been close to Times Square with its big stores, fancy hotels and bright neon lights. The Wilmott was an old-fashioned place—all pillars and potted plants—with a doorman in a frock coat and top hat and everyone in suits with *WH* printed on the lapels. True to his word, the CEO of TexChem had booked the family into the executive suite on the eighteenth floor. They had a living room, two bedrooms and a bathroom. But the wallpaper was faded, the view—across six lanes of traffic—hardly spectacular, and the beds were both smaller and less comfortable than the ones they had left at home.

I H8 NEW YRK, Madison texted to her best friend, Chelsea, before they had even taken the elevator back down for dinner. *I AM SO BORED!*

MISS U, Chelsea texted back. *WILL C CHARLIE FRIDAY. SO LAME U CAN'T B THERE!*

Thinking of Charlie made Madison all the more miserable. Worse still, she wondered why Chelsea had mentioned him. What would her friend get up to, knowing she wouldn't be there?

The family ate dinner together in the hotel restaurant. The food was good, but the Johnsons didn't enjoy the service: the waiters who kept sidling up to the table to check that everything was all right or to refill their water or to wipe away the crumbs. All in all, they would have preferred to have been left alone. But at the end of the meal, Herb made a speech. He could see the way the weekend was going and he knew he had to cheer them up.

"This place is okay," he announced. "And we can eat and drink whatever we want. TexChem will pick up the tab. After all, this is meant to be a celebration. I won the case! And tomorrow we can see the town. We can do some shopping. Macy's. Saks Fifth Avenue. Let's treat ourselves." He snapped his fingers at a passing waiter. "Waiter! Can you bring me a cigar!"

"I'm very sorry, sir," the waiter said.

"You don't have cigars?"

"Smoking is forbidden inside the hotel."

Herb's face fell.

MY DAD SUCKS, Madison texted, secretly, holding the phone under the table.

The next day, at ten o'clock, they left the Wilmott for their first day of sightseeing, beginning with the Em-

pire State Building. They hadn't been there fifteen minutes when they decided it was too hot, too crowded and
actually too tall. The weather was cloudy that day, and
when they finally got out onto the observation deck on
the eighty-sixth floor, there wasn't actually that much to
observe. Rockefeller Center also disappointed them. It
was just another skyscraper. And what was the point of
visiting Radio City, just across the road, without the Rock-
ettes? They had lunch at a deli where all the customers
were shouting and the servers were rude. In the afternoon
they took each other's photographs against the flashing
neon signs in Times Square and then walked in Central
Park until Tammy complained her feet were hurting (the
expensive Jimmy Choo high heels had definitely been a
mistake) and they went back to the hotel.

The following day was Friday and in the morning
they went to the Metropolitan Museum of Art, which
they all agreed was too big and generally too full of art. In
the afternoon they went shopping and bought new shoes,
new shirts, new skirts and new socks . . . not that they
needed any of them, but what was the point of shopping
if you didn't buy anything? That night they saw *Mamma
Mia!* . . . or at least some of it. Madison fell asleep after half
an hour and Tammy said she preferred the film, so they
left during intermission.

The trouble was that the city was exhausting them.

Perhaps if they had planned their time a little more carefully they would have been able to travel less, but they
had bounced up and down Manhattan as if they were
trapped in some sort of demented pinball machine. And
getting around wasn't at all easy. The sidewalks were
crowded and even a couple of blocks were too much to
cover on foot. On the other hand, all three of them hated
the New York cabs, which were cramped and uncomfortable with nasty plastic seats and drivers who seemed to
originate from every country in the world except America
sitting on the other side of their thick glass partitions and
never once so much as wishing them a good day, leaving
any discussion to the taped voices of TV celebrities who
urged them to "buckle up" and "enjoy the ride."

And the traffic! It seemed to the Johnsons that they
had wasted hours trapped in those yellow tin boxes, waiting for lights that refused to change or finding themselves
stuck in cross streets with everyone blaring and swearing
and policemen whistling and nobody actually moving.
Visiting the tourist sites was bad enough. Getting there
was even worse.

It was Madison who suggested on the fourth day of
their visit—it was Saturday—that they should use the
subway. They were heading uptown to the American Museum of Natural History, which, according to the guidebook, was on Seventy-ninth Street and, traveling from the

Wilmott Hotel, about as far as it was possible to go without actually leaving Manhattan itself.

"I don't want to ride in another cab," she exclaimed. She had already texted exactly the same sentiment to her friend Chelsea. "They're smelly and they're slow." Her eyes brightened. "Let's take the subway! We can be like real New Yorkers. That'll be cool."

"I don't know, sweetie pie," her mother said. "The subway's very dirty in New York. And maybe it's not so easy to find the way you want to go—"

"I think it'll be fun!" Herb Johnson was surprised to find himself agreeing with his daughter. It wasn't something that happened very often. In truth, though, he was also thinking of all the cab fares he had paid out since they had arrived in New York. It seemed they couldn't even go around the block for less than ten dollars. "You go north. You go south. How difficult can it be?"

"Herb, there are all these different lines, local stops, express stops . . ."

"We'll ask the concierge." Herb reached for his Stetson and balanced it carefully on his head. "We don't want to look like out-of-towners."

The three of them took the elevator down to the ground floor, and while Tammy adjusted her lipstick in the ladies' room and Madison texted Chelsea to find what had happened at the party and who, if anyone, had left with Charlie, Herb inquired how the three of them might reach the American Museum of Natural History using the subway.

The concierge, like his name, appeared to be French. He spoke with a heavy accent that Herb found hard to decipher. At first, he seemed surprised that any guest of the Wilmott should want to travel on public transport, but once he had accepted that Herb was serious, he raised his eyebrows and provided the necessary information. "Of course, sir. It is very simple. You can take the 1 uptown from Houston Street, which is just two blocks from the hotel. Get out at Seventy-ninth Street and walk a couple of blocks east. Or you may find it easier to head over to Spring Street, where you have the choice of the C, the E or the B—but not the A, because that's the Express, and look out for the B train because it doesn't always stop at Eighty-first Street, which is the station you need for the Museum of Natural History. The N and the R trains leave from Prince Street, which is actually nearest to the hotel, but you'll need to make a change at Times Square. Or you can pick up the same lines at West Broadway if you prefer."

"What was that about the 1?" Herb asked.

But the concierge had already turned to another hotel guest and, not wanting to look ignorant, Herb decided to let it go. He'd gotten the general idea. Lots of trains stopped near Eighty-first Street. He just had to pick the right one.

The family left the hotel, crossed Sixth Avenue and made their way into SoHo, an area of New York which was almost on their doorstep but which they hadn't yet explored. This part of the city was too old-fashioned for their taste, too cluttered with shops that were themselves too cluttered to provide a comfortable shopping experience. The Johnsons preferred the sort of open spaces that they had found along Fifth Avenue.

The New York subway was therefore the last place they would really have chosen to go. Even the entrance seemed purposefully designed to be hard to locate—they came upon it more or less by accident and saw at once that it wasn't the station they wanted. Herb had planned to go to Houston Street, but he must have set off in the wrong direction, because this was Spring. However, at least it was a name that the concierge had mentioned and the three of them set off down the steep concrete steps that led them below the level of the road. Almost at once, Herb felt uncomfortable, wishing that he had stuck to the cabs. The walls were white-tiled and grimy, like a restroom in a cheap motel. The ceiling was low. The air smelled of dust and oil. But he remembered that this had been Madison's idea. It had been the only enthusiasm that she had shown since they had left Texas. He didn't want to disappoint her now.

They bought three MetroCards from one of the machines that stood against the wall . . . or tried to. It was actually quite difficult to work out exactly what sort of ticket they wanted and how much they should pay, and then they found that Herb's dollar bills were too crumpled and the machine wouldn't accept them. Fortunately, there was a ticket seller in a booth, sitting on the other side of a dirty glass window. She scowled at them as she handed the MetroCards across—although Herb thought that he too would hardly have been smiling if he'd had to work down here all day.

The platform was another level farther down, reached through a thickly painted iron gate that seemed to turn only reluctantly. As Herb pushed his way through, he had the impression that he was being eaten alive, that he was entering the bowels of some gigantic creature. The platform was almost empty, with just a few people standing in clusters, some staring into the gloom of the tunnel, others reading the Saturday edition of *The New York Times*. There were more passengers on the other side—Herb could see them through the forest of steel girders that supported the ceiling. The light down here was hard and unwelcoming. Gusts of warm air scurried over the concrete, adding to the sticky heat.

"You know, maybe we should take a cab after all," Tammy said. She had painted her lips that morning with

Chanel crème lipstick—Lilac Sky, her favorite shade of pink. But now they formed a little O of disapproval. "It's not very nice down here."

"Well, honey, we've paid . . ." Herb didn't care about the money, but he didn't want to climb back up the steps. And anyway, it was never easy hailing a cab without the help of the hotel concierge.

"Herb, I just don't feel comfortable. Which train are we meant to take?"

"I think he said the 1," Herb replied. In truth, he couldn't remember what he had been told.

"I don't think the 1 goes from here. I'm sure we'd be more comfortable in a cab. What do you think, Madison?"

Madison, who was once again plugged into her iPod, didn't hear what her mother had said but raised her eyebrows in disdain.

Any further discussion was ended by the sudden arrival of a train, crashing out of the tunnel and roaring and rattling down the full length of the platform, a series of silver boxes scarred with graffiti and with shafts of bright white light spilling from a long line of windows.

It was the A train.

"Is this the right train?" Tammy asked.

"I guess so."

"Maybe we should ask someone."

"I don't think it matters, honeybun. They all go uptown. We might as well take it now that it's here."

The three of them clambered onto the train. Tammy stepped through the door as if she knew they were making the wrong decision but had no choice in the matter and would regret this for the rest of her days. Herb followed sheepishly behind. Madison came last, lost in the music of Michael Jackson, which echoed faintly from her ears. There were perhaps a dozen people sprawled out on the hard plastic chairs. A couple of them glanced briefly at the Johnsons, identified them instantly as tourists, and then forgot them. The doors screamed out a warning signal and then slammed shut.

With a jerk, the train moved off, then picked up speed, disappearing into the tunnel.

"This is the A train, Eighth Avenue Express, heading uptown to Inwood 207th Street. The next stop will be West Fourth Street." The amplified voice came out of speakers built into the carriage ceiling. None of the passengers seemed to notice it.

"It's the right train," Herb muttered, then called out the words a second time so that Tammy could hear.

Tammy nodded and they all sat down.

In fact, Herb had to admit, the train was a lot faster than any cab would have been. It whooshed through the tunnels, suddenly exploding into the stations and hurtling along the platforms as if it couldn't wait to be out again. It barely spent a minute at Fourth Street before the doors thudded together and it was off, racing through no fewer than ten blocks before stopping once again for breath. Above ground, the traffic would have been tied up in its usual knots—with red traffic lights, horns, piercing police whistles, angry faces. And this was an awful lot cheaper. Perhaps, after the museum, they might even use the train a second time to go back!

The A train stopped at Thirty-fourth Street and again at Forty-second. People got on. People got off. This all seemed quite normal and Herb was able to relax, knowing exactly where he was. If he got out at Forty-second Street, he would be back in Time Square, close to the theater where they had seen *Mamma Mia!* But it was then that everything went wrong. The train stopped stopping. It ignored Fiftieth and Fifty-ninth. In fact, it gave all the fifties a miss . . . and the sixties too. It seemed that the driver had gone mad! Herb saw the flashing lights of Seventy-second Street, but the train didn't stop there either. They seemed to be hurtling through the darkness as if they were going to leave Manhattan altogether.

"What station is the museum?" Tammy asked, and Herb could hear the edge of panic in her voice.

"It's not until Eighty-first Street," Herb reassured her.

"Then that must be the next stop."

But the A train didn't stop at Eighty-first Street or Eighty-sixth Street or even Ninety-sixth Street. It didn't stop anywhere. None of the other passengers in the carriage seemed at all concerned, but then they were all lost in their own worlds, nobody speaking to anyone else, so it was impossible to tell what they were thinking. 103rd . . . 110th . . . 116th . . . It was only as they arrived at 125th Street and at long last the train began to slow down that Madison looked up and unplugged her iPod.

"Are we there?" she asked.

"I don't know where we are!" her mother replied. Her lips now formed a single pink line.

The train stopped. The doors opened.

"We'd better get out," Herb said.

A few passengers had gotten off ahead of them. The Johnsons watched as they disappeared into the gloom at the end of the platform, making their way toward the stairs that would take them to the exit. The doors screamed and thudded shut. A moment later the train moved off, the windows seeming to melt into each other as it picked up speed until finally they were no more than a brilliant white blur. And then it had gone. The Johnsons were on their own.

"What now?" Tammy demanded. Her voice was a sliver of ice in the damp heat of the station.

"Where are we?" Madison asked. She had only just

begun to realize that they weren't anywhere near the natural history museum.

"Your father took the wrong train," her mother said.

"We've just come a little too far up." Herb took out a handkerchief and mopped at his forehead. It often occurred to him that, in court, he could demolish anyone. But when he was at home or with the family, he had all the power and presence of a wet rag. Sometimes he wondered why that should be. Then he told himself—it was probably better not to ask.

"One Hundred Twenty-fifth Street!" Madison read out the station name with contempt. "That is so not where we need to be, Dad."

"I know . . ."

"Let's go up to the street and take a cab back," Tammy suggested.

"I'm not so sure that's such a great idea, honey." Herb had a nasty feeling that they had left Manhattan. They had come so far north that they might be in Harlem. He didn't actually know anything about Harlem, but he had seen a number of television shows set there and nothing good had ever happened. It was bad enough being lost down here. But if they went up to street level . . . "It might not be so easy to get a cab up there," Herb said, putting worse thoughts out of his mind.

"Then what—?"

But before Tammy could finish, there was a distant rumble and a pair of lights appeared in the darkness, heading back toward them, which is to say—back south. A second later a train burst out and began to slow down. But it was on a different platform. Herb quickly looked around him, taking in the stairs leading up to a corridor that must surely cross over to the other side.

"This way!" he exclaimed. Grabbing hold of his wife, he broke into a waddling sort of run.

There were ten steps up. With Madison right behind them, Herb and Tammy clambered to the top and then, without stopping for breath, hurried along the corridor. Below them, they could hear the train come to a halt and the doors open. There seemed to be turnstiles and staircases everywhere. There were signs pointing to the A, the B, the C and the D train—and even to La Guardia Airport. Herb ignored them all. He just wanted to get his family onto this train before the doors closed again. He didn't care where it took them. As far as he was concerned, they could go all the way back to Spring Street and see the American Museum of Natural History the next time they were in New York. Why had they wanted to visit the museum anyway? None of them were interested in natural history.

They reached a staircase. Herb just hoped this was the right one. Taking a tighter grip on Tammy and checking that Madison was still with him, he hurried down. It was lucky that his wife wasn't wearing high heels today. The three of them reached the platform just as the doors signaled their alarm. They leapt on the train, the doors cutting across like guillotine blades behind them. Their clothes were crumpled. They were panting and covered in perspiration. But they had made it.

Nobody had gotten off the train. Only the three of them had gotten on.

"What train was this?" Tammy asked.

"I didn't see," Herb confessed.

"Did you see where it's going?"

"I didn't have time to look."

It was only now that they realized they were alone in the carriage.

And this train was somehow different from the one they had taken before. It was much older. The seats were brown, not gray, and the silver handrails were a different shape. Herb glanced at one of the advertisements. WINSTON CIGARETTES—FOR A FULLER FLAVOR. That was impossible! Cigarette advertising had been banned on the New York subway more than five years ago. Everyone knew that.

There was no recorded announcement. Nobody told them what the next stop was going to be. But they were going the right way. They had to be. The train flashed through a station and Herb caught sight of the street number—116. They were already nine blocks south.

"Let's sit down," he said. He was still holding Tammy's arm and he gently steered her toward the nearest seat.

"We don't know where we're going!" Tammy said.

"We're going back to the hotel," Herb responded. "And then we're going to go out for lunch and I'm going to buy you the biggest steak you can buy in this darned city. Nice and bloody—just how you like it."

"We're slowing down," Madison said.

It was true. They could feel the wheels braking beneath them, and as they entered the next station, it was obvious that they were about to stop. 107th Street. It was just like all the other stations, with a low ceiling and a sense of being squashed beneath the surface. But the walls were more ornate. The name was written in mosaic. And there were classical pillars dotted along the platform, like something out of a Greek temple.

"I don't remember a station on 107th Street," Tammy said.

"Well, we'll only be here a few minutes," Herb assured her.

The train stopped. The doors opened. Then there was silence. Nobody got on or off. The engine didn't seem to be running. They waited a full two minutes. Then the lights went out.

"What now?" Madison wailed.

It wasn't too dark in the train. The platform lights were reflecting through the windows. But it really did feel as if it was here for good, that it would never move again. None of them were quite sure what to do. Should they just stay here and wait for a guard or perhaps a driver to appear? Or was this the moment to head back up to street level? Another minute ticked past.

"There is no 107th Street station," Tammy said.

"What do you mean?"

Tammy had taken a New York guidebook out of her silver leather Prada handbag. Herb wondered why she had only produced it now. If she'd had the guidebook all the time, wouldn't it have been better to consult it while they were still at the hotel? She had opened it to the back cover. It showed a map of the Manhattan subway. "There's 103rd and 110th—but there's no 107th," she said.

"But look at the wall, honey. We're at 107th. It says it in black and white."

"And red, green and gold," Madison added.

It was true. The tiles were all different colors. But Herb scowled at her. This wasn't going to help now. "This must be a new station," he said.

"It doesn't look new."

"Maybe your guidebook's out-of-date."

"Herb . . ."

"We can't just sit here," Madison exclaimed. "This train isn't going anywhere."

"She's right," Herb said. "Maybe we can find someone to give us a little help."

But there was no one . . . not on the train, not on the platform. Even the driver, if there had ever been one, refused to appear.

"Let's find the exit," Tammy said. She was speaking in a whisper without knowing why. She could feel the emptiness all around her.

There was no exit.

No stairs led up from the platform. There didn't seem to be any signs pointing to other lines. The station could have been abandoned a week, a month or even several years ago. The air down here was sluggish. The neon lights, long rows of them, burned down, turning everything gray and white. The train they had just left seemed to have died. It was hard to believe it had ever moved at all.

"There!" Tammy shouted and pointed.

There was a single man at the end of the platform. Or it could have been a woman. The figure was too far away to be seen clearly, and anyway, he or she was concealed inside an ill-fitting coat . . . it was almost like a cloak. There was no face, no arms. Just a shape that was vaguely human, a wrapped-up bundle on legs that staggered slightly, as if drunk, toward an archway and then disappeared.

"Who was that?" Tammy asked.

"It must have been the driver."

"He didn't look well."

"Maybe that's the way out."

"I don't want to be here," Madison wailed. "I wish we'd never come."

"Hush, sweetie!" her mother crooned. "Everything's going to be fine."

Keeping close together, they edged their way down the platform, following the one other human they had seen. At last they arrived at an archway. And here was a sign. TO THE X TRAIN. About fifteen steps led down and then turned a corner. Herb looked back. As far as he could see, there was no alternative.

"Come on," he said.

"Herb. There's no X train in my guidebook," his wife muttered.

"There's no 107th Street either," Herb reminded her. "But that's where we are. You need a new guidebook."

"We need to get out of here," Madison whimpered.

"South," Herb said. "We'll take the X train south. That's all we need to do."

They followed the staircase down. There were another twenty steps after the corner, then another corner and twenty more. By the time they emerged onto another platform, they knew they were far beneath the level of the road. They could feel the great mass of earth and concrete above them. The weight of it pounded in their ears.

Another train was waiting.

"Herb . . . ," Tammy began.

Herb looked up and down the platform. The figure they had glimpsed had gone. He realized that there was no lighting at all down here. The only illumination came from the train itself. If the doors closed and the train moved off, they would be left in pitch dark. It was that thought that spurred him on.

"Get on the train," he said.

"But Herb—"

"Just do it, Tammy. Now!"

They climbed onto the train and it was as if as invisible driver or controller had been waiting for them. At once the doors closed. The lights flickered out and for just a second the three of them could imagine themselves trapped in the inky darkness, unable to see as they were carried the Lord knows where. But as the train jerked forward and began to pick up speed, the lights came back on again. At least they could see. And by the time they had plunged into the next tunnel, they were aware of two things. The track was slanting down, taking them deeper and deeper into the belly of the earth. And this train—the X train—

was like nothing that could possibly exist in any modern city. It had to be at least fifty years old. The outside had been painted dark green. The seats in the carriage were made of wood, not plastic. There were no advertisements. The wheels creaked and groaned. The whole thing looked like something out of a museum.

The journey took about ten minutes, which felt like ten hours, and during the whole time, none of them spoke. Madison sat with her head slumped, her long hair dangling between her knees, her Versace froufrou jacket drawn around her shoulders and her legs crossed. She had never looked so miserable. Herb was clinging to one of the strap handles as if he would collapse without it. He had taken his Stetson off and was holding it limply in his other hand. As for Tammy, she had already decided that she wasn't going to speak to him again for a week. Her eyes were tight little pearls of anger.

The train emerged from the tunnel. But the family saw at once that they weren't in a station. This was like nothing that could have ever belonged to the Manhattan subway. It surely couldn't belong to the real world.

A cathedral. That was Herb's first thought as he nervously poked his head out of the doors, which had once again opened. The ceiling rose improbably high above him. It was carved out of natural rock and glistened with strange crystal formations that caught and reflected the blue light that washed over the place. Where was the light coming from? There were no electric lamps, no sign of any machinery apart from the train itself.

Narrow metal walkways and spiral staircases clung to the rock face—tiny in the distance. And now that he examined his surroundings more carefully, Herb could make out doors everywhere . . . natural arches and narrow fissures in the rock with passageways leading into an inner darkness. A cathedral or a station—or even a hospital? Lower down, at the level of the train, a platform stretched out in both directions, although it had cracked and crumbled away about halfway along. A machine that might once have dispensed candy bars, empty now, the glass broken, clung to a tiled wall. And there were beds. Dozens of them. Lined up a few yards apart, some with wooden cabinets, chairs, folding screens.

"Where are we?" Tammy whispered.

Herb hadn't even noticed her beside him. He pointed at another sign, faded but still legible.

59th STREET. COLUMBUS CIRCLE.

What had happened here? It was as if an old subway station had gotten itself tangled up with a cavern out of *Jurassic Park*. It didn't belong to one world or another. Herb had once seen a movie where the world had been destroyed by a nuclear war and the survivors had huddled together in the ruins that were left. It was a bit like that here. And hadn't they been ruled over by talking monkeys or something? Herb wouldn't have been at all surprised if an ape in a suit came strolling up to them now.

Someone was indeed approaching.

"Herb . . . ," Tammy whimpered.

It wasn't an ape. It was a man, perhaps the same man they had seen at 107th Street. He was dressed in an old raincoat that might have come out of a charity shop, tied around the waist with a piece of rope and so baggy that it was almost impossible to tell if the man was fat or thin. He had a knitted hat, a scarf around his neck and mittens on his hands. He was limping slowly along the platform, and as he got closer, they saw that his head was almost completely covered with bandages. It was only when he reached them that they saw why.

His face was rotting away. What skin they could see was gray and pitted with blisters and sores. One of his eyes was covered with a patch, but the other one was in a bad way too, red and swollen with some sort of liquid oozing over the lid. Part of his upper lip had been eaten away so that all his front teeth showed, giving the impression that he was either smiling continuously or howling silently in pain. His throat had partly caved in. Herb and Tammy could see the sinews, red and glistening, stretching down beneath his chin.

The three of them stood frozen in the doorway, not

wanting to leave the train. Herb had dropped his hat. Madison was crying. And yet the man didn't seem to want to harm them. He raised a hand in greeting. Herb noticed that it was missing two fingers.

"You are welcome," the man said.

"I . . ." Herb swallowed hard. As the man spoke, his sinews visibly rose up and down as if they were the cables that controlled his voice box. Herb couldn't tear his eyes away from them.

"We're not staying!" Tammy screeched. "We're not leaving the train!"

"I'm afraid that train's not going anywhere," the man told her. "Not for a while."

"Mommy . . ." Madison was crying harder than ever. Tears streamed down her cheeks and dripped off her chin.

Two more people approached. One was dressed vaguely as a nurse—but her dress and jacket were torn, a dirty off-white. She had no nose. The center of her face was a black, gaping hole that seemed to be trying to suck the rest of her features in, like water down a drain. Ginger hair sprouted from one side of her head. The other was bulged and shaped like a cauliflower. With her was a child in a dirty tracksuit, younger than Madison, bald with bulging eyes and skin covered with boils. It was impossible to tell if it was a boy or a girl.

"Hello and welcome," the nurse exclaimed. "If you'd like to come through to registration, we'll find you somewhere to stay." She waved the stump of her arm at the row of beds. She had lost her hand well above the wrist. "I'm afraid you'll have to use the public dormitory tonight. We hate doing that, especially for a family of three. But . . . you know! The paperwork!"

"Step out, folks," the man added. "We're not going to hurt you and the sooner we get you registered, the sooner you can grab something to eat and get a well-earned rest."

Clutching hold of each other, Herb, Tammy and Madison shuffled forward. Madison was still carrying her cell phone, but of course it had no signal down here. They were aware of people everywhere, shuffling out of the mouths of the caves, standing on the catwalks, peering around the corner of the train. No—not people. These were half-people, missing arms or legs, supporting themselves on crutches or old invalid chairs, rotting away even where they sat or stood.

"Look," Herb began, struggling to find the right words. He had never felt like this before. Words were his currency. Words were his power. They were his life. "There's been a mistake . . ."

"We can sort this all out in the office," the man said. "By the way, I'm Tom Callaghan. I should have introduced myself. And this is Sister Wendy with her daughter, LaToyah. She'll be looking after your medical needs."

"Who referred you?" Sister Wendy asked brightly.

"Nobody referred us," Herb replied.

For the first time, Sister Wendy and Tom Callaghan exchanged a look of doubt. "But you came in on the X train," she said.

"We were going to the Museum of Natural History!" Tammy wailed.

There was a long pause.

"We'll talk about this in the office," Tom Callaghan said.

The office was at the end of the platform, on the other side of a huge pair of wooden doors that might have been taken from a library or a town hall. Tom Callaghan and Sister Wendy went in with the Johnsons. LaToyah had drifted away.

They found themselves in a large, square room filled with filing cabinets and lit by a dusty chandelier. A red carpet—shabby and frayed—lay stretched out on the polished wooden floor. An ornately framed picture of Michael Bloomberg, the mayor of New York, hung on one wall, with an American flag propped up in the corner. Velvet curtains hung ceiling to floor on two sides but there were no windows. A slim black man in a suit sat behind an oversized desk, facing the door. He was in his sixties, with grizzled silver hair and spectacles that hung crookedly on his face, mainly because he was missing one ear. The man had no lips. His teeth, quite possibly fake, were kept in place with two elastic bands that went all the way around his head.

"Come in!" he exclaimed. "Take a seat." It was difficult to make out what he was saying. He spoke as if he were eating a meal at the same time. "I'm Obadiah Harris. And you are . . . ?"

"Herb Johnson. My wife and daughter."

"They came in on the X train," Sister Wendy said.

"But they weren't referred," Tom Callaghan added in a low voice.

"Weren't referred?" Obadiah Harris seemed almost amused by the thought. He waved the others away. "You can leave us together," he said. "It looks like we may have some explaining to do."

"And then what?" Callaghan wouldn't give up.

The man behind the desk raised his hands. He had two of them, although not a full set of fingers. "We'll work something out."

He waited until the two of them had gone. The doors swung shut behind them. Then he examined the Johnsons. "I have to say," he muttered. "You don't look sick."

"We're not sick!" Tammy exclaimed. "There's nothing wrong with us!"

"Then what are you doing down here?"

"We took the wrong train!"

"I don't see how that's—" Harris broke off. "Maybe you'd better start at the beginning. Where you live, what you were doing in Manhattan and how you came to take the X train. Don't leave anything out. We've got plenty of time."

Herb assumed that the man was talking to him and was about to begin, but instead it was his wife who silenced him with a scowl and then launched into an explanation that began with the TexChem case, the unwanted vacation, the Wilmott Hotel, the decision to take the subway and (although she was a little muddled about what exactly had happened and where exactly they had gone) the decisions that had brought them here.

"Oh dear, oh dear," Obadiah Harris sighed. "This *has* happened before, but not for a very long time. The X train only runs once a day and at a very specific time. I'm afraid to say you people have been extremely unlucky."

"Where are we?" Herb demanded. "What is this place? Who are all you people?"

"I'm going to tell you everything you want to know, Mr. Johnson. I can understand you being upset. But please remember, we didn't invite you here."

"Where is here?"

"Well . . ." Obadiah shook his head regretfully. He

had been handsome once when he was young. But for the missing ear and lips he might still be. "I'll keep this brief because we can talk more when you've had a chance to get used to all this," he began. "But somehow you've found your way into a community of people who, not to put too fine a word on it, are pretty sick. There are over three thousand of us living down here . . . living and dying because there's plenty of that too. What we have is a disease."

"What disease?" Tammy asked. Her eyes were wide and staring. Even as she sat there, she was trying to shrivel into herself as if she could find some protection from the air around her.

"There's no name for it. Never has been. That's part of the problem. Ever since it was first diagnosed—and that was more than a hundred years ago—nobody has been able to work out what causes it . . . or if there's a cure. They say the first poor soul who caught it was a man called Lebowski, and there are those who would like to name it after him, not that he would have wanted the honor. He's been dead a long time now, buried under platform nine. But it wasn't his fault. He came from Poland; there are people who say the disease began there. Only that doesn't make any sense because nobody in Poland has it. Nobody in Europe has it. Nobody outside Manhattan has it. Just people who live here. They catch it, they get sick and they come down here."

"Why not to a hospital?" Tammy asked.

"No point going to a hospital. You see, the disease is like a rotting sickness. I can see the way you're all staring at my mouth. And maybe you've noticed my ear. Just as well you can't see what's happened to my stomach under this suit, but put it this way—if this were Christmas, I could hang the decorations on my ribs." He sighed. "Once you get the disease, you just begin to rot away, one piece at a time, and there's nothing anyone can do. And it's worse than that. The sunlight makes it worse. It's a bit like vampires." He glanced kindly at Madison. "I'm sure you've read about them. They go out in the daylight, they shrivel up. Well, with us, the sunshine just makes us hurt and it makes the illness quicken up and it makes us rot even more."

"So you've come down here . . ."

"The authorities didn't know what to do with us when the sickness first broke out. They were frightened, you see, that we'd cause a panic in the city. An illness that came from nowhere and that nobody could cure? To begin with, they kept us on Blackwell's Island just off Manhattan in the East River. Later the name changed to Roosevelt Island—but then they needed Roosevelt Island for other things, so they moved us again. That was at the turn of the century, the twentieth century, when they were building the New York subway system. They found an area specially for us and we've been here ever since."

"But what do you do here?" Herb demanded. "What do you do?"

"There isn't much we *can* do," Obadiah replied. "We look after each other and we look after ourselves. Occasionally, government doctors and scientists come visit, but they've long since given up on us. They've tried drugs. They've tried radiation. Nothing works. So they send us food and money to help us keep going, but nowadays they more or less leave us alone."

"And the X train . . . ?"

"That's how new patients reach us. Of course, the Manhattan doctors know about the disease and they recognize the symptoms. If anyone in the city gets sick with the big D, they get sent to us on the X train. We meet them and look after them just like we met you."

"But we haven't got the disease!" Tammy exclaimed. For the first time she was glimpsing a way out of this. "We took the X train by mistake!"

"That's right, Mr. Harris," Herb weighed in.

"Herb . . . ," Tammy began.

"Leave this to me, Tammy." Herb leaned forward.

"You only have to look at my wife, my daughter and me to see that we are completely healthy. We're just tourists who happened onto the wrong train quite by mistake. So if you don't want me to sue you and the people who look after you and everyone else who knows about this totally crazy situation, you'll put us back on the X train and send us back where we came from, and maybe, if you're very lucky, we'll forget that any of this ever happened."

"I'm afraid it's not quite as easy as that, Mr. Johnson," Harris replied.

"Why not?"

The older man rubbed a finger across his chin. "Well, to start with, there's the question of national security."

"What about national security?"

"I've already told you. Nobody knows about this community. Nobody has heard about the disease. You seem like a reasonable man to me, sir. How do you think the people of New York would feel if they found out that there were three thousand of us down here?"

"I don't give a damn about the people of New York! I never even wanted to come to New York in the first place! I'm going back to Texas with my family. We're never coming back here again."

"Well, that's the other problem, sir—"

"Listen." Suddenly Herb was angry. "I've had enough

of this. I don't want to talk to you any more. Just give me a yes or a no. Are you going to show us the way out of here?"

"Mr. Johnson, you must let me explain—"

"Yes or no?"

"I can't."

"Then to hell with you!"

Herb sprang into action. He was only a small man, but he could move surprisingly fast when he really had to, and he was well built after many sessions in an exclusive gym. In one movement he stood up, sending his chair toppling behind him, and grabbed hold of his wife.

"Come on, Tammy," he exclaimed. "You too, Madison. We're getting out of here."

"But Mr. Johnson!" Obadiah Harris half rose to his feet, but Herb pushed him back, using the palm of his hand.

Obadiah grunted in surprise. Herb grimaced. Beneath the shirt, he could feel the man's chest and it wasn't pleasant. It was like handling a stack of uncooked spare ribs hanging in a butcher's shop. Tammy muttered something, but Herb spun her around and propelled her to the door, jerking it open, with Madison right behind.

"Wait!"

They ignored Harris and plunged outside. Tom Callaghan was standing right there, as if he had been listening to the conversation through the door. "What do you think?" he began.

Herb pushed him out of the way and the man slumped onto his knees like a pile of hamburgers that had just been dislodged. They were out of the office. Herb stopped and looked around him . . . at the platform with the hospital beds, the train still standing dark and silent on the tracks, the rock walls and broken tiles, the crowds of people shuffling around like zombies with nothing to do. He thought about the tunnel. He could see it just ahead of him, and if he followed the tracks they would surely lead him somewhere. No. It might be a mile before the next station, and running through the darkness, perhaps with this mob behind him . . . he would never make it.

Up.

That was the only answer. They were underneath New York. But if they could just make it to the surface, there must be some way to break through to normal life. Herb could almost imagine the shoppers and the office workers streaming along the sidewalks, the cars and the cabs, a whole world going about its business with no idea of what was happening just beneath its feet. He could reach them! There had to be a way.

"This way!" he shouted, leading his family toward

the nearest staircase that zigzagged along the rock face, heading up past the cave entrances and onward into the darkness.

"You can't go up there!" A man, dressed in the rags of a police uniform, blocked his way. One half of his face was normal, unscarred. The other half wasn't there.

Herb lashed out, knocking him aside and reached the first stairs. Tammy came next with Madison close behind, her blond hair sweeping across her eyes. All around them, people were shouting and pointing, more in alarm than anger or outrage. Nobody stopped them as they began to climb. The girl called LaToyah appeared at a cave entrance, blinked at them and then turned away. Another older woman with a collapsed skull shrank back against the wall to let them pass.

The staircase led them higher and higher. It was impossible to look back now. The distance was too great. If they slipped over the handrail and fell, they would surely be killed. None of them were speaking. They were having to use every effort to keep going, to force themselves on. They came to a wide metal platform with a flight of concrete steps branching off to the left, into the rock. A row of dull yellow lightbulbs lit the way, and there was a metal door at the end. Herb thought he could feel a draft against his face. This had to be it—the exit. But what if the door was locked?

Someone shouted something behind them, but Herb didn't hear a word of what they had to say. Tammy was with him, tears flowing, crying out in pain. She had twisted her ankle, losing one of her Gucci sneakers at the same time. Madison had somehow scratched her arm. There were streaks of blood all the way to her elbow. The three of them turned off and ran the last few feet to the door. It was closed with four huge bolts, but they hadn't been fastened. Herb reached out and jerked them back. Then all three of them were tumbling forward, throwing their combined weight against the metal door. It fell open.

Fresh air. Sunlight. Bright colors. The noise of traffic. Skyscrapers soaring over them. A hot dog stand on a corner. One page of a newspaper blowing across the sidewalk.

They were back in Manhattan, standing in an alleyway between two cross streets. In front of them was a kitchen with men in white jackets unloading cardboard boxes from a van. Behind them was the entrance to a parking lot. They could see the traffic moving at the ends of the alley on either side.

Herb slammed the metal door shut. "Come on!" he shouted. He wouldn't feel safe until they were several blocks away. In fact, he wouldn't feel safe until they were back in Plano.

Somehow they stumbled out of the alleyway, down

another street and out into a wide, open area where everything seemed to be made out of glass, with two towering glass blocks looming up behind. A woman with several shopping bags had just come out of a Whole Foods and was flagging down a cab. Herb jumped in front of her as it pulled in.

"The Wilmott Hotel!" He had to force himself not to scream.

"Excuse me!" the woman exclaimed.

The cab driver opened his window. He was dark skinned, wearing a turban. "I am very sorry, sir—" he began.

"I'll pay you five times the fare to take me to my hotel," Herb said. "In fact, I'll pay you ten times the fare!"

It was too late anyway. Tammy and Madison had already pushed the woman out of the way and climbed inside. Herb bundled in after them. The taxi driver shrugged apologetically and turned on the meter. Ten times the normal fare! Who was he to argue?

Nobody said anything until they had reached the Wilmott. Herb didn't even look at the meter. When they finally pulled in, he gave the driver everything he had in his wallet, and the three of them got out.

"Good afternoon, sir. Glad to have you back!"

Herb ignored the smiling doorman, registering only that it was already afternoon. How long had they been away? How many hours had their ordeal lasted? They hurried through the plush reception with its gray marble floor, scattered tables and vases of exotic flowers. They fell into the elevator and stood there, panting, exhausted, as it carried them up to their suite on the eighteenth floor. Madison was trembling. Tammy's makeup had run. Glancing at her, with her lipstick smudged and her eyeliner running down her cheek, Herb shuddered. She reminded him of some of the people they had left behind.

Later.

Much later.

They had all showered and changed. Tammy had put antiseptic cream on Madison's injured arm. Herb had drunk six whiskeys out of the minibar. Outside, it was getting dark. The door was locked, the security chain drawn across. Their suitcases were packed.

"We should go to the police," Tammy said. She had said the same thing a dozen times before.

"We can't go to the police," Herb replied patiently. The lawyer in him was taking over. For the first time in many hours he was beginning to organize his thoughts. "They'd think we were crazy. They'd never believe us."

"We could show them."

"You think you could find that door again? It was in an alleyway, but do you remember where it was? Do you even want to look? Anyway, we saw a cop down there. You remember that? And that guy Harris said the authorities knew what was going on. For all we know, the police in this goddamn city could be in on it too."

"I want to go home!" Madison wailed, not for the first time.

"I know, sweetie pie," Herb assured her. "And that's exactly what we're going to do."

"Then why haven't we left?"

"Daddy tried to buy tickets," Herb reminded her. "But it's a holiday weekend. There are no seats. So we'll leave tomorrow, just like we were going to. We're going to eat dinner in this room and we'll have breakfast sent up too. We're not leaving the hotel until we leave Manhattan. Then we've got the limo coming for us and we'll head straight for the terminal. We're safe now. Nobody's coming after us. And if anyone even tries to get through that door, then we *will* call the cops. And tomorrow we'll fly home. Tomorrow we'll put this whole thing behind us."

They ate dinner together at eight o'clock, watched a little television and went to bed. Madison was too afraid to sleep alone, so she shared the bed with her mother while Herb slept in the next room. She thought she'd be awake all night, but the whole ordeal had exhausted her, and in fact she dropped off almost immediately. Her last thought

was of the car that would be coming to the front door
the next day. She could already see herself sinking into
the soft leather seats. The windows were tinted. Nobody
would see her as she was whisked away to the airport
and the first-class flight home. She would call her friend
Chelsea as soon as she got back. But she wouldn't tell her
what had happened. She wouldn't tell anyone. She just
wanted to forget it.

She woke up.

It was a beautiful morning. The curtains were open
and sunlight was streaming in. It actually hurt her eyes,
it was so bright. She looked at the bed next to her. Her
mother was no longer there, but she could hear talking
coming from the main room.

Her arm was itching.

Idly, she reached down and scratched it. It was itching
really badly. She scratched harder. Then stared in total,
frozen horror at what she had just done.

She had scratched away a layer of skin and flesh. It had
actually come free. It was dangling under her nails. Blood
was oozing out of the wound that she had just inflicted on
herself. Her eyes widened. She opened her mouth—either
to scream or to be sick.

Somehow she managed to prevent herself from doing
either. Numb with shock, she slipped out of bed, noticing

for the first time the clump of chestnut-colored hair lying on the sheet. She hadn't noticed it before because it was concealed by the pillow.

Her mother's hair.

She couldn't speak. She could barely walk. As if in a dream, she drifted into the room where her parents were still talking. She realized now that they were arguing in low, insistent voices.

She stopped in the doorway. A woman with a partly bald skull was standing with her back to her. It was Tammy. She was still in her nightgown. There was blood specking through the material across her shoulders.

Herb was facing her, dressed in silk pajamas and slippers.

"We have to . . . ," he was saying.

"We can't."

"We have no choice!"

Herb saw Madison come in and stopped.

"Mommy . . . ?" Madison quavered.

Tammy turned around. She was looking very pale. Red makeup was trickling out of her nose. Except Madison knew it wasn't makeup.

"What's happened?" Madison asked. But she knew what had happened. She remembered what Obadiah Harris had told them:

"*Once you get the disease, you just begin to rot away, one piece at a time, and there's nothing anyone can do.*"

Once you get the disease . . .

"I'm sorry, Madison," Herb said, and a single tear rolled down his cheek. Except that Madison saw it wasn't a tear. It was his whole eye. "Go and get dressed and finish packing your bags," he continued. "We're going to take the X train."

Seven Cuts

My name is Don Weisberg and it has been my privilege to be the president of Penguin Young Readers Group for some time now, overseeing Philomel Books, which is part of the Penguin family. Although you may not know it from the book you are reading, Philomel is actually a highly distinguished publisher of quality books for young people. They are responsible for some of my very favorite titles. Young children all over America grow up reading their bright, cheery picture books and thought-provoking novels.

I do not like horror stories.

Don't get me wrong. I'm not some old fuddy-duddy

who wants to protect children from the darker things in life. Nor do I mind violence (in moderation) in children's books. But I do sometimes think that writers can go too far and that there's really no point in producing a collection of stories that is going to give its readers horrible nightmares. At the end of the day, I am in charge of this company—and when mothers or teachers complain, I'm at the receiving end. In fact, for many years it was Philomel's policy to avoid publishing horror stories at all. Who needs bloodshed and violence in the library when there is already so much of it out on the street?

So I was very concerned when Anthony Horowitz offered us a manuscript with the exceptionally offensive title *Bloody Horowitz.*

Like it or not, Anthony has had a certain amount of success with his Alex Rider books, which are published by us. In fact, to be honest, our new, very fancy reception area was paid for entirely with the proceeds from *Crocodile Tears.* This has always been the problem with writers and publishers. At the beginning, before they are well known, they're very easy to handle. They do what you tell them. But as they become more successful, they often become more demanding. We worry about offending them. Because the sad truth is that our profits depend on them.

Now, I'm not saying that Anthony has become big-headed. But the point is, I was worried about upsetting him. At the same time, I was very reluctant to publish the collection which you now hold in your hand.

So why, you are asking, did I go ahead?

Well, after I'd read the manuscript, I called Anthony's editor and publisher into my office. Michael Green had been with Philomel for more than twenty years and had worked with Anthony for almost as long. He had also read the horror stories.

"What did you think of them?" I asked.

"I hated them," he said with a shudder. Michael is quite a small, nervous man, with wire-frame spectacles and thin lips. Although he is in his forties, he looks much younger. "That one about the boy who was electrocuted in a field. Or that poor little girl who was eaten alive . . . I don't know what kind of mind could think up such things. And as for the story about Darren Shan being killed . . . he's quite a famous author! Would it even be legal to publish a story like that about him?"

"I agree," I said. "What do you think we should do?"

Michael thumped his fingers nervously on my desk. For a moment he looked like a piano player trying to find a tune. "I suppose we have no real choice," he said at length. "If we don't publish them, somebody else probably will and we'll not only lose the profit, we'll upset Anthony. But I really don't think we can let them go ahead as they are. We're going to have to make some cuts."

"What cuts do you think are needed?" I asked.

"I have them here." Michael opened his leather briefcase and took out a sheet of paper. He unfolded it and set it in front of him. "There are seven cuts I have in mind," he said. "They're simply too violent and unpleasant. They'll have to go."

"May I see?"

He turned the piece of paper around and this is what I read.

> You Have Arrived: The severed limb on page 90 is almost certain to give young readers nightmares. The story will work just as well without it.
>
> The Cobra: Charles wetting the bed on page 109. This is very distasteful. Is it really necessary?
>
> The Mechanic: Description of Dennis Taylor's eyeballs exploding. This strikes me as highly unlikely and quite disgusting. Suggest we remove.
>
> Bet Your Life: All the deaths in this horrible story are dwelled on in far too much

detail. I think we need to cut the machine-gunning of Raife Plant and also the electrocution of Richard Verdi. Both made me feel sick.

Power: Another electrocution, again described with far too much detail. We can certainly make a cut here. And why do we have to mention Craig losing his underpants on page 272? Completely out of place in a children's book.

I counted up the number of cuts that Michael was demanding. There were seven of them, just as he had said. I thought for a moment. "If we were able to persuade Anthony to make these cuts," I asked, "do you think we would be able to publish the book?"

Michael paused before speaking. I could see that he was reticent to answer my question. "I suppose we could slip it out without anyone noticing," he admitted. "Perhaps if we published it just after an Alex Rider book . . . without advertising it."

"But what if he refuses to make the cuts?"

"Then I think we'd be putting our reputation on the line. Honestly, Don, I think it would be a mistake."

It was almost lunchtime. The Penguin offices are at the southern end of Manhattan, with SoHo a five-minute walk away. We have some of the best food in the city close at hand, and as it happened, I had been invited to a brand-new Tex-Mex/Japanese fusion restaurant, the only place in the city where the sushi came deep fried. I was hungry and eager to be on my way.

"Well, you'll have to go and talk with him," I concluded.

Michael went pale—and he had never been what I would call deeply colored to begin with. "I really would rather not," he said.

"Why is that?"

"Well . . . I know this is a terrible thing to say, but . . ."

"Come on, Michael! Spit it out!" I didn't know whether to be annoyed or concerned.

"It's just that Anthony worries me. If you really want the truth, Don, I sometimes wonder if he's right in the head."

This was news to me. I sat back in my chair, astonished. Michael went on.

"He sits on his own all day in an apartment in London. I've heard it's right next door to the Smithfield meat market. It's like a crematorium with great slabs of raw flesh hanging on hooks. Apparently he has a human skull on his desk. It was given to him when he was a boy. And there's a horrible spider in a glass case . . . I know he can be very pleasant when he wants to be, but sometimes I look into his eyes and I see something strange." He took a deep breath. "Be honest. You've read these stories. Don't you think you'd have to be a little bit disturbed to write something like them?"

"Lots of authors write horror stories," I responded. "Look at Stephen King. And Darren Shan for that matter. Are you saying they're all crazy?"

"No. I'm just saying they have a dark side, and with some of them you can't be sure where that fictional dark side ends and the real one begins."

This was going nowhere. I decided to draw the meeting to a close. "Listen," I said. "All we're doing is asking Anthony to make seven cuts in a book that will be three hundred pages long. I can't see that he'll complain. I'm sure that he'll be delighted that we're publishing the book at all."

"He's very precious about his work, Don. You don't know him the way I do. His books are full of death. And you haven't spent hours with him, arguing . . ."

"I want you to go over to London and see him. Don't look so gloomy, Michael. I'm in a generous mood. I'll give you two days' vacation. Maybe you can visit Buckingham Palace or something. See some theater." I got up and opened the door for him. "Just make sure you're back here in a week with the changes settled."

Michael flew to London to see Anthony the following Tuesday. His meeting was at 2:30 P.M.

He did not call the next day. Nor did he e-mail. I figured he must be jet-lagged. And then, to be honest, I forgot all about him. Maybe that was wrong of me, but I'm a busy man.

The first I knew that something was wrong was when I got a telephone call from his wife, Elece. Michael's return flight had been scheduled for Tuesday night. He hadn't been on it. No one had heard from him. Elece had reported him as a missing person to the police.

I'm not quite sure what I thought about this. Editors, even the best ones, can be highly-strung people and I wondered if Michael hadn't simply taken off for a tour of Europe. The last time I had seen him he had, after all, been in a state of nervous excitement. The police actually came to Penguin to investigate. I spoke to a nice detective and I was relieved that he didn't seem to be too worried. He was sure that Michael would turn up.

He did, two days later.

In London.

Floating facedown in the River Thames.

It seemed that he had been attacked by a maniac. The

killer had taken a knife to him. He had been stabbed repeatedly and then thrown off the Waterloo Bridge. I saw the headlines in the daily paper that night as, dazed and distressed, I made my way home.

CHILDREN'S EDITOR RECEIVES SEVEN CUTS

Seven cuts. . . .

I'm sure it was just a coincidence. I mean, I'm not suggesting that a bestselling author would descend into madness and murder to defend his work. Absolutely not. And I can promise you that Michael's unfortunate death played absolutely no part in my decision.

But in the end, I went ahead. I decided to let the stories appear exactly as Anthony had written them. I didn't want to upset him—that's all. Perfectly understandable, don't you think?

I just hope you enjoyed them more than I did.